THE COACH'S WIFE

Books by Barbara Casey

The Coach's Wife
The House of Kane
Just Like Family

For more information
visit: www.SpeakingVolumes.us

THE COACH'S WIFE

Barbara Casey

SPEAKING VOLUMES, LLC
NAPLES, FL
2021

The Coach's Wife

ISBN 978-1-64540-435-4

I dedicate this book to my parents,
George and Charlotte Woods,
who shared in the joy of winning the
NCAA National Basketball Championship -

and to all the loyal fans who have
yet to experience that joy.

Foreword

There has probably never been a time when I didn't enjoy sports on some level. As a young child it was with the innocence and wide-eyed excitement that goes hand-in-hand with competing and winning a prize. Later, the rewards were less material and somehow more spiritual in nature. When I married Willis Casey, however, my enjoyment and appreciation of sports, especially collegiate sports, took on a totally new and deeper meaning. I could no longer be satisfied to just sit on the sidelines and cheer. I quickly became aware that there were other factors involved in the so-called game of sports—factors that played a critical role in the over-all scheme of things as they existed within a university.

Willis was the director of athletics at North Carolina State University in Raleigh. It was through his eyes I learned that collegiate sports was not "just a game," and that a winning athletics program was much more far-reaching than I had ever imagined. It influenced things like student enrollment, scholarships, donations, accreditations, standing within the community, and even the personal development of young men and women. As I became more involved, I began to experience the ever-changing and often volatile emotions that existed with each game played, or each event. If a team won, the exhilaration was unreal; but if it lost, there was only the feeling of despair. With time I adjusted. I allowed myself to be interested, but not so emotionally involved that it spilled into all the other areas of my life. I thought I was in control. Nothing, however, prepared me for that season when the men's basketball team went to Albuquerque and won the NCAA National Championship.

Under the direction of a highly emotional, super-charged Italian coach by the name of Jim Valvano, this team game after game seemed to lose, only to pull out a win in the last seconds of regular play or in overtime. It managed to survive the regular season, and as underdog, the Wolfpack team took not only its fans but the entire country by storm and marched into "The Pit" as it was called at the University of New Mexico to pull off one of the biggest upsets in the history of collegiate basketball. It is still talked about today as though it just happened.

Willis and I were sitting in the stands at center court that final game as we watched the winning dunk shot. The entire coliseum exploded. Willis pulled me through masses of cheering fans, past the security guards and onto the court. The Wolfpack players were laughing and crying and piling on top of each other in a heap. Coach V, as he was affectionately called, was running around wild-eyed, flailing his arms, searching for someone to hug. He found Willis. Then he found me. The overwhelming joy of the Wolfpack fans was so strong that time seemed to momentarily stop so that the enormity of what had just occurred could catch up with reality.

The Coach's Wife is not reality. Nor is it a replay of an unbelievably thrilling event that took place during Willis's tenure as athletics director. It is a story that is simply the product of my imagination brought to life on a printed page. Within that story, however, is a spirit that reflects something that is real—that one glorious moment when winning the NCAA Basketball National Championship became a reality for the Wolfpack.

Barbara Casey

Prologue

Everything you can imagine is real.
                                    —Pablo Picasso

Marla Connors wrapped her full-length, black mink coat tightly around her and sat back in the rich brocade chair—one of a matching pair—that faced the ivory damask sofa. She had chosen this particular chair in the lobby because it allowed her full view of the front entrance of the hotel as well as the bank of brass-framed elevators located off to the right. She watched a group of noisy Seawolf supporters get off one of the elevators, all of them wearing red and white and carrying an assortment of pompoms, banners, and other displays of school spirit to wave during the basketball game. Several other people, also Seawolf fans who had waited to see if State would make it to the NCAA semifinals, were trying to check in at the hotel desk.

Even though Marla could easily see anyone coming into or leaving the lobby of the hotel through the massive glass doors, as well as anyone using the elevators, she for the most part was hidden from view by a tall palm and several smaller potted plants placed around the seating area. And even if someone did notice her sitting there, no one would recognize her—not with the wig. The shoulder-length blond hair and heavy makeup, as well as the coat, made her look older than her thirty-three years.

Another group of loud fans clamored out of an elevator. Charlie Morgan, the new athletics director, and his assistant, Ray Knox, were among them as well as Stuart Simmons, one of the assistant coaches. The Piedmont State University Seawolf team was scheduled for the

first game of the semifinals in the NCAA National Championship basketball playoffs, and many of the fans had already started drinking.
Their boisterous and obnoxious behavior was only a mild indication of
what they would be like during and after the game.

He entered through the glass doors and stood for a moment in the
sunlight that was scattered on the thick maroon carpet. Tall, muscular,
erect, his sixty-year-old body looked like a poster ad expounding the
benefits of keeping in shape. He had probably been doing a pre-game
interview outside for one of the television networks. His thick graying
hair was slightly wind-blown giving him a boyish look, and he still had
on the sweats he had worn to practice that morning. Marla crossed her
legs and when she did the coat opened slightly, exposing her bare leg
and thigh. She smoothed the blond hair with her hand and licked her
lips. Other than that, she made no movement. He would see her. He
always did.

She watched him as he glanced around the different seating areas
in the lobby while retorting with his famous one-liners to the team's
well-wishers who were waiting to board the buses that would take them
to the coliseum.

"How'd practice go, Coach?"

"Too bad it wasn't the finals. We would have won."

Everyone laughed. He kept moving forward toward the elevators,
all the while glancing around, searching.

"Hello, Coach." A heavy-set woman wearing bright pink lipstick
and dark blue eye shadow came out of the crowd and kissed him on the
mouth. The fans nearby hooted and did various imitations of the wolf
howl.

"How are you, Jean?" He pulled away from her, not waiting for an
answer. Someone yelled from the crowd, "Hey, Jean, how about
spreading some of that over here." There were more wolf howls.

"Coach, is Miller going to be able to play with that groin pull?"

"If Doc says he can. If Doc says he can't, we'll get a new Doc."

Again, laughter from the crowd. They loved him—even when he didn't win. But especially when he did. The Seawolfers, that loyal, obsessed group of fans who followed and supported the University's basketball team, couldn't seem to get enough of his New York sense of humor and street-smart style, and the fact that he not only was a winner, he was a flashy winner. Now, after twenty years as head basketball coach at State, he was still winning. And as far as the fans were concerned, Neal Connors was a water-walker.

And then he saw her. His eyes lingered for a moment on her exposed leg and followed it up to where the coat once again concealed her bare skin. Slowly she stood up, deliberately readjusted her coat, and walked toward the elevators.

Neal tossed out several more wisecracks as he made his way through the crowd. He reached the private elevator just as the doors were closing. He shoved his hand between the doors, and they reopened.

"Going up?"

She was alone.

"Yes, but this is a private elevator. It only stops at the Presidential suite."

He entered and the doors quietly closed behind him.

"I don't mind if the President doesn't."

He moved toward her until she was pressed against the reflective glass wall of the elevator. Then he gently cupped her face in his hands and kissed her fully on the lips. As his tongue explored the depths of her mouth, his hands slowly moved from her face and down her neck, parting the folds of the coat as he did. His hands continued searching, caressing her soft skin. He pushed the coat off her shoulders and onto

3

the floor, fully exposing her naked body. His face burned with excitement and desire. He kissed her throat and breasts and as he did his fingers stroked her clitoris, at first tentatively, and then, when he felt the warm wetness, with more urgency, thrusting them deep into her vagina.

She untied the single drawstring holding up his sweat pants and slipped her hand inside, feeling his stomach and thigh and then the penis she knew and loved. He was hard, aroused for her. The elevator stopped but before the doors opened, Neal reached over and held the "close door" button. With his other hand he pushed his penis into her warm vagina, all the while groaning in ecstasy.

Marla began biting and sucking his neck, his shoulder, his arm to keep from screaming with pleasure. And then she felt the explosion of warm liquid blending with her own. She threw back her head, unable to control her emotions. Neal immediately covered her mouth with his own, stifling her scream, and thrust forcefully the last of his cum into her body.

The buzzer sounded. Someone else was wanting to use the private elevator. Carefully Neal pulled out and yanked up his sweat pants. Then he picked up the coat and put it back on Marla. The elevator doors opened. Neal and Marla got off and walked to their suite, one of three on the fifteenth floor that had been reserved for Piedmont State's dignitaries. The school's chancellor and the athletics director were staying in the other two suites. Neither Marla nor Neal spoke. That wasn't part of the ritual. They would shower and dress in silence, and then Neal would leave to ride with his team on the charter bus to the coliseum. Marla would follow on another bus carrying Seawolf officials and the wives of the players and coaches.

Before Neal left their suite, he looked over the clothes Marla had picked out to wear to the game. The gold pin shaped in the image of the Leaping Seawolf, the team's mascot, was already fastened to her red dress. At the door he paused in front of the beveled, gold-framed mirror and adjusted his red and white striped tie. Then he felt for the rock inside his right pants pocket. It was there. He fastened the top button of his gray pinstripe suit jacket. This was the semifinal game, which meant he had to wear the gray pinstripe. He had worn the brown suit in the quarterfinals. The navy blue suit he would wear to the finals; that is, if they made it that far. And considering how they had been playing since the first round in the Regionals, they stood a good chance.

Neal believed he would keep on winning just so long as no one interfered with his pre-game rituals. Wearing the brown suit, followed by the gray pinstripe, and then the navy blue was part of the ritual. Getting all of the team to rub a rock his father had given him before he died was also part of it. And making love to his wife in the elevator. The 14K gold pin was Marla's own superstition, but he didn't make fun of it. As long as he continued to win, he wasn't going to give up any of it.

Reaching the lobby, Neal confidently stepped off the elevator and pushed his way through the noisy Seawolfers to the waiting bus.

Chapter One

Another deafening roar exploded from the coliseum, and when it did Marla threw down her partially smoked cigarette and ground it into the polished tile floor with the toe of her shoe. Quickly she reached for another cigarette from the opened pack in her small red handbag. She lit it, sucked the smoke into her mouth, held her breath, coughed, and then slowly released it. Marla didn't smoke, but when she paced up and down the hallways of basketball coliseums, puffing on cigarettes seemed appropriate. It gave her something to do with her hands, and it helped keep her sane.

"God, how I hate this." Gale Simmons, the gray-haired woman pacing in the same direction as Marla, was married to one of the assistant coaches at Piedmont State. She, along with several other women—also wives of coaches, some of them wives of players—were known as the hall walkers. They were the women who met on a regular but unscheduled basis the last two minutes of every game, pacing the halls, smoking, or pretending to in Marla's case, and trying to give each other encouragement. Unable to watch the most crucial time of the game—that last two minutes—they paced in heart-pounding agony, listening to the fans erupt in cheers or boos, and to the announcer scream out the play-by-play over the public address system.

It didn't matter which team they supported. The bond they shared went beyond the game and winning or losing. It was after the game that most mattered. If their team won, it meant going through the torture one more time, but at least their husbands would be happy. If their team lost, it meant their husbands would go through weeks of depression and as their wives they would have to put up with an impenetrable wall of silence broken only by an occasional negative outburst—

usually directed toward them. Each of the hall walkers had experienced it. And it was that experience more than any other that cemented the friendship between them.

With thirty seconds to go, the score is 76 all. This is a hot one, folks. Let's see what the Seawolf pack is going to do. Sydney Rob makes an inbound pass into the back court to Jerry March—the clock is moving, folks. Jerry lobs the ball back over to Rob. Rob passes it over to Miller in the right court.

Interception by Darrell Washington! Holy cow, sports fans! The Seawolf's Sydney Rob loses the ball to the Demon Deacons. Wake Forest has the ball. Washington bringing it down court. Fifteen seconds on the clock.

Marla stopped pacing. Her whole body was trembling. Lydia Rob, Sydney's wife, rushed over to Marla and began frantically rubbing the gold pin on her dress. The other women just stood frozen in disbelief.

Gale Simmons, the assistant coach's wife who had been pacing with Marla earlier, glared at Lydia as though she had been the one to lose the ball to the opposing team, not her husband. "Son of a bitch," she muttered.

Deacons have the ball. Washington over to Moser. Now Moser back over to Washington, and Washington wants a time out. Ten seconds left to play in the NCAA National semifinal ball game. The score is tied at 76, and the Wake Forest Demon Deacons call time out.

The eight women supporting the Seawolf team huddled together in the hall not daring to say anything. A long ash fell unnoticed from Marla's cigarette. Her head was pounding so hard she thought she was suffering from an aneurysm.

Lydia stopped rubbing Marla's gold pin and wrapped her hand around it instead. "Oh, please, Lord, don't let it end like this—not with Sydney throwing the ball away."

The noise erupting from the vomitories of the coliseum and into the hallway was ear shattering. Marla could imagine what Neal was doing. Squatting on the floor with the players hunched around him, he would be scribbling plays and moves on a pad of yellow paper, giving each member of the team a position to play, an order to focus on, a magical move that would somehow win the game for them. She had seen him do it so many times. She doubted if the players even knew or under-stood what he was telling them. Even if they were able to understand him, they couldn't possibly hear him over the noise of the screaming fans. But they went through the motions, nodding, grabbing hands in a sweaty, spoke-wheel fashion, and doing some high-fives with the bench-warmers before rushing back out onto the court. They believed in Coach. He had told them this was their year to win. They were the Cinderella Team, the Team of Destiny. They were the Dream Team, and he wouldn't lie to them. He loved them. For many of the players, Coach was the only father-figure they had ever known. They wouldn't let him down. They couldn't.

Deacons in the backcourt. Ronald Carrie with the ball. Seven sec-onds. And he's fouled. Seawolf Derrick White has fouled Deacon Ronald Carrie. Seven seconds to go, and Carrie will go to the free-throw line. Deacons call a time-out. Seven seconds left. Seawolves with 76. Demon Deacons with 76. Hold on to your seats, folks. It ain't over yet.

The women stood in the middle of the hall, clutching hands, unable to speak. Sue Trepak, the girlfriend of Stilt, the Seawolf's big center, came rushing out of the stands past the group of women toward the restroom. Marla knew that kind of fear. To be so afraid of losing that it made you vomit. Marla had done it in the beginning. Before she became a hall walker. Sue would learn—that is if she stayed around the team any length of time. She would become a hall walker, too.

Carrie of the Wake Forest Deacons to the free-throw line. Two shots coming to Carrie. Seven seconds left, 76-76 the score. The first one from Carrie hits the back of the rim, rolls around the rim, and out. One more coming now. A little more important. Seventy-six a piece. Carrie throws it up—and misses! Seven seconds to go and the Seawolves have the ball!

"I think I'm going to pass out," Gale said to no one in particular. Marla dropped her burned-out cigarette and crushed it with her shoe. She heard one of the other women scream the word "shit," but the noise level around them was so great, Marla didn't know who screamed it.

Delaney Miller will put it inbounds for the Seawolves. Stanley Bentley at six foot eleven inches for the Deacons is right in front of him. Deacons straight up, man-to-man. Delaney has to throw it over six feet eleven inches, and Bentley isn't going to make it easy. Miller gets it in to Derrick White. Seven seconds, six. White has to hurry. Time's running out. He gets the ball across center court. Four seconds, three. He has to hurry. White gets the shot off. Two seconds, one—and he scores! Derrick White scores, and there's no time left on the clock! Coach Neal Connors and the Seawolves have won it! They will be playing in the NCAA Championship game. The final score, Piedmont State Seawolves, 78; Wake Forest Demon Deacons, 76.

"One more time, girls." Tears were running down Lydia's face from the relief she felt—not because the Seawolves had won the game, but because her husband hadn't lost it on an intercepted pass. The women who had been supporting Wake Forest quickly offered their congratulations. Several of the women hugged each other. A few of them cried. Then they disappeared into the crowd of people that was rapidly filling the hall. For them, the season was over until next year.

"Let's get out of here." Marla walked quickly toward the nearest exit to find the bus that would take the women back to their hotel. Neal would return later—after talking to his players and after the press conferences. Probably after the second semifinal game between Purdue and Houston. Maybe this night they could have a late, quiet dinner in their room—just the two of them—without the constant interruptions from inebriated fans and insensitive reporters.

People poured out of the stands and pushed their way through the halls. Marla felt someone yank on her arm.

"Hey, aren't you the coach's wife?"

Marla turned around and faced a small birdlike woman, arms and elbows protruding like wings, and a tall, overweight man. Both were wearing red tee-shirts with a picture of State's mascot, the Leaping Seawolf, sprawled across their chests in black.

Someone else bumped Marla from behind. "Hey, little lady." It was another Seawolf fan. Marla remembered seeing him hanging around the basketball office. He had a beer in one hand and a red cardboard sign with the words GO STATE! in the other. He put his arm around Marla, spilling beer on her hair and dress. "Whatever you're doing for Coach, keep it up. You give him anything he wants, ya hear? We don't want to lose now." He winked and tightened his grip around her. She could smell the foul odor of beer on his breath. Gale pulled Marla away from him. As they squeezed through the crowd toward the exit Marla heard the birdlike woman screech, "She only married him for his money, you know. He's old enough to be her father."

Once outside, the two women walked part way around the coliseum passing several chartered buses until they found the one that would take them back to the hotel. It was parked in a reserved area close to the building and several of the other wives were already on board.

Gale sat down next to Marla. "Are you O.K.?"

Marla nodded. "I'm just so drained."

"Don't worry about what those idiots said back there. You know how the Seawolf fans love to talk."

Marla found a tissue in her purse and tried to wipe the beer out of her hair. The smell of it was making her feel sick. It wasn't just the rude comments or what the fans thought of her. She had been feeling tired a lot lately and, as before whenever she got tired, it caused her to remember the things she was trying so hard to forget. Her marriage to Martin and the eight long years of abuse she suffered had been a living hell. Fighting for her divorce—for her life. And the nightmares—so real and so terrifying that the images of them stayed with her for days afterwards. She thought she had gotten over all of that when she married Neal—that it was buried in the past. But lately she had started remembering. The rawness she associated with Martin still hurt. And the nightmares—they hadn't stopped. Maybe it was the tension surrounding the games. Or because she had been away from home for so long. She didn't know.

Marla closed her eyes and rubbed her forehead, trying to erase the headache. The smell of stale beer wasn't helping any. There was something else as well—another fear that was apart from her ex-husband. She first became aware of it right after she divorced Martin. She believed at the time that it was her fear of him that caused it. Then it went away. Lately, though, she had been feeling it again. Even though she couldn't identify it, she knew it was there. It was something dark and evil, just under the surface where she couldn't see it or touch it, and it gave her a terrible sense of danger.

A couple more wives got on the bus and sat down near the back. Marla could feel Gale watching her. "Gale, do you ever think something bad is going to happen to you, but you don't know what?"

Gale laughed. "All the time, honey, all the time. Why? Is that what you are thinking now?"

Marla nodded. "Once when I was in college I was chosen along with one other art student to exhibit one of my paintings in the school's private gallery. It was a tremendous honor, for it meant that my painting would be on display with several world-famous works that the college had acquired over the years." Marla smoothed the tissue on her lap and refolded it. "I was married at the time, living off campus, and attending classes as a day student. I wasn't even an art major, but the faculty on the jury who evaluated the submissions felt that 'my artistic ability was noteworthy'. That's academic jargon for 'they thought my picture was pretty'." Marla wiggled her fingers in the air indicating imaginary quotation marks.

Gale nodded her head and grinned. "I can color inside the lines. And I did a paint-by-number painting on velvet one time. I bet they would have loved my stuff."

"I had chosen a nightscape, something that had been extremely difficult to execute because of its unusual composition and delicate coloring. I put a lot of thought into my decision to submit this particular painting because of the importance of the event. I called it *Moonset*; it was my best work." Marla twisted the tissue in her fingers as she recalled her painting. All of her other paintings had been done simply to fulfill class assignments. But *Moonset* was different. It was the first work she had gotten emotionally involved in. She had spent weeks on it, trying to create the exact image she wanted—a moon illuminating russet tones muted by the dark, wind-swept clouds of a threatening night storm. It wasn't just the amount of time and work she had put into it. It became an extension of herself—something she was able to project from her own imagination and actually bring to life. Finding out that there were professional artists who saw beauty and merit in it as well made her love *Moonset* that much more.

"Go on," said Gale.

"The day before my painting was to be taken to the gallery, someone broke into the room on campus where my painting was being kept. Nothing else in the room was disturbed except for my painting, and that had been ripped and slashed to pieces. It was so brutal. I didn't even realize that it was my painting, *Moonset*, until I saw a small piece of the canvass with that russet color on it. Other than that, nothing was left of it that could even be identified."

"My god," Gale shook her head. "Did you find out who did it?"

"No." At the time, some people blamed the other student who had been invited to exhibit. They theorized that when he saw my painting, he didn't feel that his own work was good enough, and the fear of ridicule and failure was more than he could stand. Apparently he had a history of emotional problems. But it could never be proved." Marla looked away. She couldn't bring herself to tell Gale that it had been her husband who had destroyed her painting. He admitted it to her several months later. By then it was too late to tell anyone. The other art student had already graduated, and another student's painting had been selected to replace *Moonset*. She wouldn't have told anyone anyway, she was so terrified of Martin.

"How awful," said Gale. "That must have been a huge disappointment for you."

"It took me a long time to get over it. It was almost as though I was being suffocated. Finding my painting so horribly mutilated and not knowing why, I felt like I was the one who had been mutilated. I felt violated and frightened that something else bad would happen to me." Marla took a deep sigh and looked down at the twisted tissue in her hands. "It was terrible. I wondered if I was an unwilling pawn in some wicked game that I had no control over. I lost my sense of direction and proportion. I had nothing on which I could anchor. And there were moments when I even felt guilty that maybe I had done something to make someone hate me so much."

"And that's the way you feel now?"

Marla nodded and looked out the window at all of the cars starting to exit the parking lot. That was what she was feeling now, only this time it was worse. She would wake up during the night trembling and overcome with a heightened awareness that something terrible was about to happen. Like before, she couldn't see it or touch it, but she knew there was something evil getting closer to her, surrounding her, and eventually there would be some horrible evidence of it—just like her painting. She hadn't even been able to talk to Neal about it. How could she when she didn't know what it was? Yet, she knew it was near her, and she felt helpless to do anything about it.

"I guess I'm just being silly." Marla smiled at Gale wanting to change the subject. She wished she hadn't even said anything. It was her problem, after all, and she knew no one could help her with it—just like before.

"No. You're not being silly at all. It's just these damn basketball games. They make us all a little crazy. It will soon be over now though." Gale reached over and patted Marla's hand. "And then we can go home. Thank god."

Of all the wives Gale was the oldest and had been a coach's wife the longest. She knew all of the ups and downs of being a coach's wife. Her husband was the assistant coach Neal most relied on. In fact, Stu Simmons was an assistant coach before Neal came to State and had applied for the job of head coach when it came open. But he was passed over along with about thirty other candidates wanting to head up State's basketball team.

"I've been following that shit'n basketball around the country for thirty-five years," Gale announced to everyone on the bus, "and I still hate it."

"Come on, girl." Lydia Rob yelled back. She was stretched out on the back seat of the bus, her arm resting across her eyes, completely exhausted. "You know you don't."

Marla shuddered. She couldn't imagine being the wife of a basketball coach for that long.

"If you start complaining again about Stu being only an assistant coach, I'm going to make you get off the bus," one of the other wives said.

Marla glanced over at Gale to see if she was going to answer back. Everyone was feeling the stress that comes with the end of the season. But she knew what the woman meant. When Marla first started traveling with the team right after she and Neal got married, she felt uncomfortable around Gale. Gale brought up the fact that Stu was just an assistant coach so often that Marla wondered if she somehow blamed Neal for being head coach, even after so many years. But now that she knew Gale better, she was used to her outspokenness. Whatever Gale's feelings were, she apparently managed to put them aside as far as her friendship with Marla was concerned, which was more than anyone else associated with the athletics department had done. Like those fans who had grabbed Marla when she was leaving the coliseum, they all seemed convinced that Marla was only interested in Neal's wealth and a good time. After all, who wouldn't like to travel all over the country and occasionally out of the country with one of the top-ranked college basketball teams in the nation? But if she took care of Neal's sexual needs and didn't cause any problems, then they would put up with her. What they didn't understand was that in the short time she had been married to Neal, Marla had grown to hate being the coach's wife. The constant disruption of her life, living out of suitcases, hotel food, hours spent on airplanes, and the head-throbbing emotions experienced in each game. And the seemingly unending social obligations she and Neal simply couldn't avoid even though neither of them liked parties of any kind. The only reason she went along was so she could be with Neal. Because as much as she hated all of it, to be separated from him would be even worse.

"Remember the Carolina game last year in the Dean Dome, Marla?" Gale rummaged through her purse until she found the pill bottle she was looking for. She opened the cap, dumped out a bilious green capsule, and swallowed it.

"I will never forget it." Marla grimaced. "I was so nervous I was sick." She watched Gale swallow a couple of more times. She looked pale. "How can you take that thing without water or something to wash it down? What is it, anyway?"

"Just something to settle my stomach. It's nothing." Gale took a deep breath and let it out slowly. "The score was tied 89 all with fifteen seconds left on the clock. Remember? It was in overtime, and it was Carolina's ball. Of course I was walking the hall, and you came running past me, your face about the same shade as oatmeal, and into the ladies' room."

"You followed me in and held my hair back while I threw up," said Marla shaking her head. "I knew then that you and I were going to be friends."

"That was when I told you about the hall walkers."

"I don't know which gave me more relief—throwing up or finding out that I wasn't the only one who couldn't take the pressure of losing a silly basketball game."

Gale smiled. "Up until then you had been hanging in there until the end of all of the games. We had a bet on as to when you would start joining us, you know."

"You mean you and the other hall walkers?"

"That's right."

"My gosh." Marla glanced around at the other women on the bus and then back at Gale. "So who won?"

"I did, of course. I figured that if you cared anything about State's basketball team at all, you wouldn't be able to take the stress of the Carolina game. It was a good thing you did join us. It sort of human- ized you. Up until then the other wives thought of you as some sort of prima donna."

"Who married Neal only for his money and so I could go with him around the country having heart attacks and migraines at all of these basketball games."

"People do get wild notions about what fun is, don't they?" Gale laughed and looked out of the bus window. It was starting to snow. "Do you think we will ever play a game that doesn't go down to the wire on some last second, shit-ass shot or into a fucking overtime?" Gale sighed deeply and leaned her head against the back of the seat. Cheering fans could still be heard from inside the coliseum. Others were pouring out of the exits, eager to get back to the hotel where they could start partying. Only in the bus was it eerily quiet as it slowly maneuvered out of the gigantic filled parking lot toward the highway leading back to the hotel. "Well, we're in the finals, girls," Gale added after a moment. "Either against Houston, with its seven-foot-four-inch giant disguised as a center, or Purdue, with the two fastest forwards in the country. Shit!"

Marla watched the snow as it gradually started covering the ground. She didn't even want to think about it. At least the finals were going to be played in the same coliseum. They wouldn't have to pack up and travel to another state. And everything considered, the hotel where they were staying was pretty nice. The management had done everything possible to insure their comfort. But she missed home. She had been traveling with the team on and off since the beginning of March when she went to Charlotte for the ACC Championship.

Spring was such a beautiful time of the year in North Carolina. The dogwoods and red bud were in bloom, and all of the azaleas she had planted last fall had been ready to open when she left. They would probably still be in bloom by the time she got home, but she had already missed the best part—when they first started showing their colors. Just two more days. After having Sunday off, State would play in the Championship game on Monday night. And then they could go home.

Chapter Two

"Coach, we might have a problem."

Neal carefully pulled his arm out from under Marla to keep from waking her and turned closer toward the telephone. The clock next to it showed 2:13 a.m. in glaring blue. He had just barely gotten to sleep. He watched Houston pound the shit out of Purdue in the other semifinal game, and didn't get back to the hotel until after midnight. Marla had waited up for him so they could order room service.

"Is it serious?" Neal didn't have to ask. For Stu to be calling at this hour, it had to be. Stuart Simmons was the most laid back, understated human being he had ever known. That was why he was such a great assistant coach. He was a perfect stabilizer to Neal's volatility, and he was good around the players. If they felt Neal was being too hard on them, they would go to Stu. He could always smooth things over. If they were having girlfriend problems, grade problems, or money problems, Stu would take care of it. But that was also why as long as Neal was around, he would never be head coach. Neal could excite his players and energize them to a playing level that no other coach could. But Stu didn't have the balls it took to be head coach. When it came to making the difficult decisions or acting under pressure, he couldn't do it.

"It might be." The answer was casually spoken, indicating no hint of urgency. But Neal knew better.

"You'd better come to the suite rather than discuss it on the phone."

Marla raised up when Neal got out of the bed. "Is anything wrong?"

"Nothing to worry about. Stu just wants to go over some new play or something." There was no need to upset her until he knew what it was all about. Neal leaned over and kissed Marla. He smelled the sweetness of her hair and body and immediately felt a tingling sensation in the pit of his stomach and a surge of heat through the shaft of his penis. He wanted to make love to her, but it would have to wait. "You go back to sleep."

"I love you." Marla reached out from under the sheet and tenderly touched his face and then turned over on her side, exposing the bare skin of her back.

Neal hesitated a moment, wanting her, loving her, and then gently covered her with the sheet. He grabbed the sweat suit off the chair where he had thrown it earlier and went into the living room, quietly closing the bedroom door behind him. A few minutes later he heard a light knock. Stu came in carrying two cups of coffee.

"I got these from the coffee shop downstairs. It stays open all night." Stu waited as Neal dumped two sugar packets and three artificial creams into his cup. He knew Neal didn't like coffee. But he enjoyed the ritual of drinking it. And the only way he could do that was to kill the coffee taste with sugar and cream.

"What's up?" Neal finally asked after he had finished stirring the muddy white mixture.

"I caught Stilt doing drugs." One thing about Stu, he didn't try to gloss over the facts. If he had something to say, he came right out with it.

"Holy shit. When?"

"About an hour ago. The night watchman was walking his rounds and heard a woman screaming. He went to investigate, and it was Stilt's girlfriend. Apparently he had gotten high and started punching her around."

"Of all the stupid, fuck'n . . ." Neal was out of his chair. "Why?"

"Who knows. He said he was under a lot of stress. The tournament, and knowing he's got final exams facing him when he gets back on campus."

"My god! That's what a student athlete does, for crissake. He plays in tournaments, if he's lucky, and takes exams." Neal ran his hand through his hair. "I don't believe this. You know we can't play him in the final game. Not with the NCAA doing drug tests on the players. So we have a fuck'n team without a center to play the most important game in our lives."

"I know."

Neal sat down and immediately jumped back up again. "My god. You don't think he took some before the Wake Forest game? Because if he did, we will be disqualified."

"No. He said this was his first time."

Neal grabbed a fringed cushion off the sofa and slammed it to the floor. "Yea, but do we know that for sure?"

"All the drug tests came out negative. His was one of them."

"Goddamn it! What could he have been thinking? Where in the hell did he get it?" Neal knew it was a stupid question. There was always someone around willing to "help out" an athlete. Neal sat back down and stared at Stu. Then he remembered what else Stu had told him.

"What about his girlfriend? Is she all right?"

"Doc took care of her. Some bruises and a cut under one eye."

"Is she going to file a complaint?"

"I don't think so. She really loves the guy, and apparently he's never done this kind of thing before."

"Thank god for that. All we need is to have the press pick it up, and Piedmont State's so-called Dream Team will take on a whole new meaning."

Neal swallowed some coffee and grimaced. "Shit. I can't believe this. Does anyone else know about it?"

"No. Only the night watchman, and I don't think he's going to say anything. I gave him two tickets to the finals." Stu watched Neal take another gulp of coffee. "Are you going to tell Morgan?"

Charlie Morgan had been athletics director for only a few months. Against all the advice from Neal and the Athletics Council, the chancellor had hired an old classmate from his alma mater in New Hampshire to replace the former director of athletics, retired after twenty-five years at State. Morgan didn't have a background in athletics and knew absolutely nothing about what it took to run a successful program. In the short time Morgan had been on campus the head football coach had already quit, and several of the other coaches were talking about leaving. Neal just tried to avoid him.

"No."

Stu nodded. He didn't say anything else. Of all the things that could happen to the team, short of a mass outbreak of the flu, this was about the worst. One game away from the NCAA Championship, and they lose their center.

"O.K. Here's what we'll do." Neal leaned forward. As always, he had a plan just as Stu knew he would. "Get Stilt on the next flight out of here and back to Raleigh. I don't want anyone talking to him. I want him checked into the college infirmary when he gets there. Send one of the assistant trainers—Hoskins will be good—along with him to make sure nothing else gets fucked up. When the press starts asking questions, tell them he's sick and we felt it was necessary to send him back to Raleigh where he could be taken care of. It will probably be best if his girlfriend goes back with him. I don't want anyone asking her any questions either."

"I'll take care of it."

"Now all I have to do is figure out how to win a basketball game against Houston without a center."

When Stu left, Neal was sitting on the glass-enclosed balcony off from the living room scribbling on his pad of yellow paper.

* * *

Ray Knox pulled the collar on his coat up tighter around his neck and ears and shoved his hands deep into his pockets. He cursed under his breath when he saw a group of drunks, probably Seawolf fans, coming his way. It was too dark to see who they were, but if they were Seawolfers, he was sure they would recognize him if they saw him. And even if they were blind drunk, they would wonder what in the hell he was doing hanging out in a service entrance doorway of the coliseum at three o'clock in the morning. Christ. That was all he needed. He pushed his back against the cold metal door as far as he could hoping he wouldn't be seen. The five men burst into an off-key rendition of the Piedmont State Fight Song and staggered past the doorway, oblivious of the cold and of him. One of the men tossed an empty beer can onto the pavement, creating even more racket. Knox listened to it roll several yards until it finally stopped and then heard the pop and hissing sound of another can being opened.

Christ it was cold. A blast of frigid air whistled around the door frame. He cursed again. At Morgan for getting him into this situation and at himself for doing it. This had to be the low point in Knox's career. Hanging out in darkened doorways in the middle of the night waiting to make a pay-off. To make it even worse, the guy he was supposed to meet was late. He had told Knox 2:30. Unless Knox got the directions mixed up. But the guy had said the service entrance on the east side of the coliseum. And that's where the hell he was.

23

Freezing his ass off and dodging drunken Seawolf fans so he wouldn't be seen.

Knox pulled out a wadded up handkerchief from his hip pocket and wiped his nose. He was probably getting sick. Morgan was going to make up for this big time if he expected Knox to keep doing his dirty work for him. No more cheap presents or token salary increases. Shit, he had enough TVs and cameras and electronic gadgets. Cheap toys from Morgan. He wanted some big money—security for when he decided to retire. And the way he was feeling now, he was ready to retire.

Knox heard footsteps, the empty beer can being kicked, and someone—a man—cuss. Knox leaned out slightly from the doorway and peered into the darkness. He smelled him—the rancid odor of nervous sweat—before he saw him.

"You got something for me, heh?"

Startled that the man was so close, Knox stepped out of the doorway wanting to get more space between them. Pressed into the doorway like that, he felt trapped. Like some kind of shit'n rat. The man was wearing a long heavy black coat. A scarf covered most of his face. What it didn't hide, the knit cap did.

"It's about time you got here. Is it taken care of?" Knox asked. He realized much to his irritation that he was shaking, and it wasn't just from the cold. His voice sounded soft and weak.

"It's taken care of, heh."

Knox reached into his breast pocket and pulled out an envelope. "This is what we agreed on," he said. "If State loses the game, you'll get the other half."

The man didn't take the envelope. Instead, he pulled out a cigarette lighter and flicked it on. "Open it," he said.

Knox tried to pry the sealed flap on the envelope open, but it was difficult since he was wearing gloves, and besides that his hands were trembling. He yanked one glove off with his teeth and ripped the envelope open. The man held the lighter next to the envelope so he could see its contents. Satisfied, he took the envelope and moved the lighter closer to Knox's face. "You Houston fans must have a real hard-on about winning the National Championship, heh."

Knox took a step back, wishing he had thought to wear some sort of disguise. He didn't say anything. If the guy thought he was some half-crazed Houston supporter, so much the better.

"Tomorrow night. Same time, same place." The guy flicked off his lighter and shoved it back into his pocket along with the envelope.

Knox stood in the doorway until he was sure the man was gone. Then after checking to see that no one else was around, he walked briskly back toward the hotel. He was sweating in spite of the cold, and he had to take a crap. He always had to crap when he got nervous. Maybe the guy hadn't been able to get a good look at him. After all it was pretty dark. He probably couldn't see that much with just his lighter. Knox quickened his pace when he felt his lower intestines start to cramp. Morgan owed him big time for this. Otherwise he was getting the hell away. He wasn't cut out for this kind of shit. Morgan could just do his own goddamn dirty work.

* * *

"You messed up, Stilt. Now you have to take responsibility for it like a man." Stu had been talking to Stilt while Hoskins called the airlines to make plane reservations for himself, Stilt, and Sue Trepak, Stilt's girlfriend. It would take time for all of the effects of the drugs to wear off. Whatever drugs were left in Stilt's stomach he vomited up when Stu told him he wouldn't be playing in the final game. After that he got angry; then he begged. Now he was just sitting on the sofa

25

crying. Sue sat next to him with her arm around him. Considering what Stilt had just put her through, she was holding up remarkably well.

"Is Coach really mad at me?" he asked, not looking up.

"I don't think he is mad. Just disappointed. He was counting on you. After all, you are one of his key players. All of his plays were designed with you playing center position. Now he'll have to figure out something else. You put him in a hell of a spot, Stilt."

Stilt rubbed his head. "Oh, god. I didn't mean it. I swear I didn't mean it."

Sue looked at Stilt and rubbed his back. There was a bandage under one eye, and her left cheek was bruised and swollen.

"Well, we're all set." Hoskins put the phone down and walked over to where the three were sitting. "We need to leave now, though, so we can get our luggage checked in."

"You know what to do when you get back to Raleigh," said Stu. "Take Stilt directly to the infirmary. I have already talked to Dr. Courin. He will be there to check him in and take care of him. If anyone asks you any questions, tell them they will have to wait until Coach gets back in town. All you know is that Stilt is sick."

Hoskins nodded.

Stu watched them get into the taxi that would take them to the airport and then went to the elevator to go up to his room. He looked at his watch. It was 4:37 a.m. He hadn't even been to bed yet. It had been one hell of a night, finding Stilt like that. He still didn't know who had given him the stuff. Normally Stilt was such a gentle guy. But drugs had a way of changing people. They sure had changed Stilt. No telling what would have happened if the night watchman hadn't come around when he did.

Stu pushed the card into the door lock until the little light turned green and quietly opened the door to his room. He hoped Gale was sleeping. She had been getting up during the night a lot lately. She said it was just indigestion, but he had made her promise him she would go for a physical as soon as they got home. If it was an ulcer or something like that starting to act up, he wanted her to get it taken care of. There was no sense in putting it off. After all, at this stage in their lives, they couldn't be too careful. During all the years they had been married, he was the one who had always gotten sick with colds, or hay fever, or the flu, or some goddamn thing. Gale had taken care of him, clucking over him like a mother hen. And those times when she couldn't, she insisted on taking him to the doctor. So now he was doing the insisting. Just as soon as this tournament was over, he was going to take her to the doctor.

Gale was in bed, apparently asleep. Stu tiptoed into the bathroom and shut the door. Neal had told the team and coaching staff that he wanted them downstairs for breakfast at seven o'clock. They would go to the coliseum afterwards for their morning warm-ups and practice session. Stu debated whether he should even go to bed; he knew Neal wouldn't. After thinking about it, he decided to undress and try to get some sleep. A little would be better than none at all. And at the rate things were going, he might be up another night if anything else went wrong.

Afraid he might disturb Gale, he carefully lifted the pillow from the bed and grabbed an extra blanket off the top shelf in the closet. Then he lay down on the small love seat that was positioned in front of the single window in the room with his legs dangling off the end. He felt so tired, but his mind wouldn't turn off. It had been such a long season. How in the world Neal had managed to accomplish what he had with these players, Stu didn't know. Even at the beginning, they had been a lackluster team at best. Totally unmotivated. Plagued with injuries and illness. Coach even had to get full-time tutors for several of the players to help them make the grades in order to stay in school. On top of everything else, their star forward came down with mono three weeks into the season. They finished the regular season last in the Conference, which was no big surprise. But then something happened. Slowly they began to peak. They wound up winning the Atlantic Coast Conference Tournament which gave them an automatic invitation to the Nationals.

Still it was a struggle. Every game ended in an overtime or double overtime, or on some last-second shot. But somehow they managed to win. He doubted if they would ever have another year as exciting as this one had been. He was glad he had been a part of it, even with all the problems that had come up. Stu sat up and rubbed his legs. They felt numb because the circulation had been cut off, dangling off the sofa like that. He turned over on his side and drew his knees up toward his chest.

A couple of the players, Derrick and Sydney, told him their mothers wouldn't be able to come to the game; they couldn't afford the air fare. But they would be watching it on television. Stu would get them to call their mothers after the game. Win or lose. It was always good to keep the mothers happy. And it would make Derrick and Sydney feel good.

He hoped Neal was doing the right thing by not telling Morgan about Stilt—not that he blamed him. Morgan was such an unpredictable son of a bitch. It would be just like him to forfeit the game if he was told. In the long run, it probably wouldn't matter anyway. They didn't stand a chance of winning. Not with Stilt out. Still. Stu sighed and closed his eyes. In a few minutes, he was asleep.

Chapter Three

Marla ran her hand across the bed, and when she didn't feel anything she opened her eyes. Neal wasn't there. The sun was just starting to filter through the window overlooking downtown Albuquerque. Outside everything was blanketed in white. She put on her robe and wandered into the living room. Neal was sitting on the balcony. Prisms of light reflected from the many panes of glass enclosing the area, and the noises from outside were muffled by the late-night dusting of snow. She went up behind him and put her arms around him, kissing his ear and neck.

"Good morning," she whispered, licking his ear and gently blowing in it. Neal tossed the pad down and reached around for his wife, pulling her onto his lap. She kissed him on his mouth and then pulled back to look at him. "Did you get any sleep at all?" She stroked the stubble of beard on his face with the tips of her fingers. His face felt warm.

"Enough," he answered.

She continued looking at him. "Can you tell me what's wrong?"

Neal gave her a quick account of what had happened. He had never been able to keep anything from her. Besides, it always made him feel better when he told her what was going on. She had a remarkable way of putting things in their proper perspective. That, and her belief in him to always do what was right, gave him added confidence to work through his problems, which seemed to have tripled since Morgan became athletics director.

Before he met Marla, he hadn't given a shit whether anyone agreed with what he did or not. And he certainly hadn't needed anyone. Basketball was his life, and there simply wasn't room for anyone or anything else. There had been the usual casual involvements, of course.

Being such a popular figure, there were always women coming on to him. Most just wanted sex. Others wanted more. That woman, Jean, in particular had been difficult—calling him at home and at his office all the time, showing up in his hotel room when the team was playing a game out of town. But he had finally convinced her he wasn't interested. Basketball was his only interest in life. The women were just occasional, temporary distractions. But that was before he met Marla. And now facing his sixty-first birthday in a couple of months, he found he needed her support, her strength, and her love more than he ever needed anything in his life.

"Oh, Neal. I am so sorry. I know how important this game is to you." Marla held Neal closer to her. "No one believed you would be able to bring the team this far, and you did. I'm sure you'll be able to come up with something, whether Stilt plays or not."

"I'm afraid that means I won't be able to spend much time with you today. With the game being tomorrow night, I was hoping we could do some sightseeing. But now . . ."

"Don't even give it a thought. I'm sure Gale and I can find something to do. All you need to do is concentrate on the game tomorrow night. Right? We'll have our time together later."

Neal buried his face in Marla's hair. "What do you remember most about the first time we met?"

"I remember how intense you were. You had nothing on your mind but that unfortunate loss to William and Mary." Marla gently rubbed her finger across Neal's bottom lip and smiled. "And I remember noticing your tie and thinking it was the sexiest red and white tie I had ever seen."

Neal laughed and thought back to that night. He had just watched his team lose, a rare occurrence for the Seawolves, to a non-conference school out of Virginia. Losing the game to a weak team had been bad enough, but it was the way they lost it that tore Neal up. On a free throw for a technical foul that shouldn't have been called in the first place. The Seawolf fans had been ruthless, saying that the Pack played William all right, but couldn't handle Mary. That loss knocked them out of the number one seed going into the ACC Tournament. Marla was in her car waiting in a long line of cars to exit the parking lot. Neal was so disgusted about the way the officials had called the game, he didn't bother looking before he backed out of his reserved parking space. He rammed into her car causing a rather loud noise and a big dent in the left rear door panel of her car. Normally he would have merely exchanged insurance information and forgotten about it. But she was so damned beautiful. For some reason she was also very frightened, so he insisted on following her home to make sure she arrived safely. Two cups of coffee and a hefty slice of lemon pound cake later he found out she had been working on campus for only a short while in the chancellor's office. She had moved from Red Oak, a small town fifty or so miles east of Raleigh. The next day Neal found out with the help of someone who worked in personnel that Marla was thirty-three years old and recently divorced.

"What do you remember about our first meeting?" Marla asked.

"Thinking that you were the most beautiful woman I had ever seen. And there was a certain vulnerability about you."

"I should think so. You had just crashed into my car," Marla teased.

"No, it was more than that. All I know is, from the moment I first saw you I wanted to protect you and love you—forever." The night of the accident Neal thought he was the reason that Marla was so frightened, stupidly crashing into her car the way he did. It was only after he got to know her that he realized she was still carrying the emotional scars from her first marriage. More than anything he wanted to help her forget all of the ugliness from her past. He loved her so much. If there was any possible way to do it, he would.

Marla rested her head on Neal's shoulder. "I was so happy when you followed me home that night and then called me the next day to ask me out."

Neal grunted. "I thought I was being clever, taking you to all of the out-of-the-way places so we wouldn't be recognized."

"I think everyone knew." Marla kissed the top of Neal's head and gently curled a lock of his hair around her finger. "That's all right though. We had a good time."

Neal's infatuation with the chancellor's new administrative assistant had been the main topic of conversation around campus and everywhere else. All of the sports bars near campus had bets on as to how long it would last. Those who knew Neal figured it wouldn't. After all, here was a man who had never been married, who was obviously set in his ways, and whose only interest in life was winning basketball games. Besides that, he was almost twice her age. Only Stuart Simmons recognized the situation for what it was. Neal was a man totally and completely in love. When Neal and Marla were married six months later, no one quite believed it, or wanted to. At least none of the Seawolfers. Neal was the coach after all. They didn't want him to have anyone or anything else in his life that could distract him from winning the basketball games. Stu believed it though. He had seen the change in Coach. Basketball was no longer Neal's first priority. It had been replaced by something else, and that something else was named Marla.

"I only wish I had met you sooner. Not now when I'm already an old man."

Marla took Neal's face in her hands. "Hush. You aren't even close to being an old man. Besides, basketball means so much to you I doubt if you would have given me a second look a few years ago. It's all I can do to get your attention away from it now." She pouted at him teasingly and gently rubbed her hand between his legs."

Neal's reaction was immediate. Never had anyone given him so much pleasure and happiness. Marla had become such a big part of him that even basketball had lost its importance. The amazing thing was that he didn't particularly care. Things were changing in collegiate sports. Basketball was no longer just a game, and it was no longer particularly fun. Proposition 48 that had been pushed through by the NCAA was making it impossible to get the good players out of high school if they had poor grades. Unless they carried a C average and scored a minimum of 700 on the SATs, even if a sliding scale was used, they could forget college basketball. That and the financial incentive to be on national television just added to the stress of winning. Having to work for an athletics director with a background in animal husbandry or some goddamn thing that had nothing to do with college sports didn't help either. Not only that, Neal simply didn't like the bastard. And now with the worry of drugs—Neal sighed heavily and stroked Marla's long, dark hair, feeling its silkiness and smelling the sweet scent of her body. If he could just get this Championship. He would take some time off and he and Marla could go to the Cottage. Damn, how long had it been since he had even seen the ocean?

He was feeling depressed, and that was the last thing he needed if he was going to make the team believe they could do the impossible— win the NCAA National Championship without a center.

Marla slipped off his lap. "Come on, I'll cook you some breakfast."

"We don't have a kitchen."

"I'll improvise." She pulled him to his feet and led him back to the bedroom.

* * *

"Marla, I didn't wake you, did I?" It was Gale. Marla knew she would probably call and had gotten up as soon as Neal left to meet with the team.

"Hi, Gale. No, of course you didn't. I was hoping you'd call. Neal isn't here, and I am up and dressed with nothing to do. You want to go shopping or something?" Marla carried the phone over to the window. "I see cars moving on the streets so I guess it didn't snow enough to make it too slippery. I really would like to get out of here for a while." Marla gave up her job at the University when she married Neal so she would be able to travel with him. But between the practice sessions, coaches' meetings, team meetings, press conferences, and spending the necessary quality time with each of the players, Neal had to be gone a lot, leaving Marla alone. And now that this problem with Stilt had come up, Marla didn't know when he would get back. He had told her before he left that morning not to expect him until she saw him.

"I figured you were probably on your own. Stu was already gone when I woke up this morning. Isn't this thing with Stilt a bunch of shit? I was still up when the night watchman called Stu about it. I sure hope the press doesn't get hold of it."

"I know. Gosh I'll be glad when this tournament is over. Neal looked so tired this morning when he left."

Gale was a lot older than Marla, but Marla felt closer to her than to the other younger wives she had met. They all seemed to be busy having babies or involved in their own careers. Gale didn't have either. She had focused her entire married life on Stu and his interest in collegiate athletics. She knew what it was like to spend long empty hours in some hotel room miles from home with nothing to do but wait until the next basketball game. Now that Marla was married to Neal and traveling with him, Gale had become a good friend and was someone she could do things with. Since Neal and Stu were usually tied up with the team, Marla and Gale would take off on their own, touring whatever town it was where they were staying, shopping at another mall, eating their meals together, and just killing time between basketball games. Gale was also someone Marla could confide in.

"Gale, I didn't want to ask Neal since he is already so upset, but has anything like this ever happened before? I mean, a problem with drugs?"

"Never with drugs. There have been other problems, of course, like when Coach got a couple of the players, both of them starters, thrown out of school because they broke into some of the dorm rooms and stole some stuff. He really caught hell from the Seawolfers for that one."

"You mean because he had them expelled from school?"

"That's right. The Seawolfers were afraid that by losing two of our starters, we would lose the ACC Tournament. It was going on at the time. Neal was right, of course. Those boys didn't have any business being on the team or in school. And there have been players suspended from the team because of bad grades. But there's never been anything about drugs."

"I find it so hard to believe that it was Stilt caught using the drugs. He is so religious."

"Yea, I know. A Born-Again-Christian. A member of the Christian Athletes of America. All of that. I find it hard to believe, too. But it happened. Probably someone got to him and convinced him that he needed it to win. There's nothing we can do about it now. Look, we don't need to be brooding about this. How about if I meet you down in the lobby in ten minutes. We can get a taxi over to the historical part of Albuquerque if you like. I understand there are a lot of unusual things to see there—museums, wampum venders on every corner, Indian boutiques—are there such things? Oh well, and some great restaurants. A guy down at the front desk told me about some place that serves home-made pumpkin bread baked in a clay flower pot. We certainly don't want to leave Albuquerque without eating some of that."

After Marla hung up the phone she checked her purse to make sure she had everything she needed and put on the red leather jacket that matched her skirt. She always wore red and white—the school colors—for their tournaments. The gold seawolf pin was attached to her white pullover sweater.

She was just about to leave when someone knocked on the door. She tried looking through the peephole, but she couldn't see anything. Whoever it was had covered the hole. There was another knock.

"Who is it?" she asked. Maybe Gale had decided to meet her at the suite instead of the lobby. Or it could be an overly zealous fan wanting to tell Neal how to win the game.

"It's Charlie. Charlie Morgan."

Marla hesitated. She didn't like the new A.D., the way he looked at her, and the way he always seemed to find a reason to touch her. "Neal has already left to meet with the team," she said without opening the door.

"I know. I want to talk to you. May I come in?"

Marla glanced around the room. From where she was standing she could see the rumpled bed where she and Neal had made love a short while earlier. She walked over and pulled the bedroom door closed.

"What can I do for you, Mr. Morgan?" Marla stood in the doorway, blocking his entrance.

He pushed past her, stroking her arm with his hand as he did.

"Call me Charlie, please, and I hate carrying on conversations in hotel hallways. You never know who might be listening."

Marla watched him cross the room and for a moment she thought he was going into the bedroom. He hesitated just outside the closed door and then walked back to where she was standing.

"Red suits you." His eyes wandered up and down her body. "It compliments your blue eyes and brown hair."

He reached out and touched Marla's hair, tracing a lock of it down her shoulder to where it stopped on her breast. "I bet you would look good as a blond too."

Marla stepped back, away from his hand. So that was it. He must have seen her in the lobby waiting for Neal and recognized her.

"If you are so interested in women's hair, why don't you discuss it with your wife?"

Charlie laughed and moved closer. "My wife wouldn't understand. I think you would though." He grabbed Marla's shoulders and roughly pulled her to him, forcing his mouth on hers. Marla struggled to free herself from his hold, and when she finally did, she slapped him across the face as hard as she could. The force of it stung her hand and brought tears to her eyes. He smiled cockily.

"Marla?"

Charlie turned quickly. The door was partially open, and Gale was standing in the hallway.

"I thought I would come to your suite so we could go down to the lobby together. I mean you never know who or what might be lurking around in the hallways." She paused and looked at Charlie standing off to one side still holding his face.

"Well, I won't detain you two ladies. I'll catch up with Neal later, Mrs. Connors." He walked past Gale and down the hall.

"My god." Gale handed Marla a glass of water along with a valium she retrieved from one of the bottles of pills in her purse. "Stu told me Morgan is a bastard. I can see why." Marla tried to drink the water, but she was shaking so much most of it spilled on her leather outfit. And her lips felt bruised. Gale took the glass out of Marla's hands and held it to her mouth so she could drink it. "That son of a bitch. But what can you expect from someone who gets a Master's degree in watching animals screw."

"Promise you won't say anything, Gale, to Stu or anyone. I'd just as soon Neal not know about this—not yet—with the big game tomorrow night and with everything that's happened."

"I know, honey. I know. Don't worry. I'm not going to say anything." She took some tissue from her purse and mopped the water off Marla's suit. "I think you'd better tell Neal as soon as you can, though. I have a feeling that piece of shit will try it again."

Marla looked at Gale in horror. Gale put her arms around Marla and held her. "We'll deal with it. Don't worry. I've learned a lot more than defensive and offensive moves on the basketball court these past thirty-five years. Being in such close proximity to men's locker rooms all the time, you tend to get educated. And believe me, if that bastard thinks he can get away with crap like this, he'll soon find out otherwise."

Gale picked up Marla's purse from the nearby table and handed it to her. "Are you all right now?"

"Yes. I'm fine."

"Maybe we can find a tomahawk for you from one of those wampum dealers. That would slow him down."

Marla stood up and walked to the door. Gale didn't know all of the reasons she had divorced her first husband. Whenever Gale asked her about it, Marla explained it by saying that she and Martin had simply grown apart. Only Neal knew of the mental and physical abuse she suffered, the terror she had lived in, the long struggle to get her divorce, and, of course, the nightmares.

She had wanted so much to make the marriage work. Martin had been thorough in making her believe that she was to blame for his violent outbursts and bizarre behavior. She thought she just needed to try harder. Maybe if she dressed differently, or cooked better, she would somehow be a better wife. And then he would be happy. She remembered reading in the newspaper about a young woman who was gunned down by her husband in the hospital parking lot where she worked as a volunteer. Everyone who knew her said the same thing: that she was the most loving and unselfish person they had ever known. Even as she was being rushed into surgery, blood streaming out of her body, dying, she thanked the doctors who were trying to save her and told them that she loved them. And yet, only moments earlier, the man she had been married to for ten years filled her body with bullets, all the while yelling that she was incapable of loving anyone. For Marla, it wasn't the constant threat of death that made her finally leave. It was the undermining of her self-confidence—Martin always questioning and ridiculing her motives about everything she said and did. It was the realization that if she continued to stay with Martin, she would lose all of her own identity and self-respect—what little was left. That, and knowing that if Martin physically hurt her one more time, she would kill him.

When Gale jokingly mentioned the tomahawk, it spun her back once again into those buried memories—the image of a knife—the feel of the smooth wooden handle and the long, cold shining blade. Martin laughing. The fear that she wouldn't be able to use it to defend herself, or worse, the fear that she would.

* * *

"Just remember. This is our tournament. We are champions, and we are going to play that game tomorrow night like champions. Nothing is going to stop us from winning. And if I hear anyone on the team say otherwise, he'll be sent back to Raleigh on the first available flight. We aren't going to quit yet; it's too soon. Do I make myself clear?"

Neal had been talking to his players for the past hour. Stilt had gotten sick and wouldn't be able to play. That was all he said. It would be up to them to make up Stilt's absence on the basketball court, and he knew without any doubt whatsoever that they could do it, he told them.

He had arranged for his players to practice in the coliseum first thing that morning and again later on in the afternoon. He looked at his watch. They still had two and a half hours of court time before Houston was scheduled for practice. "All right, let's get out on the court, and I want to see some sweat."

Dejectedly the players moved toward the basket at the far end of the court, talking among themselves. Neal had decided to alternate between two players—Allen Chapman and Ron Mashburn—in the center position. Chapman, or Chappy as he was called, was a freshman and inexperienced. Mashburn was a transfer student from a junior college and also inexperienced. But both of them were big and strong. And that's what Neal needed—strength in the center post. "I said I want to see some sweat," yelled Neal. A couple of the assistants began running the players through their warm-up drills. "What do you think?" Neal asked Stu. "Did I sound convincing?"

"You convinced me," said Stu. "In fact, I am so convinced we're going to win this Championship, I'm ready to go in and play center for you."

Neal watched his players move listlessly up and down the court. He would talk to them after practice and again this afternoon. Somehow he would have to make them believe that they could win. After all, they had the talent. They had already proved that. But they needed to believe, or all the talent in the world wouldn't get them a win.

A loose ball came bouncing toward Neal. "Derrick, what in the hell do you think you're doing? The idea is to catch the ball and pass it to either Sydney or Jerry. You don't turn your back on the ball. You think you can remember that? Because if you can't, I'm sure I can find someone who can." Neal was being deliberately hard on his players. But he needed to do something to shake them out of their lethargy, even if it meant getting them angry at him. "Miller, I've seen little old ladies out hustle their blind, three-legged dogs better than you're out hustling Chappy. Now get with it."

Miller muttered something under his breath and glared at Neal.

"Take the bench, Miller. Mash! Replace Miller."

One of the trainers tossed Miller a towel, even though he didn't need it. Miller grabbed it and stalked off to the sideline.

"Does anyone else have a problem?" said Neal.

No one answered.

"Then let me see some action."

For the next two and a half hours Neal drove his players. He ridiculed them and belittled them to the point where he knew they were ready to fight him. Then he praised them only to start tearing them down again. After five minutes on the bench, he had let Miller back on the court, and immediately the pace picked up. If Neal's instincts were right, and they usually were, Miller would be the one to lead the team in the final game. He had the nerves of steel. That was why the other players called him "Steel Man." If he could get Miller to believe, the rest of the team would follow.

* * *

Marla stripped off her red leather skirt and jacket and white sweater and pulled the soft doeskin dress over her head. Then she hooked the silver and turquoise belt around her waist.

41

"O.K. I'm ready to come out now. How about you?" Marla could hear Gale grunting from the dressing room next to hers.

"I swear. It's a good thing this tournament is almost over. Many more meals on the road and I'll never get back down to my normal size."

Marla giggled. Gale was determined that they were going to have a good time and had insisted that they try on some hand-sewn Indian clothes in one of the small boutiques before having lunch. "We still need to buy something to take home with us as a reminder of Albuquerque. Besides, trying on clothes is the best thing in the world for getting our minds off ass holes like Charlie Morgan," she said.

She was right. Marla had almost forgotten about Charlie Morgan. Almost. She came out of her dressing room and stood in front of the full-length mirror. Gale vocalized a little bump and grind music and sashayed up beside her wearing a fringed, tan leather pair of pants and matching jacket. In spite of what Gale said about gaining weight, the outfit hung loosely on her. The two women stared at themselves in the mirror not saying anything. Just then Marla saw the reflection of a man pass behind her causing her to jump with fright. She quickly turned around, but no one was there.

"Hey, Marla. Are you all right? I mean we don't look that bad." Gale held Marla by the arm and gazed back into the mirror. "Or do we?"

"It's these red high heels," said Marla after a while. "I don't think they really add anything to the Native American look. Do you?" She smiled at Gale in an attempt to force the image she had just seen out of her mind. But it had looked so much like her ex-husband. "You, on the other hand, can carry it off," she said lightly. "That fringed leather looks great on you." Marla took a deep breath trying to steady the panic she felt.

Gale made a face in the mirror obviously not convinced. "I don't think so." She finally settled on a Western hat and Marla bought the silver and turquoise belt. Once outside they wandered around Old Town Square until they found the restaurant that had been recommended to Gale by the hotel desk clerk. It was a large, stucco adobe-style building, beautifully landscaped with cactus plants and other desert flowers. Apparently the hotel desk clerk had recommended it to everyone else who was staying at the hotel as well. It was full of Seawolf fans.

They were eventually seated and given menus as large as coffee table books and just as heavy. "I think I'm hungry for chicken salad and maybe a bowl of hot soup," said Marla flipping through the menu. "And a nice glass of wine." Now that they were surrounded by a lot of people, she felt better. It had just been her imagination. That's all. Martin wouldn't have had any reason to be in Albuquerque. He had never been interested in sports of any kind.

"That sounds good," said Gale looking over the top of her menu, and then she nudged Marla. "Oh oh," she said under her breath. "Don't look now."

"Well, hello, Marla. Where have you been hiding?" It was Anne Morgan, Charlie's wife. Several women Marla recognized as wives of employees in the athletics department were with her.

"Hello, Anne." Marla waited for her to speak to Gale, but when she didn't, "You know Gale Simmons, I believe?" she asked. Anne glanced at Gale without saying anything and then back at Marla. "I'm afraid you let us down, Marla." The waiter, probably a college student working part-time, came up to the table to take their order, and Gale disappeared behind her menu. Anne continued to ignore Gale as well as the young man as he began rattling off a memorized list of daily luncheon specials while impatiently drumming his pencil against the order pad.

"Salmon croquettes cooked Cajun style on a bed of black beans and yellow rice . . ."

"How did I let you down, Anne?" Marla asked.

"Coach didn't come to the party last night in our suite. All of the major contributors were there." Marla watched Anne's nostrils flare when she said the word "major."

"There is also blackened tuna with creamed spinach wrapped in filo dough, fried chicken gizzards in a special garlic . . ."

"Everyone was expecting to see Coach there. Charlie was especially disappointed, and quite frankly, it put me in a rather awkward position. I mean, anyone else would have felt privileged to even be invited." Anne seemed totally unconcerned that she was interrupting anything or that several people sitting nearby were listening.

"Yes. I'm sure it was a lot of fun." Marla noticed that Anne didn't mention the fact that she hadn't gone either. Marla had always detested parties of any kind, but especially ones that were simply an excuse for people to get drunk together. Fortunately, Neal felt the same way. The thing at Morgan's suite had been nothing more than a gathering of wealthy Seawolfers who had paid, mostly through large contributions, for the privilege of getting drunk with the athletics director. *Some privilege*, Marla thought.

"Or for a lighter fare we are offering a delicious lobster bisque cooked in a creamy golden sherry or homemade vegetable soup . . ."

"Look, do you mind?" Anne glared at the waiter. "We are trying to carry on a conversation here."

"Now is that a golden sherry or a red sherry?" interrupted Gale as though she hadn't heard Anne's rude remark to the waiter. She surfaced from behind the menu smiling and fluffed her short, gray hair with a flip of her fingers.

The waiter looked at Gale appreciatively. "It's a delicious golden sherry. Or if you are hungry for pasta, there is a wonderful veal marsala in a light tomato sauce," the waiter continued enthusiastically, ignoring Anne's hostile glare. "And we also have chili, if you'd like something hot and spicy."

Anne turned her back to the waiter and continued talking to Marla. "You really ought to do something about socializing that husband of yours," she said somewhat acidly. "After all, you are the coach's wife now and you should act like it. You need to make sure he attends these important functions since it is the Seawolfers who support the program."

Marla looked at Anne in disbelief. If it weren't for the fact that Anne was practically in tears with anger, she would have passed the entire conversation off as some sort of tasteless joke. "I'm sorry, Anne, but I don't tell my husband what he has to do or where he has to go."

Gale closed the gigantic menu. "He does have other things on his mind right now other than carrying on small talk with a bunch of drunk fans. There is, after all, the National Championship to think about. "I'm sure even you and Charlie can understand that. Certainly, as the lowly wife of a lowly assistant coach, I do." Gale looked up at the waiter and winked. "I mean, that is the reason why we are all here now, isn't it?"

The waiter who had finally finished his recitation took the menu from Gale and smiled. "Go Seawolfers!" he said in open admiration of Gale.

Anne continued to ignore Gale and the waiter. The other women with her all seemed to find something fascinating to stare at in the vicinity of their feet. "Yes, of course. Well, we'll see you tomorrow evening at The Pit." The Pit, formally named Dreamstyle Arena, was the University of New Mexico's adobe arena where the NCAA Championship games were being played. "By the way, Charlie and I will be hosting another little get-together, hopefully a celebration of our win, in our suite following the Championship game. I expect to see you and Coach there."

"I expect to see you and Coach there," Gale said mockingly after Anne and her entourage left.

"What in the world do you suppose brought that on," asked Marla. "I haven't done anything to that woman that I know of."

"It isn't you, Marla. It's because she's married to that bastard. It makes her mean and ugly. The only women she can get to hang around with her are wives of some of the staff who work for Charlie, and that's because they are afraid if they don't do things with her when she calls them, their husbands will lose their jobs. I should have told her she needs to do something about castrating that horny husband of hers instead of worrying about whether Coach attends her stupid parties or not. Can you imagine the nerve of some people?" Gale smiled at the young man who was still waiting to take their order. "Bring my friend and me two glasses of Merlot, your chicken salad plate, lobster bisque, and that pumpkin bread that's baked in a clay flower pot you are so famous for. Is that all right with you, Marla? All of a sudden I feel hungry."

Gale didn't eat much of her lunch. Mostly she picked at the bread, and that was because it was such a novelty. "I'm just getting a head start on the diet I know I'll have to go on when we get home," she said when Marla asked her about it. Marla didn't eat much either, partly because of being nervous about the upcoming game between State and Houston, and partly because the sense of danger she had been feeling seemed closer than ever. It made her jittery. Like thinking she had seen Martin standing behind her in the dress shop. It had just been some man walking past the window outside the shop. That's all. And his image had somehow been reflected in the mirror. She tried to shrug it off, blaming it on the unpleasant encounter first with Morgan and then with his wife, as well as her over-active imagination. But just like before, she knew it was more than that, and it frightened her.

When they got back to the hotel, it seemed like every Seawolfer who had made it to Albuquerque was in the lobby. And they were all talking about the same thing—the Piedmont State basketball team had lost its center. Marla saw Neal off in one corner answering questions from several reporters. She pulled Gale over closer to where they could hear.

"So just how important is winning the NCAA National Championship, Coach?" a reporter asked.

"I would be lying if I said it's just another game," Neal answered. "The truth is, winning the NCAA Division 1 Basketball Championship has been my dream ever since I got my first coaching job thirty-five years ago. I was at Elsworth College then, a small, no-count school in up-state New York, fifty miles from where I was born. In three years I was able to build the Elsworth basketball program to its first winning season. When I did, I immediately accepted an offer to coach at a larger school, also with a losing record, and also in New York." The reporters had all heard the story before, but they never got tired of it.

"Wasn't it easier back then, Coach, being that they were smaller schools and not so many NCAA rules to worry about?" another reporter asked.

"Not at all. It was tremendously difficult. Recruiting was impossible with a next to non-existent budget. And no one wanted to play on a losing team—no one who was any good. The players who were already there had such a poor attitude, I could barely get them down the floor in a practice game let alone in a game on their schedule."

Marla glanced around at the reporters. They were eating it up. They knew they could trust Neal to be up front with them. Many of them had been following the team ever since Neal was first named head coach at State. And besides that, everything he told them made good copy.

"So what did you do?" the same reporter asked.

"I signed up Rick Lacomb. I'm sure most of you have heard of him. He was a six-foot-seven-inch guard out of Bunting, Georgia. He had been named All American, was MVP of the prestigious McDonald's High School All-Star Game, and was rated among the top ten prospects in the nation. Rick had such an uncanny shooting eye that he was being recruited by Duke, Carolina, Houston, and Kentucky—all basketball powerhouses." Neal looked around at the reporters and smiled. "But he signed with me. Lacomb was just the first of several after that, and eventually I was able to turn a losing program around to a 20 - 9 record. It also got us an invitation to the NCAA's, the school's first in twenty-five years. We didn't win the Championship title, but at least we got to play in the NCAAs. After that was when Piedmont State offered me a job to head up the Seawolves, and you know the rest of the story."

One reporter who hadn't said anything spoke up. "You said that you sent Stilt back to Raleigh because of illness. Isn't it true that he isn't sick at all, but that he failed the drug test required by the NCAA, and that's why he's not playing in the game tomorrow night?"

The hotel lobby suddenly got quiet. Everyone had heard the rumors, but no one had dared to ask Coach. "Oh, no," Marla whispered squeezing Gale's hand.

Neal looked directly at the reporter. "I can honestly say that Stilt has passed every drug test he has been given." Neal paused and looked around at the other reporters. "He was caught violating the drug rule, however, which, as you know, goes against the NCAA zero tolerance policy as well as my own. It was my decision to suspend him from the team and send him back to Raleigh where he could receive medical treatment. Does that answer your question?" Neal asked, looking back at the reporter.

Embarrassed, the reporter looked down at his empty notepad. He had asked what he wanted to ask. Now he could report back to whatever rag sheet he worked for.

"Last question, guys. I have had a full day today and expect to have another one tomorrow in order to get ready for the game." Neal glanced around the room. He was angry. His team was demoralized enough knowing that Stilt wouldn't be playing in the game. But when they found out it was because Stilt was caught using drugs, it would make it even worse. Someone had somehow found out about it and passed the information on to that half-assed reporter. Neal wanted to know who.

"Do you really think there is any chance that you can win the game against Houston without Stilt?" someone asked from the back.

Neal clenched his fists and started to walk away without answering the question. Then he stopped. "At the other schools where I coached I managed to build winning programs. At State, not only have I managed to build a winning program that has put us in the NCAAs every year, twelve times in the Sweet Sixteen and ten times in the Final Eight, this year we have a chance to go all the way. I didn't come this far to lose it all now. So why don't you just stick around until tomorrow night and find out."

After the group of reporters broke up, Neal took Stu aside. "I want you to find out who that reporter was who knew about Stilt and where he works. And I want to know where he got his information."

"You got it," said Stu.

Gale looked at Marla and let out a deep, shaky breath. "It's going to be a long night."

Chapter Four

"Whoa, check this one out." Lydia Rob tossed an eight-by-ten glossy in full color out onto the table. It was a photograph of a woman, possibly in her late twenties or early thirties, blond, shapely, and wearing nothing but a tan line, a red hair ribbon and red stiletto heeled shoes. "The note with it says, 'whenever you're in Miami, Neal, look me up'. Then she gives her address and phone number. Her name is Candy." The women sitting around the large table laughed. A makeshift workroom had been set up in one of the hotel's smaller meeting rooms for staff members of the Piedmont State Athletics Department. They were answering the hundreds of congratulatory letters and telegrams that had already started coming in to Coach Connors and his team on having made it to the Finals. Marla and Gale and some of the other hall walkers were also helping. With the Championship game being played that night, everyone was feeling nervous. Sorting through the mail at least kept them occupied.

So far, they had answered about two hundred or so letters and they hadn't even put a dent in the ones that were still unopened. Another pile of letters like the one Lydia read, along with an assortment of photographs, most of them of women in various stages of undress, several condoms, and one pair of red thong panties that had been sent to Coach by female admirers, filled a trash container placed near the table.

"Get a load of this one," a secretary from the basketball office said giggling. She raised her eyebrows and held up a snapshot of a woman, this one tremendously overweight, wearing a flowered bikini, lounging on a wicker chaise. It was a selfie taken with a smart phone. "On the back it says, 'I can give you as much as you want, Coach'. From the looks of her, I would say she has enough for Coach and everyone else on the basketball team—maybe even both teams." All of the women laughed but Marla. She knew that Neal had a lot of fans, especially women. He was so well known, and being attractive along with it, women were always flirting with him. She thought she had gotten used to it. But this was too much. She hadn't realized how crude and aggressive the women could be. She didn't doubt that Neal loved her and no one else, but she couldn't help feeling a little jealous and insecure.

Marla tried to smile when she noticed Gale looking at her. But she felt like her insides were twisted in a knot. She excused herself and went to find the ladies room. Once there, she began to cry.

"I should have warned you," said Gale following her into one of the stalls. She yanked off some toilet paper from the dispenser on the wall and handed it to Marla.

"Warned me about what?" Marla sniffed and blotted her eyes with the paper. She felt embarrassed and petty for even letting something like those ridiculous letters bother her.

"About those hussies who like to write letters. They see your husband on television or read about him in the paper and they get a wide-on. All of a sudden they become brazen, men-crazed barracuda. It might make you feel better to know that Neal isn't the only coach who gets this kind of attention. Even Stu has gotten his share of it and, god knows, he isn't even good looking. I mean, let's face it, I love him dearly, but he is no Greek god."

"Has it ever bothered you? These women, I mean?"

"Only one time. It was the year before Neal was named head coach. We had just won the second round in the ACC Tournament, and Tom Nelson who was head coach then had already announced his retirement. So Stu was doing all of the post-game interviews. The letters I could pretty much laugh off, but this one bitch started calling him at home."

"My gosh. Didn't she know Stu was married?"

"Oh, yes. But that didn't stop her. She always had some half-assed reason to call—usually about tickets or location of seats or the game schedule—something like that. And then I started noticing that every time I stopped by the Athletics Department, there was a young coed there, sitting in a chair just outside Stu's office."

"Was she the same person who was calling him at home?"

"The same. She usually had on one of those cropped tee-shirts, the kind that shows your midriff? And a mini skirt. And she had this long, black wavy hair. You see how I look now. Well, even back then my hair was short and gray. Sometimes I think I was born with short, gray hair."

"What was she doing there?"

"The best I could tell, she would talk to the secretaries, trying to find out things about Stu, like his favorite color, his favorite food, stuff like that, and just wait around for him to pop in or out of his office so she could get a look at him."

"What did you do?"

"One day Stu called me and asked me to come by the office so we could go out to lunch together. When I got there she was sitting in the chair outside Stu's office wearing her damned tee-shirt and mini skirt with her legs crossed. And, of course, that head of hair. And I suddenly noticed she didn't have any underpants on."

"Oh, my gosh."

"I know. I really think it was that long, black hair that pushed me over the edge rather than seeing her with no underwear on, though. I was so fucking jealous I grabbed a handful of her hair and yanked her out the basketball office and out of the building. I told her that she was spreading germs all over the department with her cunt, and if she didn't start behaving, I would tell her parents. And if she didn't have parents, she would have to deal with me."

Marla started laughing. "I can just see you now," she said.

"I know," said Gale laughing with her. "I must have really looked like a wild woman. That's not the best part, though. Later on at home I asked Stu if he had been messing around with her. I mean, after all. What man wouldn't be flattered to have some young pussy going after him. I thought our marriage was strong, but who really knows. And you know what? He didn't even know who I was talking about. That's Stu for you; he is so focused on basketball. Apparently he never even noticed her."

Marla leaned back against the sink. "Oh, Gale. I don't know if I am cut out for all of this."

"Of course you are. Remember, I have had a few more years dealing with all of this shit than you have. You just have to keep your sense of humor about everything. Believe me, Neal doesn't see anyone but you. He adores you. Surely you know that."

"Yes, I do." Marla smiled and hugged Gale. Thanks, friend." Marla fixed her makeup and washed her hands. "By the way, whatever happened to that coed? Did she leave Stu alone after that?"

"She as sure the hell did. The last I heard, she was in Oregon somewhere practicing medicine—gynecology. Can you believe it?"

When Marla and Gale returned to the room, Marla noticed that the trash can with all of the graphic letters and other junk had been emptied.

"We considered having a contest," said one of the secretaries when Marla asked about it. "Like the most crude, the ugliest, the most unbelievable proposition—you know, that kind of thing. But then we decided there was enough excitement surrounding this tournament. Besides, it probably would have gotten leaked to the press, and that wouldn't be too good for State's image."

"Thanks, ladies," said Marla.

Gale left around three, saying she wanted to go to her room and take a nap. Marla and the rest of the women finally quit working a little before five o'clock. It had been a long day for them, and they still had to eat and get ready to go to the game.

"You want to join us, Marla?" Lydia was headed for the hotel restaurant with several other hall walkers to get an early supper.

"Thanks all the same. I think I'll just order something from room service. I'll meet you down in the lobby at seven." That was when the buses were scheduled to leave for the coliseum.

Marla checked by the front desk to see if Neal had left any messages. He hadn't. Several of the basketball players were roaming around the lobby, though, so that meant they were back from their afternoon practice.

"There you are, Marla. I've been looking for you." Doc put his arm through Marla's and walked with her toward the private elevator. "I've just given Neal an antibiotic and sent him to bed," he said lowering his voice.

Marla stopped and turned toward Doc. "What's wrong with him?"

"It looks like the flu. He has a temperature of 103. No telling how long he's had it. You know Neal. He just keeps pushing and he won't tell anyone when he's feeling bad. He's a sick man, Marla. I don't mind telling you, I am worried about him."

Marla hurried toward the elevator.

"He needs to stay in bed and not even go to the game tonight, but he's going to do whatever he wants no matter what I say. See if you can convince him to stay in bed, Marla, at least until it's time for him to go to the coliseum. And make sure he takes the rest of the medicine I left with him, too."

Marla nodded and got on the elevator. She couldn't tell Neal not to coach the most important game in his career, no matter how sick he was. He had to make that decision. All she could do was to be there for him and support his decision. Neal had been so sure that this was his year to win the National Championship. But with so much going wrong—she couldn't help wondering if there was a connection between the fear she had and what was happening to the team. The elevator came to a stop and the doors quietly opened. Maybe Gale was right. Maybe what she was feeling came from the stress of the basketball games and knowing how much Neal wanted to win the tournament.

Marla hurried down the corridor to the suite and unlocked the door. The curtains had been drawn closed so that the bedroom was semi-dark. She could hear Neal breathing and he was turned on his side. The medication Doc had given him must have put him to sleep. Quietly Marla took off her clothes and slipped under the sheet next to Neal. His body felt hot and dry. She pulled the blanket up around his shoulders and positioned her own naked body next to his.

"Marla, make sure I get up no later than 6:30."

"I will, my darling." So he had made his decision. No matter how sick he was, he would coach his team in the final game of the NCAA National Championship.

"I love you."

"I love you too." For the next hour and a half Marla lay next to Neal, watching him sleep, watching the clock, and willing him to miraculously get well.

* * *

"Did you see that article in today's *Washington Post*?" Lydia Rob was sitting directly behind Marla. All of the hall walkers had seats near one another in the stands. It didn't keep the Houston fans from harassing them, but it helped for all of them to be near one another. Marla noticed that Anne Morgan was sitting in the same row as Marla but across the aisle.

Houston had outmuscled Purdue in an explosive offensive display in the other semifinal game. That win gave Houston their twenty-sixth straight victory and an unchallenged number one rank. No one gave Piedmont State a chance. All of the experts had said from the beginning that if State did make it to the Finals, no matter who it was against, it would be a mismatch. Now with State's center gone, it would be a rout. The mismatch story line and the loss of Stilt provided a great opportunity for the sports writers to unleash their wit. Nothing, however, had been mentioned about Stilt getting caught using drugs. Apparently Neal's answer had satisfied the reporters—for now, at least.

"It said elephants would tap dance before State would win, and that State was going to its execution."

Marla turned around and looked at Lydia. "Ever hear of the twelfth-hour reprieve?"

"Yea."

"Well, that's what we're going to get."

"And if elephants can balance on those large rubber balls, they can tap dance," someone sitting next to Lydia said.

The other women agreed, but no one really believed it.

The Houston basketball team ran out onto the court and began warming up. It sounded like an explosion in the coliseum as the enthusiastic Houston fans erupted in loud cheers and yells. Gale nervously glanced at the clock.

After a few minutes Lydia tapped Gale on the shoulder. "Gale?" She sounded worried.

"I know," Gale said staring in the direction of the men's locker rooms.

"What is it," asked Marla.

"Our guys aren't on the court yet. They should already be warming up." After ten minutes, she leaned over to Marla. "Something is wrong. Our team should be on the court warming up. I'm going to see what I can find out."

"I'll go with you," said Marla.

The two women left their seats and started making their way around the inside perimeter of the coliseum toward the teams' locker rooms. When they got there, several basketball officials, two highway patrolmen, and a representative of the NCAA were talking in the hallway. Marla recognized Doug Stone from the NCAA office. She introduced him to Gale.

"Piedmont State's team bus hasn't gotten here yet, Marla." Doug explained. "We've got people out looking for it now."

"What do you mean it's not here yet?" asked Gale. "It left the hotel right before our bus did. It was in front of us, wasn't it, Marla? And it had an escort—the highway patrol!"

Marla nodded her head. "The team bus left a few minutes before our bus, around seven o'clock," she said. "The buses bringing the fans were scheduled to leave the hotel a half hour later." She couldn't believe this was happening. How could a bus disappear?

One of the highway patrolmen spoke up. "Even though the roads have been scraped, they have a tendency to freeze up once the sun goes down. With that snow we had last night, there's a possibility the bus is stranded somewhere—or it might have skidded off the highway."

Marla felt dizzy and put her hands up to her face. She hadn't been concerned when they arrived at the coliseum that she didn't see the other bus since the team bus always parked in a different area.

"Did anyone question our driver?" Marla asked. "He might have noticed something."

"Look, I don't think we have anything to worry about," one of the other men said. "It isn't that far from the hotel to the coliseum, and it's a pretty direct route. If the bus did happen to go off the road, it will be found."

"What about the game?" It was the station manager from one of the television networks. He looked at his watch. "It's scheduled to start in eight minutes. Even if they arrive in the next two or three minutes, the players still have to warm up, and that will delay the game by at least fifteen minutes. That's going to mess up television air time."

"I think television air time is the least of our worries," said Gale angrily. "Here we are talking about the possibility of an entire basketball team and its coaching staff being involved in an accident, maybe someone being killed, and you are worried about TV air time?"

Doug put his arm around Gale. "Gale is right. Let's take one thing at a time, and the first thing is to find that bus."

Just then another highway patrolman came rushing toward them. Melting snow dripped from his uniform. "We found them," he said. "About a mile from here. The bus went into a ditch. Communications got jammed. Everyone is all right. Another bus had already gotten there when I left them, so they should be arriving in just a few minutes."

"Thank god," said Gale. She put her arms around Marla and held her. "Honey, this is one hell of an initiation for you into your first NCAA Tournament."

Marla searched through her purse until she found a piece of paper and pen. *I love you. Good luck*! she wrote.

"Would you please give this to my husband," she asked one of the officials. He took the note and disappeared into the men's locker room.

By the time the two women got back to their seats, the Seawolves were on the court going through their warm-up drills. Marla was so nervous, she couldn't sit down. Neal looked up at her in the stands and waved. He had her note in his hand. He was all right.

"O.K. So he's all right," said Gale watching Neal walk over to talk to the officials at the scorer's table. "And Stu has that constipated look he always gets just before a big game, so he's all right."

An announcement was made explaining the reason for the delay of the game, and once again the coliseum shook from the fans cheering. The game clock was reset. At the end of fifteen minutes, the introduction of the two teams and head coaches was made. Chapman from the Seawolf team went to center court to match up with Houston's tall center. Houston got possession of the tip-off and immediately began their dominating offense. For the next fifteen minutes, they maintained complete control over the ball and the game.

"Well, the first half could have gone a lot worse," said Gale. "No one on the team broke his leg." None of the other women said anything. State was down by twelve points. Everyone had predicted that Coach Connors would hold the ball—delay the game in order to run down the clock—since, with Stilt out, he couldn't run his usual plays. But he had surprised everyone by running the ball and substituting often. All things considered, they were lucky to be down by just twelve points when the buzzer sounded ending the first half. And if Coach was feeling bad, he didn't show it.

"Come on, girls," said Gale, getting slowly up from her seat. "We might as well go get something to eat."

Refreshments were set up on tables at each end of the private dining room. The hospitality room as it was called was sponsored by the host school and was available only to NCAA dignitaries, administrators from the schools who had made it to the Final Four, and , of course, the wives and girlfriends of the coaches and players. Even here the women huddled together, not wanting to separate for fear it might bring bad luck to their Team of Destiny, as if their luck could get any worse.

"There is something about that guy that I just don't like," said Lydia as she jammed a cracker smothered in smoked fish into her mouth. She was looking at Charlie Morgan.

Marla sipped a glass of Chardonnay. She was too nervous to eat anything. She glanced at Morgan and then took another sip of wine.

"You and everyone else who knows him. Even his wife acts as though she doesn't like him," said Gale in her usual outspoken manner. She absent-mindedly stirred the few peanuts she had put on her plate with her finger.

"As far as that goes, I don't especially like her, either." Lydia put another cracker in her mouth, this one covered with pimento cheese. "Look at him," she whispered looking back at Morgan, "acting like he had something to do with the team making it to the Finals. What a jerk."

Charlie Morgan was working the room like a glad-handing politician. With his wife, Anne, lagging along behind him, he was laughing and joking his way around the room as though he were the star attraction at a circus performance for kids. And maybe he was. After all, to most people from outside the Athletics Department, or in his case, who simply didn't know any better, the NCAA Basketball Championships were just that—a performance. They had little or no understanding of the emotional and physical price that had been paid to reach this point, or what it would mean to the winning school and its basketball program.

When Marla noticed Morgan start to walk toward her, she grabbed Gale's hand. "Let's get out of here."

"I'm right behind you." The rest of the hall walkers quickly followed.

The women returned to their seats in the coliseum and listened to Piedmont State's band play the Fight Song and the fans cheer the Sea-wolf team when it came back out on court to warm up for the second half of the game. In a few minutes the buzzer sounded, and the players took their positions.

"Please, sweet Jesus," Marla heard someone behind her say. She took a deep breath and smiled at Gale for encouragement.

Going up at midcourt Piedmont State's Allen Chapman against Houston's Clyde Wood. Both teams in red and white. And the tap is going to the Seawolves. Chappy shoots from the corner. He misses, and the rebound is grabbed off by Barton of Houston.

Marla dug her fingernails into the palms of her hands as she watched the Seawolves struggle without success to make up the twelve-point deficit. It was hot in the arena, and the players were perspiring heavily. Neal was substituting often in order to give them water, but the heat was wearing them down, and the Cougars managed to outscore the Seawolves 17 - 2 at the opening of the second half.

Marla watched her husband leap from his chair over and over again yelling instructions, pumping his players, trying to give them hope. Doc stayed near him. The Houston Cougars continued to pound past State with their driving dunks. Their seven-foot-four-inch Nigerian sophomore center was killing Neal's team. He was super quick for such a big player, and he was tough in the middle of the court.

With a twenty-two point lead and six minutes left on the clock, Houston went into a stall. Neal countered by having his players delib-erately foul. When the Houston players kept missing the free throws, State slowly began to come back. With two minutes, fifteen seconds left, State had miraculously made up all but four points. The score was Houston 52, State 48.

Houston's freshman point guard went to the free-throw line and missed. State got the ball and, with two minutes left in the game, called time out.

"You want to leave now, Marla?"

All of the other wives had already gone out to the hall. Only Gale and Marla were left in the reserved seats.

"I think I'd like to ride this one out, Gale. You go ahead and join the others if you want."

"I think I'll stay, too. After all, I might not ever get this close to a National Championship again."

Marla watched Neal frantically scribble on his pad. He looked flushed, and Doc handed him a damp towel to wipe his face with. The players were breathing hard, many of them bent over and pulling on the elastic waists of their shorts to make it easier for them to fill their lungs with air. Sweat poured from their bodies leaving small puddles of water on the floor around them.

The buzzer sounded but the fans were yelling so loud no one could hear it on State's bench. The Seawolf team had ten seconds to get back on court or they would lose possession of the ball. One of the officials was counting off the seconds.

"Son of a bitch!" screamed Gale jumping out of her seat. "Coach didn't hear the buzzer. We're going to lose the goddamn ball!"

Just then one of the assistant trainers saw the clock and rushed over to tell Neal before the time ran out.

So this was it. The final two minutes. It had been six months of basketball. Starting on October 15, and the pre season practice before that. Six months of basketball all concluding in this one final game. There was the hand clasp, the high fives, and the Seawolves ran back out onto the court with only two seconds to spare.

Houston applied hard pressure. Mashburn, the junior college transfer, couldn't get the ball into Miller, State's best shooter, and wound up
lobbing it to the far corner under Houston's basket. Their center got
the ball, but before he could dunk it, Sidney Rob fouled him. Houston's
center went to the free-throw line and missed. State got the ball and,
with forty-five seconds left in the game, called their last time out.

"Oh, my god." Gale clutched Marla's hands. Once more they
watched the players surround their coach who was kneeling on the floor
with the ubiquitous yellow pad in his hands. Marla saw Doc lean down
and say something to Neal, but Neal shook his head and continued
scribbling and shouting instructions.

*So this is it, folks. With forty-five seconds left on the clock, the score
Houston 52, Piedmont State 48. The Seawolves have taken their last
time out.*

*The horn has sounded and both teams are back on the floor. State's
Bobby Holden substituting for Derrick White passes the ball in to Jerry
March. Jerry March comes down the court and passes off to Sydney
Rob. Rob passes it back to March who slams it home on three Houston
defenders. Houston 52, Piedmont State 50. Thirty seconds left to play.
Just hang on to your seats, sports fans. As a great philosopher once
said, it ain't over 'till the fat lady sings.'*

Unable to move or speak, Marla and Gale watched Houston pass
the ball in and down the court toward their basket. The noise from the
screaming fans was absolutely deafening.

*Houston's Franklin into the front court with a jumper, misses,
grabbed by Sydney Rob and he's fouled. That's four fouls on Rob and
Houston will be on the free-throw line. Franklin on the line, tosses up
the ball, and he misses. Bobby Holden of the Seawolves comes down
with the ball. With fifteen seconds to go, Holden throws the ball down
court to Miller. Miller goes to the corner, tries a popper and it's*

blocked. Holden gets the rebound. Eight seconds. Holden fires the ball into the middle to Sydney Rob out above the top of the key. Rob lets it fly from thirty feet, but it's short. Miller picks it off near the basket and dunks it home. And he's fouled. The score is tied 52 all with two seconds left on the clock. And Piedmont State's Miller will go to the line.

Gale let go of Marla's hands and ripped through her purse until she found the bottle of valium. "You want one?"

Marla shook her head. Gale dumped two out into the palm of her hand, pushed them into her mouth, and swallowed. Then she grabbed Marla's hands again. Both teams lined up around the free-throw line.

Miller has two shots. He throws up the first. It hits the back of the rim and bounces out.

Gale bent over and put her head between her knees, unable to watch. Marla wrapped her arms around her.

Miller bounces the ball, two, three, four times, takes a deep breath, and throws up the ball. And it's good! Piedmont State 53, Houston 52. Two seconds left on the clock.

Franklin of Houston takes the ball out of bounds. Rob and Miller trying to block the inbounds pass. Franklin lobs it the length of the court. The clock doesn't start until the ball is touched by another player. Houston's Roy Cox catches the ball, bounces it, and sky hooks it toward the basket. Two seconds, one. It is no good! And there's no time left! The Piedmont Seawolves have done it! The Cinderella team has won! The glass slipper fits! The Team of Destiny has just won the NCAA National Championship!

Gale and Marla jumped up and down, laughing and hugging each other. The other wives came rushing into the stands from the hall crying and screaming. It was absolute bedlam on the basketball court. People poured out of the stands and onto the court wanting to touch the players, the coaches, each other. Marla looked for Neal. With so much confusion she couldn't see him. And then he was there, standing next to her, holding her.

The sight in The Pit is unbelievable, sports fans. Sydney Rob and Jerry March have started cutting down the net. Delaney Miller, Bobby Holden and the rest of the Seawolf team are running around the court hugging everyone. Assistant Coach Stuart Simmons is jumping up and down with Assistant Coach Kevin Burns. The Piedmont State team doctor is dancing with the trainers. And Head Coach Neal Connors is in the stands kissing his wife.

* * *

"So, Coach. How do you like Albuquerque?" It was the first question asked at the press conference following the game. Neal and his five starters, actually six since Mash and Chappy had shared the center position, were sitting at the podium. All of them had big grins on their faces except for Miller who showed no emotion. He was still being the "Steel Man." Microphones, tape recorders, and other electronic devices cluttered the table in front of them. Neal heard the question but really couldn't think of a good answer. With the excitement of having just won the National Championship, his impatience to be with Marla, and the flu that was wrecking havoc inside his body, he couldn't concentrate. It was a dumb question besides.

"I think Albuquerque is the greatest city in the world," he managed to answer. If we hadn't just won the Championship, however, I might feel otherwise." The reporters laughed.

"When did you realize that you had this game sewed up?" Neal recognized the reporter. He was one of the old-timers who had followed the Seawolves for as long as Neal had been coach.

"When we won the ACC Tournament back in March." Everyone laughed, including the players. It wasn't the snappiest come-back, but it would have to do. Neal looked around the crowded room. The reporter who had asked him earlier back at the hotel about Stilt using drugs was standing in the back.

Another reporter from one of the local television stations stepped forward. "Do you mean there was never a time that you thought you weren't going to win the Championship?" A cameraman started filming.

"Never. It was just a matter of getting the players to think it, too."

"Now that you have won the National Championship, what is your next goal?" It was the reporter who had asked about Stilt.

"Get a good night's sleep, starting as soon as I get back home. Thank you, gentlemen." Neal and his players got up and headed for the showers. The press conference was over. As far as Neal was concerned, he had already said everything there was to say. Not only that, he had backed up his words with action.

"Were you able to find out anything about that reporter, Stu?"

Neal and Stu were the only ones left in the locker room. The basketball team had already showered and dressed and were loaded on the bus waiting to be taken to the airport. Coach didn't want them hanging around the hotel any longer than necessary, especially after winning the National Championship. It was too easy for them to get into trouble. There would be enough celebrating to do once they got back to Raleigh. The coaching staff was going back with them, as well as Neal and Marla. Stu and Gale would return the next day in order to give Stu a chance to close out the account at the hotel and settle any other problems, financial or otherwise, that might have cropped up. Stu and Gale would also attend the Athletic Director's party he and his wife were giving in their suite that night. Gale had told Marla she was planning to wear her new Western hat, the one she had just bought on their shopping trip in old town Albuquerque, just to give Anne something else to bitch about besides Coach not attending her stupid party.

"His name is Al Nance. The best I could find out, he's supposed to be a pretty good reporter, writes mostly about sports. He works part-time for the *Albuquerque Tribune*. He's a freelancer the rest of the time. He sells his stuff wherever he can get the biggest buck. And he's written a book, a history on the NCAA. When I asked him where he got his information on Stilt, he pulled that confidential source bull shit. For some reason, though, I had the feeling he really wanted to tell me but was afraid to."

"Why do you say that?"

"Well, you know how cocky these dumb-ass reporters can get sometimes. This guy was different. He seemed O.K. In fact, he was almost apologetic. He mentioned having a sick kid, like maybe he needed the money or something and that was why he was doing it."

Neal nodded. "Well, what's done is done. I guess it doesn't matter now."

"There was one strange thing about my conversation with him," said Stu. "After he told me he couldn't reveal his source, he suddenly asked me, sort of out of the blue, how well you knew the Athletics Director."

"Morgan?"

"Yea. It just seemed a little strange, that's all. Totally unrelated to what we had been talking about."

Neal thought for a moment. "Morgan probably pissed him off in an interview or something, just like he does everyone else."

"Yea, maybe."

"Well, I'm going to collect Marla, she's waiting for me in the hospitality room, and head for home. I don't know about you, but I'm ready to spend some relaxed, quality time with my honey." Neal didn't want to think about Morgan now. He just wanted to think about Marla and celebrate with her the most exciting win of his coaching career, even if it meant celebrating it in bed with the flu.

Neal put his arm around Stu's shoulders, and the two men headed out the door.

* * *

"Listen up, guys." The plane was about five minutes out of Raleigh-Durham. Overall it had been a quiet flight. Neal, with a temperature still climbing, had slept most of the way. Even the players had been subdued. Whether it was the shock of winning or just simply fatigue, it didn't really matter at this point. They would soon be back in Raleigh and hopefully life would return to normal. "There might be a few fans waiting to greet us at the airport. I want you to behave like gentlemen. Be courteous. Show a little class. But get your asses loaded on the bus as quickly as possible so we can get back to the campus. Any questions?" Neal glanced around. No one said anything. Neal sat back down next to Marla and held her hand. "God, I'm tired. I can't wait to get home."

Marla leaned over and kissed him. "I know. As soon as we get home, you are going to bed." Neal looked at her and smiled. "And no fooling around either," she added. "I just want to take care of you and pamper you until you get well."

When Neal entered the terminal, there were so many people cheering and yelling, he thought there must be some kind of national emergency. But then he saw the red and white signs and banners welcoming the winning Seawolves back home. "My god," he said taking Marla's arm. He held on to her as he worked his way through the crowd of fans.

"Coach, I just heard there's going to be a pep rally at the Brick Yard when we get to the campus." It was one of the trainers. "Everyone is asking if you will be there."

"I thought there was supposed to be a pep rally tomorrow." Neal held on to Marla and managed to push his way through the doors exiting the terminal lobby. The team bus was parked just outside in a loading area.

"There's going to be one then, too. In the Coliseum. This one is for all the fans who are waiting on campus now. The streets have already been closed off—on campus as well as the city streets around campus." The trainer looked at Neal hopefully. "The fans will really be disappointed if you don't go."

Neal looked down at Marla. "I'll go along with anything you want to do," she said.

When everyone finally got loaded on the bus and they left the airport headed on the interstate toward the University, not even Neal was prepared for the welcome they got. Fans in their cars, trucks, and every other kind of transportation lined the interstate with their headlights on. The noise from honking horns could be heard from every direction for miles around. People stood on the side of the road waving to the team; many stood on the tops of their cars and vans. When the bus got to the campus, the Raleigh police escorted it by motorcycle to the Brick Yard, that brick-paved area on campus used for outdoor entertainment, lectures, or other student events. A huge bonfire was burning in the center of it, and thousands of cheering fans crowded around wanting to see the team that had given Piedmont State its first National Championship. Everywhere people were yelling, "How 'bout them Seawolves?"

"We couldn't have done it without you." Neal stood on a makeshift platform and spoke into the microphone. "It was your support and belief in us that enabled us to bring home the National Championship."

The fans went wild. Neal stepped down and handed the micro-phone to one of the cheerleaders. Then he steered Marla out of the crowd with the help of two police officers to a waiting patrol car that would take them to the Athletics Center where his car was parked. He needed to go home. When they found the car, Marla got into the driver's seat. Neal was simply too sick to drive. The two police offic-ers escorted them home.

Chapter Five

The Cottage, as Neal had unpretentiously named it, was an old abandoned Coast Guard station located on the east end of Portsmouth Island, just off the North Carolina coast from Morehead City. The island itself was inaccessible except by boat or small aircraft. There was a grass runway located one hundred yards or so behind the Cottage which the federal government continued to maintain. Other than the four families who still owned properties on the west end of the island that had been purchased under the original land grant laws by their ancestors, Portsmouth Island was deserted. With no telephones and no mail service, it was a place where one could truly be alone.

That was what Neal had loved about it. When he learned that the Coast Guard was going to dismantle the station, he made an offer to buy it. If it had been anyone else other than Neal, the offer wouldn't have even been considered. But being a high-profile winning coach of a major university tends to open doors that normally would be closed. There is always a wealthy supporter of the team willing to pull the necessary strings just so he can call the coach a personal friend and maybe pick up some choice tickets at tournament time. In this case it had been the Governor.

Neal got his cottage and spent whatever time he had during off-season or whenever he had a few days to himself fixing it up. It was where he took Marla the first time they went away together for a weekend. She was as enchanted with it as he was. No matter what problems were going on around them, the problems became virtually non-existent once they reached the island. The trouble was, since Marla and Neal had been married, they simply hadn't found much time to go there. That would change once Neal retired, of course. But until then they would have to settle for those rare occasions when Neal could leave the team, the basketball office, and the athletics department behind. The two weeks following the NCAA Basketball Championship was one of those occasions.

"It's a silver dawn." Marla leaned back into Neal's shoulder and body. They were standing on the wide veranda that wrapped around the Cottage, sipping coffee, listening to the wildlife of the island's marshlands awaken, and watching the sun slowly inch its way over the horizon.

"A silver dawn?" Neal asked in a teasing tone.

"Yes, as compared to the golden dusk." Marla sipped her coffee thoughtfully. "It isn't something that is easily defined. But you know it when you see it."

"Very interesting." Neal reached under the tee shirt Marla was wearing—his tee shirt—and tenderly caressed her left breast.

"It's when everything sparkles with a clearness and freshness in a light that is soft—and silver. Everything looks and smells and sounds new. It's beautiful."

"Then you are my silver morning."

They continued looking out over the island, absorbing the natural beauty around them. It had been a glorious eight days of uninterrupted freedom. The caretaker had everything ready for them the day they arrived. They ate when they felt like it. They listened to Marla's collection of classical music. They read books they didn't have time to read during the basketball season. On some days they explored the inland parts of the island, following trails left behind long ago, probably by the wild ponies that had once inhabited the island. Other days they walked along the miles of sandy white beach that encircled the island like a string of pearls.

Because it was off the track from the other larger islands that faced the mainland, Portsmouth Island held an untouched wealth of beautiful shells and sea vegetation that continuously washed up on its shore. Marla had a vast and varied collection of Scotch bonnets, conchs, moon snails, marsh periwinkles, and other gifts offered up by the sea which she displayed on every flat, horizontal surface she could find in the Cottage as well as outside. Marla and Neal talked, never running out of things to say to one another. And they made love, spontaneously and with complete abandon. Marla had never felt such complete happiness. Everything was perfect—except for one thing.

She hadn't told Neal yet about Charlie Morgan coming to their suite the morning of the Championship game. It wasn't that she was intentionally keeping it from Neal. There just never seemed to be the right time to tell him. He had been so ecstatic after winning the final game and his team being National Champions. She didn't want to darken that moment for him. Afterward, there had been all of the post-game celebrations to attend. When Neal was finally too sick to go on, he went to bed and stayed there for five days recovering from the flu. By the end of the fifth day, however, he was eager to go to the island, and she didn't have a chance, not with the packing and all of the arrangements that had to be made. Not really. And here on the island, it just seemed inappropriate to cloud the beauty and perfection which surrounded them by something so distasteful. She would tell him once they returned home. But until then, she would keep it to herself, cramming it back into that hidden dark corner of her mind whenever it tried to reveal itself.

Neal and Marla were so wrapped up in each other and the early-morning beauty surrounding them, they didn't hear the sound of the helicopter the first time it circled high above them. It was only when the tee shirt Marla was wearing started to flutter from the draft of the propeller blades that they noticed it even then.

Looking skyward, his hand shielding his eyes from the glaring sun, Neal saw the University helicopter with Piedmont State painted in bright red on the side. "Oh damn," was all he said.

"I'll get dressed," said Marla and she went inside to put on a pair of shorts and a halter top. Neal watched the helicopter land on the grassy runway behind the Cottage and then waited for whoever it was that felt it was so urgent to find him to emerge. It was Ray Knox, the ass-kissing assistant that Charlie Morgan had brought with him from the University of New Hampshire when he took the job as Athletics Director at State.

"Charlie wants to see you immediately. I'm to take you back with me."

There was no hello, no preliminary small talk. Just this five-foot-four-inch piece of shit trying to make himself heard over the deafening noise of the chopper.

"What does he want to see me about, Ray?" Neal made an effort not to punch Ray in the nose. Marla came back out, dressed, and slipped here arm through Neal's.

"There's a big problem and you need to get back now." Ray was enjoying the fact that he was disrupting the vacation plans of the Connors. It made him doubly pleased because he knew what the big problem was, and Neal was going to catch hell for it. Maybe even lose his job. He had always been too cocky anyway, all over a few wins in basketball.

Neal didn't like Ray's body language or his self-satisfied smirk. "I'll ask you one more time, Ray. What is it about?"

Marla felt Neal's muscles tighten in his arm. She didn't move.

Ray knew Neal's temper. He had seen it displayed on the basketball court enough times. He glanced nervously back at the chopper.

"There's a big scandal. All the papers are full of it. Pictures and everything. About how the team took drugs the night before the Championship game, and how you covered it up. There will probably be an NCAA investigation. Charlie has already talked to the Chancellor about it. It's in all the papers," he repeated as though that would give what he was saying more weight.

"My god." Neal glared at Ray. "Why didn't Stu come to tell me?" He would have added, "instead of you," but it wasn't necessary. The meaning was clear enough.

"He's at the hospital."

"The hospital?" Neal could feel himself losing control. "What's wrong with him?"

"It's not him. It's his wife. She has cancer or something."

Marla gasped and clutched Neal's arm tighter.

"Christ, if I had known you were going to be so interested, I would have brought you the medical report. But quite frankly, I didn't think she was much of a friend by the way she spread all of those stories about how your wife only married you for your money and all that other crap."

Marla stepped back, trembling all over. Gale was more than her friend. She had been an ally when no one else wanted to accept her as the coach's wife. She wouldn't have said those things. Maybe some of the others did, but not Gale.

Ray squared his shoulders and smirked. "Besides, if I were you, I'd be more concerned about this other thing."

In one quick movement Neal grabbed the front of Ray's shirt and yanked it with Ray in it towards him. Marla covered her mouth in fright.

"Listen to me you insensitive, shit-eating toad. Stuart Simmons has devoted thirty-five years to Piedmont State, twenty of those years as my assistant. And you didn't think I would be interested in knowing that his wife has cancer?" Neal let go of the shirt, and Ray stumbled backwards visibly shaken. "I think you've been hanging around our Director of Athletics too much."

"Well, from what I hear, I'm not the only one who's been hanging around our Director." Ray looked at Marla and then quickly away, all the while trying to smooth the wrinkles from his shirt.

"What in the hell do you mean by that?" Neal glanced at Marla who had backed against the porch railing.

"Ask you wife, Coach."

Ray had found Neal's vulnerable spot—his love for Marla—and he was going to enjoy causing him pain.

"Marla?" Neal continued looking at her.

"I was going to tell you about it when we got home, Neal. I didn't want you to be upset." This was coming out all wrong. "I didn't mean for you to find out like this. Believe me, it was nothing."

"Tell me what?" Neal's hands were clenched white.

"He made a pass at me the morning you met with the team before the Championship game. He came to our suite and tried to start something. But nothing happened, Neal. Except that I slapped him and told him to get out. Gale was there. She can tell you. Nothing else happened."

Marla watched Neal's face, praying that he would understand, that he would believe her. "I wanted to tell you before, but it just didn't seem like the right time." Neal turned away. "Please, Neal." She reached out and touched his arm.

"That's not the way I heard it." Ray had regained his composure. He had wounded Neal and he knew it. Now he wanted to rub salt in the wound.

Neal looked at Ray. "You bastard." And then he smashed him in the face with his fist. "Get the fuck out of here."

Blood squirted from Ray's nose. He grabbed a handkerchief from his back pants pocket and held it to his face. He pulled it away and looked at the blood, and then pressed it back against his nose. Without saying anything he turned and quickly walked to the waiting helicopter. If Connors wasn't going to fly back with him, it was Connors' ass in a sling, not his. He had done everything he was told to do. He pulled the handkerchief from his nose and looked at the blood again. Christ. He might even press charges against the son of a bitch.

Neal and Marla watched the helicopter lift off the runway and disappear into the distance, its noise destroying what was left of the magical island sounds. Marla hadn't moved from the porch railing. She felt sick. The way Neal looked at her when she told him about what had happened with Morgan. And then Ray saying that Gale had spread those stories about her. He must have made it up. Not Gale.

"We'd better get packed." Neal opened the screen door to go inside.

"Neal?" Like the beauty of the morning, Marla's heart felt shattered.

"You should have told me, Marla," he said slamming the screen door behind him.

Chapter Six

Marla and Neal made the three-hour drive from Morehead City back to Raleigh in silence. After packing, they had left a message for the caretaker that they were cutting their vacation short. He would see to whatever needed to be done about closing up the Cottage. Then they had taken the skiff they had rented to use while on the island across the channel and checked it back in. After retrieving their car from the storage lot, they headed for Raleigh.

Neal drove directly to the hospital. Whatever was wrong in the Athletics Department could wait until he found out about Stu and his wife, Gale. And Neal knew that Marla was frantic with worry over her friend.

They found Stu wandering toward the hospital cafeteria when they got there. His eyes were dark and sunken. Several days of beard growth covered his face. When he saw Neal, he started crying. The two men found a table off in one corner of the dining room, and Marla went through the line to get them coffee and something to eat. When she got to the table Stu was telling Neal about how Gale had kept the biopsy of a breast lump a secret from him. "She didn't want me to worry during the National Championship," he said. Neal glanced at Marla. "Apparently she had known about it for a couple of months. She wanted to wait until after the NCAAs to schedule the surgery." Tears spilled down his cheeks. Marla reached over and held his hand.

"The doctors didn't even do anything. They just cut her open and sewed her back up. They said it had spread too far."

Marla wiped the tears from her face with her napkin. How could she not have suspected anything? She thought of Gale taking all of those pills. The valium and those ugly lime green capsules. Marla had teased her about the green ones being nuclear pills—that they probably made her glow in the dark. Gale had told her they were for an upset stomach. What had they been—pain killers?

"This morning she told me to go home and get cleaned up and rest. She said I look like a bum." Stu ran his fingers through his uncombed hair distractedly, as though that would accomplish what Gale had told him to do. "I just can't leave her here alone," he whispered.

"I'll stay with her," said Marla. "Gale is right, you know. You need your rest, Stu. You need to take care of yourself so you can be strong for her."

Stu nodded. He looked as though the weariness he felt made it impossible to talk or even think.

"Oh god, Neal. Have you heard what's happening in the Athletics Department?" Once again Stu's mind was racing, this time on another track.

"We'll talk about it later."

"I didn't tell anyone about Stilt. I swear I didn't."

"I know, Stu. We'll get it straightened away. There weren't any NCAA rules broken. Stilt was caught using drugs. As head coach, I suspended him from the team. It's that simple. The reporters are just trying to sell newspapers."

"Morgan wants your ass." Stu glanced at Marla. "Excuse me, Marla."

"That's all right. Look, why don't I go see Gale now and the two of you can talk in private."

Marla got Gale's room number and left.

* * *

Room 363 was to the right of the nurses' station, two rooms down, an orderly told Marla. But he must have been mistaken. Marla didn't recognize the old woman with IVs in each arm and an oxygen tube up her nose. It was only when she started to leave and the woman said her name that Marla realized it was Gale.

Avoiding the bandages that wrapped Gale's chest and the various plastic drips, Marla pressed her face against Gale's, holding her the best she could. "Why didn't you tell me?" she whispered.

"Oh, right. As if you didn't have enough to worry about in that pretty head of yours." Gale's voice was weak. Her skin felt like paper.

"Nothing matters more than you. You're my best friend." Marla knew her tears were soaking Gale's hospital gown. She couldn't help it. "Besides, don't you know that every time you tell someone your problem, that it divides that problem by one-half?"

Gale made a sound from her throat. It wasn't a laugh, but it would have been if she hadn't been bandaged and connected to so many tubes. "Then I shouldn't have a care in the world," she said, "with so many people knowing I have cancer now. Did you know Lydia Rob has put me on some kind of list at her church? It's a Holiness Baptist or Primitive Voodoo or something, and all the members there pray for me every day. I don't even know those people, and they are doing that for me."

"That counts," said Marla. She moved one of two chairs in the room next to the bed and sat in it. Then she gently stroked Gale's bruised arms and hands.

"Isn't that something?" Gale looked down at the bruises. "When they go after your blood in this place, by god, they intend to get it." Gale closed her eyes. After a few moments she opened them again. "See that gismo on this tube here?" She wiggled her right hand.

Marla nodded.

"That's so I can control my own pain. Gone are the days when a patient has to grope for the suitable adjective to describe the severity of his pain to a doctor in order to get drugs. I mean, after all, what can you say after excruciating and butt-wrenching? Right? So if I feel pain, I squeeze that gismo and, presto, no more pain." Gale drifted off again. Marla didn't know if it was from the surgery, the cancer, or the gismo she controlled with one finger. Marla stayed with her.

"Did you tell Neal about that?" Gale asked some time during the afternoon.

"Yes, he knows." Marla didn't explain about Ray coming to the island or what he had said. Gale simply wouldn't have said those things about her. And if she did, Marla didn't want to know.

"Good," answered Gale without opening her eyes. "You two have something wonderful going. You don't need an ass hole like Morgan messing it up—not that he could, even if he wanted to."

Marla rubbed hospital lotion on Gale's hands and arms and legs. She got her a pitcher of ice and water. And when Gale pushed the gismo for the third time in an hour, Marla talked about the island—the sunrises and the sunsets, the sounds of the birds at dawn, and the waves of the ocean breaking just beyond the marshes separating it from the Cottage. And she told her about the scents—those natural, sweet smells emitting from the mangroves and live oaks, the sea oats and the Devil's cane. And the Jobellflower, that wonderful orange-yellow flower that grows in great drifts in the sand of the flats.

When she thought Gale had at last fallen to sleep, she stopped talking, but she didn't leave her. Instead, she continued to sit by her bed, holding her hand, and praying that Gale wouldn't have to suffer long.

Neal found Marla like that—sitting with her friend and holding her hand. He had finally convinced Stu to go home and get some sleep. Then he had driven over to the Athletics Department to see Morgan. Morgan's secretary told Neal that he was in a conference. So Neal made an appointment to see him the next day. It was probably better that way. He needed time to calm down before he met with the bastard.

Stu came in a short while later. Marla couldn't tell if he had slept any or not. She suspected he hadn't. But at least he had shaved and showered, and the clothes he had on were fresh.

"I'll come back and stay with her tomorrow," said Marla, kissing Stu on the cheek. "That will give you time to take care of other things."

Stu nodded. "Thanks, Marla." And then looking at Neal, "I'll come into the office tomorrow."

"Only if you want to. There's nothing there that can't wait."

Stu was sitting in the chair bent over his wife when Neal and Marla left. When they got outside, Marla was surprised to see that it was still daylight. Dawn on the island seemed so long ago and so far away. That silver dawn of early morning.

* * *

Marla watched Neal get out of the shower and dry off. He had said very little to her since they had gotten home from the hospital. She had unpacked, thrown in a load of clothes to wash, watered the house plants—all of it busy work, and none of it particularly satisfying.

The azaleas were still in bloom, barely. Most of the blossoms were starting to turn brown, especially the white ones. Soon all of the blossoms would turn brown, die, and fall to mold. Death.

Marla sat in front of her dressing table and stared at her reflection in the mirror. Wearily she rubbed cream on her face and brushed her hair. Then she got in bed, suddenly feeling very sad, alone, and needing desperately for Neal to hold her. This thing with Morgan was like a steel wedge between them. It was something that hadn't happened to them before, something she and Neal hadn't experienced. And Marla didn't quite understand why it was happening now. She had thought it was because of her love for Neal that she hadn't told him about Morgan. But maybe without realizing it she had been afraid that he wouldn't believe her. Or maybe she had been afraid he wouldn't be able to handle it. Somewhere deep down inside his confident, assured self, maybe there was a vulnerability that had not shown itself before now. Because it hadn't been tested—before now. And maybe she had sensed this all along. Tears trickled down Marla's face and wet the case on her pillow.

Neal turned off the bathroom light and climbed into bed. Only the pounding of Marla's heart disturbed the dark silence around her.

"I think I understand why you didn't tell me."

Marla was in his arms, kissing him, touching him with her face, her hands, her body, and her tears.

"I promise you, I'll never keep anything from you again."

He pulled her on top of him, caressing her back and tiny waist and the roundness of her hips, embracing her, feeling the warmth of her body, the softness of her breasts. She straddled his lean, muscular body and guided his erect penis inside her. She wanted to be filled with all of him and feel herself inside of him. Neal groaned and rolled over, gently positioning Marla's arching body under his own. And then with an urgency that he hadn't experienced before, he thrust inside her until she let go. Only then did he allow himself the release that he had been holding back.

Afterwards they lay in each others arms too spent to say anything, yet feeling the enormity of the trust and love that each felt for the other. They didn't talk about what had caused the wall between them. It wasn't necessary. It was no longer there. Marla listened to Neal's steady breathing and felt his arms relax around her. He was asleep. He had believed her. Nothing would ever get between them again. Marla felt safe and happy. She turned her face toward the window. It was dark outside and she could see the moon's dull reddish glow from be-hind some storm-darkened clouds. So similar to something she had painted many years ago when she was studying art in college.

Chapter Seven

Neal's appointment with Morgan was scheduled for nine o'clock. Stu was already at the basketball office when Neal got there. He had spent the night at the hospital and left when the nurse's aide came in to sponge-bathe Gale. Marla had called while he was still at the hospital to tell him she would be there at eight-thirty.

"Are you sure you want to be here today?" Stu had followed Neal into his office.

"I'm sure," answered Stu. And then after a pause, "I think I'll go absolutely crazy if I don't get my mind off it. Gale being sick and all. Does that make sense?"

Neal looked at his friend and co-worker of over twenty years. During all that time, it had been Stu to keep things calm and on a steady course, even those times when everything was a struggle. The early years when there was very little money in the budget, poor facilities, and losing teams. Now, seeing him in such a fragile state, it frightened Neal. Just as his own reaction to the thought of another man touching Marla had frightened him. Everyone had a weak spot, and it had taken Neal sixty years to find his.

"Yea. It makes sense. I'm meeting with Morgan this morning at nine. Why don't you come with me. You can help me explain the facts of life to him."

"I don't trust the son of a bitch, Neal."

"That makes two of us."

Morgan kept Neal and Stu waiting, much to Neal's irritation, for fifteen minutes in the outer office. When the secretary finally told them Mr. Morgan was free, the two men went in. Ray Knox was sitting in a chair opposite Morgan's desk. A strip of flesh-colored tape stretched across the bridge of his nose.

"Neal. Stu." Morgan nodded his head without smiling in the direction of the two men. "Well, Neal, it looks like you have really fucked us up here."

Ray sniggered.

"Oh really? And how have I done that, Charlie?" Since Morgan hadn't asked Neal or Stu to be seated, Neal crossed the large office and sat down in a plush velvet wing-back chair. When Morgan first arrived at State, it had been written up in the campus newspaper about his fetish for the velvet chair. Apparently it was something that had been in his family, and it was one of those antique ornamental things that was supposed to be admired from a distance, but certainly not sat in.

Stu pulled up an arm chair next to Neal.

"My god, Neal. Where have you been, on the moon? Don't you get the newspaper on that island of yours? It's the worst scandal ever to hit the University. How could you allow something like this to happen?"

Neal watched Morgan shuffle some papers on his desk and waited for him to finish.

"It seems to me the only choice I have is to announce the disqualification of the basketball team as National Champions. The NCAA is going to do it anyway. And, quite frankly, I don't see how I can keep you on as head coach. Even with that, the NCAA will probably take away most of our basketball scholarships."

He stopped shuffling and looked anxiously at the antique chair, then at Neal. "Well, what do you have to say?"

Neal clenched his teeth and silently counted to ten in order to keep from flying off the handle, a technique his father had taught him.

"First of all, there isn't going to be an NCAA investigation. One of the players was caught using drugs by a member of the coaching staff. I suspended him from the team. Then I reported it to the NCAA basketball official prior to the Championship game. It was his ruling, as the representative from the NCAA, that nothing else needed to be done.

"As far as the stories in the newspapers go, I'll be glad to hold a press conference and explain the situation fully—including how you have decided not to keep me on as Piedmont State's head basketball coach and that you want to relinquish the National Basketball Championship title. I'm sure the Seawolf fans would be interested in reading about that. And I can think of a few other things involving tickets and expense accounts coming out of your office for the basketball office to pay that they would probably like to read about as well. So if that's all you want to discuss, I'll go back to my office now and make the necessary arrangements. Does four o'clock this afternoon sound all right to you for the press conference? That way it can be broadcast on the WRAL TV six o'clock news as well."

Morgan sat down at the point when Neal mentioned he had reported the incident to the NCAA representative. The red flush that spread over his face was the only indication of the rage he was feeling. Ray cringed in his chair. When Neal finished talking, Stu looked at him and smiled. He would have given him a high-five if it hadn't been for the fact that Neal might have gotten out of the chair to do it. And he liked seeing Neal sitting in that fucking chair.

"I want a complete written report on this matter on my desk before I go home today." Morgan's anger couldn't be disguised any longer, even though he tried to hide it by smiling.

Feeling he needed to do something to help Morgan out, Ray jumped up and flipped through the leather-bound appointment book on

Morgan's desk. "It's time for your next appointment," he said pointing to something.

Neal didn't move. "I just have one more thing to say. Stu, if you and Ray will excuse us."

Stu got up and went to the door. "Ray, are you coming?"

Ray looked at Morgan not knowing if he should leave him alone with Neal. He didn't want to appear disloyal, but, after all, he had already gotten a taste of Neal's temper. It didn't take him long to decide he didn't want to risk it again. He touched the strip of tape on his nose and followed Stu out of the office.

Neal got out of the chair and stood in front of Morgan's massive walnut desk. He knew he wouldn't be able to control himself, no matter how many times he counted to ten, if he didn't keep something between them.

Morgan stood up and cleared his throat. "Well, I'm glad we got this little matter cleared up." The smile was still frozen on his mouth.

"I'm only going to say this once." Neal rested his hands on the edge of the desk. "If you ever so much as even sneeze in the direction of my wife, I'll kill you." Neal took a great deal of pleasure out of watching the smile on Morgan's face disappear. Then he turned and walked out the door.

* * *

The nurse on duty looked up at the blinking light on the monitor. It was room 363 again. "I honestly don't know where she is getting the strength," she said to one of the other nurses. "This is the third time she has wanted something in the last twenty minutes." She got up from the desk from where she was working. "I'd better go see what she wants this time."

"I need to have something notarized," Gale said when the nurse opened the door. She had a piece of paper—the stationery the nurse had gotten for her earlier—in her hand. The nurse knew it wouldn't do any good to argue with Gale. As sick as she was, she was determined to take care of something as soon as possible. It would be easier on both of them if she just went along with her.

"I'll get someone from the business office," she said.

"I'll need you here to witness it, too," said Gale.

The nurse nodded and went in search of a notary.

Gale lay back on her hospital bed completely exhausted. She was in so much pain, but she didn't dare push the button that would release the pain-killer. She had to be alert to do this. Once she got this signed and sealed, then she could take the medication.

A short while later the nurse returned with a man following behind her. "Mrs. Simmons, this is Mr. Burke. He is a notary, and he can take care of what you need."

Gale handed him the piece of paper in order that he could put his seal on it. With a trembling hand she signed the paper, whereupon the nurse and the notary each signed below her name.

"Fold it and stick it in that envelope you brought to me, will you please?" Gale asked the nurse.

"Of course. Do you want me to seal it too?" the nurse asked.

"Yes. And just put it in the drawer," said Gale motioning to the table next to her bed. Gale pushed the button to release the medication. She never knew anything could hurt so much. The cancer and the surgery. But no matter how much pain she was in, she had to do this. She owed Marla that much. Now she wouldn't have to worry about it anymore.

* * *

Gale was sleeping when Marla got to her room. Marla had stopped by the hospital cafeteria and picked up a cup of coffee to take with her. She sat by Gale, looking at her, and sipped the hot black liquid from a white Styrofoam cup. The oxygen hose going to Gale's nose had been removed, but the IVs were still hooked up to both of her hands. The bandage around her chest had been changed. This one didn't have blood stains on it.

Someone brought in a breakfast tray and left it on the portable bed table. The beige plastic lids covered a plate and several smaller dishes. Marla wished she had brought something to read, but just then Gale opened her eyes. "I thought you'd be here." She smiled at Marla and closed her eyes again. She sounded drowsy, and her words were a little slurred.

Marla reached out and held her arm, avoiding the plastic drips that snaked around it. "How are you feeling?"

"Great. Absolutely great," she mumbled. "The doctor said I can go home tomorrow."

Marla looked at her friend in disbelief. Maybe it was the medication Gale was taking, and she didn't know what she was saying.

Gale opened her eyes again and looked at Marla. "I'm electing not to take any treatment, Marla." Her voice was a little stronger. "All they can offer me is chemotherapy and radiation. What's the point?"

"Oh, Gale. Are you sure?" Marla caressed Gale's other arm, plastic drip and all.

"I'm sure. Honey, all it would do is make me feel sick. In the end, it wouldn't cure me. It might extend my life a month, or possibly two, but I'd be sick as a dog the whole time. By not taking it, I will at least have some good days left. And I won't lose my hair. Even if it is short and gray, I've gotten sort of attached to it. Right now most of my pain is from the surgery. But that's getting better every day. As far as the pain from the cancer goes, they can give me pills for that, and I can take those at home. And Lydia gave me this to wear." Gale fumbled for the red coral amulet attached to a gold chain around her neck. "Lydia swears this will keep me pain free."

Marla nodded and immediately burst out crying. "How can you be so brave about this?"

"I have a feeling you have been brave about some things I never could have faced."

Marla wiped her tears with the back of her hand and took a deep breath. "What do you mean?"

"I know about that son of a bitch you were once married to. I guess everyone does. When someone as pretty as you comes along and snatches up the most confirmed bachelor in the history of athletics, there are bound to be people to do some snooping. You know how these Seawolfers are. You were probably the most investigated person since that cousin who was accused of keeping Kate Smith prisoner in her own home."

"Oh, god." Marla stared out the window.

"Don't worry. You passed muster. Of course, Neal never knew about it. He would have had a flying fit if he had."

Marla felt sick and yet strangely relieved all at once. The thought of people digging into her past horrified her. But at least she no longer had to worry about someone finding out. Apparently everyone already knew.

"Just forget about it. People are only human, and they couldn't help but be curious. I need to tell you something else. I'm afraid I was curious too, Marla. And I said some things that I'm ashamed of now. Things that weren't true. I guess I never got over feeling resentful because Stu wasn't given the chance to be head coach, and I wanted to take it out on you. But that was before I got to know you. You are a good friend, Marla. And I know you are the best thing to ever happen to Neal. Can you forgive me?"

"I guess we do what we have to do."

"That's right. Hopefully with a little dignity, but if not, no one is going to be around long enough to give a purple shit anyway. I don't think I could have lasted these past few months without your friendship, Marla. Please remember that." Gale shifted uncomfortably. "I want to tell you something else. Stu couldn't have won the National Championship even if he had been head coach—not with this team. I'm glad Neal could do it."

Marla dug for a tissue in her purse, but couldn't find one. Gale handed her the corner of her sheet. "What are a few tears and a runny nose between friends?"

Marla wiped her face with the sheet and then stood up. "You think you can eat something now?" She moved the table with Gale's breakfast on it closer to Gale and adjusted the bed to a more upright position. The food wasn't hot, but it was still warm enough to be edible.

"I'm going to need your help getting through this," Gale said suddenly. At first Marla thought Gale wanted her to cut up something or open one of the several cartons cluttering the tray, but then she realized Gale was talking about something else.

"Whatever you need, I'm here for you."

Gale nodded. "I knew you'd feel that way." She pushed her partially eaten breakfast away. "When I get out of here, I don't want Stu hanging around the house with me and worrying. I know he means well, but it will drive him crazy and me along with him. He needs to keep going to the office and working. And when Neal starts recruiting, I want him to take Stu with him, just like always. For a while at least. I'll know when it's time for him to be with me."

"We'll work it out. I'll stay with you whenever and for however long you want me."

"Thank you, Marla. Now I won't worry." Gale closed her eyes. "I feel so sleepy. It's all this medicine. Did I tell you they are going to take the IVs . . ." She didn't finish.

Marla moved the bed table away and replaced the covers on the dishes. She wiped her face once more with the edge of the sheet and tried to fix her makeup. She would tell Neal what Gale had said. He would get Stu to travel with him when he started recruiting. She just hoped she would be as strong as she needed to be for Gale. She took a deep breath. She would have to be, that's all.

* * *

"Of all the meetings I have attended at State in the thirty-five years I have worked here, this morning's has to be the most memorable." Neal and Stu were walking across campus heading back to the basketball office. "Seeing the look on that bastard's face was absolutely priceless when you started telling him what all you would say at the press conference. Are you going to give him that written report he asked for, Coach?"

"Hell no!"

Stu grinned recalling what had taken place. "What in the fuck did you say to him when Ray and I left the room?"

"I told him I'd kill him if he ever bothered Marla again—in a nice way, of course."

"Goddamn." Stu shook his head still grinning. "I bet you left no doubt in his mind." Stu thought for a moment. "Do you really want to hold a press conference?"

"Yes. Not for the reasons I told Morgan, but I need to get the facts—the true facts—out to the press. Otherwise it will only get worse."

"I'll notify everyone when we get back to the office," said Stu.

"Make it for four o'clock in the conference room. That ought to make Morgan shit all over himself. Make him think I'm setting it up for Channel 5, which I am, because I want them there too. Also, I want a telephone conference hookup with Doug Stone in the NCAA office."

"The NCAA representative at the finals?"

"That's right. They are an hour behind us here, so it will be three o'clock in Mission Bay, Kansas. He should be in his office then. I want him to be available to answer questions so there won't be any doubt left in the minds of these reporters. And we'd better have some refreshments sent over for the press too. Sandwiches, cookies, that kind of thing. Food always makes them easier to get along with."

"You got it. Anything else?"

"Yea. I want to see Stilt's ass in my office as soon as you can locate him."

* * *

"What about next season, Coach? You going to let Stilt play?"

The conference room for the basketball office was crammed full of reporters, TV cameras, and photographers. Stilt had just made an official public apology. A buffet table had been set up in back of the room that was sagging under the weight of roast beef and chicken sandwiches, a variety of salads, and brownies. Two enormous urns, one with hot coffee and the other with iced tea, cups, glasses, and a large bowl of ice covered the surface of another smaller table off to one side.

"I will make that decision next season. Stilt hurt the team, the game of basketball, and, most importantly, he hurt himself by making a stupid mistake. I think he's learned his lesson, but he'll have to prove it."

"Just let me add here," Doug Stone from the NCAA office could be heard over the speaker phone, "Coach Connors is to be commended for showing such direct and immediate action under the circumstances. I'm not sure how many other coaches would have suspended their center from play right before the final game of the NCAA National Championship."

Some reporters wrote rapidly in their notebooks. Others clicked recorders on and off while stuffing their mouths with food.

"How do you explain the misinformation we were fed, Coach?" It was the sportscaster from WRAL TV, channel 5. Neal was expecting this question.

"I would say someone doesn't like us very much and is doing whatever necessary to destroy the basketball program it has taken me twenty years to build, and the National Championship team along with it." He smiled at the men around the room. "I would think you bright fellas can answer that question better than I can. After all, you were the ones who reported on what was fed to you. Just check your sources, guys."

Just then Charlie Morgan came striding into the room with Ray hustling along behind him. Morgan who always practiced being late like it was an art form because he mistakenly thought it somehow made him look busy and important couldn't have timed it better if Neal had choreographed it. A hush fell over the room. And Neal knew then, just as sure as he was standing there, who had been responsible for the false stories.

"That's all I have to say. If any of you gentlemen have other questions, you can make an appointment with my secretary. In the meantime, there's still plenty of food, so help yourselves." Neal walked around the far side of the room, avoiding the Athletics Director and his side kick, Ray Knox.

"Coach? Can I talk to you for a minute?"

It was Al Nance, the reporter from Albuquerque who had first written the story about Stilt using drugs and implicating the rest of the team.

"You're a long way from home, aren't you?"

The reporter nodded. "The *Tribune* paid for my trip to Raleigh so I could do a follow-up story on the NCAA Champions."

Neal studied the reporter's face. "So, what can I do for you?"

"I just want to explain why I wrote the story I did, and tell you that I am sorry. I reported the information the way it was given to me by an official of Piedmont State. Even though that person was in the position to know and shouldn't have had any reason not to tell the truth, I knew he was lying. After all, I have been around the newspaper business long enough to know when someone isn't being straight with me. But I reported it anyway, and I am ashamed."

"If you thought it was a lie, why did you report it?"

"I got paid $25,000 for that story from the tabloid that printed it. That money paid for the operation my six-year-old daughter needed. Believe me, I have regretted it ever since. I dishonored my profession, and I dishonored myself. If I had it to do over again, I wouldn't. I would find another way to get that money. I just wanted you to know that I am sorry."

Neal watched Nance walk toward the door. He could understand why Stu had thought he was an O.K. guy. Nance didn't come on with that "freedom of the press" and "the people have the right to know" crap, whether it is the truth or not, like so many of the reporters he had dealt with. "Al."

Nance walked back over to where Neal was standing. "How is your little girl?"

Nance broke into a smile. "She's fine. Just fine. Of course, there will still have to be some additional procedures, but they will be done when she is older, and they will be minor. The doctors say that the worst is over."

Neal smiled. "I'm glad to hear it."

"Well, I've got a flight to catch." Nance started to offer his hand, but hesitated.

"Good luck," said Neal shaking his hand.

"Thanks." Nance glanced at Morgan across the room. "Be careful who you trust, Coach," he said looking back at Neal. Then he left.

Chapter Eight

It had been three weeks since State's big win in the National Championship, and everyone was still talking about it as though it had happened only yesterday. Neal finished recruiting in state, and he was preparing to go out of state to Virginia, Maryland, and New York. He knew the coaches from several of the high schools in those areas, and that they produced quality players as well as good students. Stu would go with him.

Marla was spending most of her days at the hospital. The doctors had decided to keep Gale another week before releasing her. Getting Gale home from the hospital was a nightmare. Marla originally planned to go over to Stu's and Gale's house and clean it up some that morning Gale was to be released. Stu hadn't touched it since getting back from Albuquerque other than throw wet towels in a corner of the bathroom and stack the sink with dirty dishes. Also, Marla wanted to be there to help Gale get settled in when Stu brought her home from the hospital. Marla was vacuuming the living room when Stu called saying he needed her to come to the hospital. Apparently there was a problem he couldn't handle. This man who had organized teams, equipment, schedules, and other people's lives for over three decades suddenly couldn't make a decision on such a simple matter as what to do with all of the flowers and plants people had sent to Gale. There was also the question of all the cards and letters. What finally threw him into a panic was when he tried to help Gale get into the car, she started feeling faint. The doctor said it was weakness due to inactivity and her illness. It was to be expected. But Stu was beside himself. So he called Marla.

"Marla, I'm just afraid to drive with Gale feeling so bad. I mean, what if she passes out or something?"

"I'll leave right now, Stu. Just try to keep Gale comfortable until I get there."

Marla shoved the vacuum cleaner back into a hall closet and drove to the hospital. Calmly she helped Gale climb into her car, picked out three plants and put them in the backseat, and gave the rest to the hospital volunteer on duty to pass out to other patients. She let Stu keep the cards and letters since he already had them in his car stuffed in a paper sack. As they were leaving, Stu put his car in reverse rather than drive and backed into Marla's car. It didn't do any damage, but it was just one more thing to fray everyone's already fractured nerves. So Marla took the lead, and Stu followed close behind back to the house.

"When does Neal go out of town?" Gale's head was pressed against the back of the seat and her eyes were closed. The doctor had given her something for nausea before she left the hospital, but she was deathly white.

"Tomorrow. He'll be gone a couple of weeks on that three-state swing he does. He's already told Stu he needs him to go with him."

"Thank god. I love that man, bless his soul, but he is absolutely no good around sickness."

Marla glanced in her rearview mirror. Stu was right behind her. She hoped he wouldn't hit her from the rear. "We're almost home now. Two more blocks."

Gale opened her eyes and looked around her. "The azaleas have finished blooming."

"Yes. But we have the day lilies to look forward to."

Gale didn't say anything.

* * *

One reason Piedmont State was rated highly as a basketball power was because of Neal's success as a recruiter. Neal could talk, and talk he did—to the young men he wanted on his team, and to their mothers. He knew if he could convince the mothers that he was interested in their sons' welfare, he would be able to get them to play for him. His players were culled from top prospect lists in the national basketball magazines. Neal went after only those players who could contribute to the team, for he believed that it was the team who won the games, not the individual—no matter how good he played.

The players came because Neal sold The Dream: to play on a National Championship team. And now with a fresh National Championship win just behind him, The Dream was even more believable.

Starting in Virginia, Neal's first big score was in convincing Glenn Adams, a six-foot-four-inch forward from Richmond to join the Seawolves. Adams had led Richmond High to two straight championships and was being courted by several schools in the Ivy League. Adams' mother had died several years earlier, so with no mother to talk to, Neal recruited Glenn's father, convincing the senior Adams that he would build his new team around the quickness and agility of his son. It worked, and Glenn Adams agreed to enroll at State.

Once Adams signed up, Neal was able to recruit a bruising young six-foot-ten center with a body of granite by the name of Jeff Cornwell. Cornwell, a senior at Salem High School, averaged 29.5 points a game. Neal assured both Adams and Cornwell that as freshmen at State they would get plenty of playing time.

From Virginia Neal and Stu went to Maryland to see their friend and head coach Richard Matha of Cardinal Newman High School, just outside of Baltimore. Matha's teams were annually rated among the top in the nation, and he had a reputation as a molder of young men. Two of Neal's starters on the Championship team had been Matha's boys. Neal was able to sign up two more players: Frank Whit, one of the greatest penetrating guards ever to come out of Cardinal Newman, and Terrance Terrell, a long-range shooter.

So far it had been a successful trip. These four players—Adams, Cornwell, Whit, and Terrell—would go a long way in replacing the five seniors, two of them starters, who would be finishing up their eligibility at the end of the semester. Back in their hotel room Stu was already writing follow-up letters to the kids and their families he and Neal had visited, and Neal was going over the list of players he still wanted to talk to in New York. There was one kid who especially looked good and would complement the team he was building.

The telephone rang startling both men. "It's kind of late to be getting a phone call, isn't it? said Stu looking at his watch. He answered it on the second ring. It was Kevin Burns, the other assistant coach who was taking care of things in the basketball office while Neal and Stu were away.

"You'd better listen to this." Stu handed Neal the phone and went into the bedroom to pick up on the extension.

It was obvious from Kevin's tone that he was upset. "What's up, Kevin?" Neal had his yellow pad.

"Morgan called a meeting with the Athletics Council, and he's gotten them to agree that new academic rules need to be made for the athletes. Apparently he's going to the Chancellor with it next."

"What kind of academic rules? You mean over and beyond what the NCAA has already established?"

"That's right. He wants to eliminate freshman eligibility for one thing. Not just for those athletes who are accepted under Proposition 48, but all freshmen athletes. He also wants to do away with the Seawolf Booster Club. No more Seawolfers."

"Where in the hell does he think we're going to raise money for our athletic scholarships?" Neal's anger was slowly starting to build.

"He apparently thinks we don't need it to run a sound program. He has also recommended that the University admit athletes based on their academic qualifications and not on their athletic ability—no exceptions."

"The son of a bitch. What the fuck does he think he's doing?"

"There's one more thing. He's going to push for immediate suspension of any basketball player with below a 3.0 average, retroactive to the beginning of this semester. You know where that leaves us, Coach. Over half of the team will be dropped."

"I should have known something like this was coming. The bastard. He must be completely insane. When is he talking to Chancellor Boyd?"

"Tomorrow morning. Ten o'clock. I think he figured with you out of town, he could get his old buddy to agree with him." Kevin paused. "Of course I don't need to tell you, if he does get the Chancellor to agree to this, we can just hang up our jock straps."

"We'll get the first flight out of here tomorrow morning. I'll be at that meeting. And Kevin, if for any reason the flight is delayed, you attend it and stall things until I get there."

"I'll do my best, Coach."

Neal hung up the phone and went back into the living room where Stu was making notes on everything Kevin had said. "Well, my friend, this might mean the end of my coaching career in basketball, but I'm going to take that bastard down if it's the last thing I do."

Chapter Nine

With Neal and Stu out of town, Marla moved in with Gale. It just made it easier not to have to keep running back and forth. And she wanted to be there if Gale needed anything.

Gale wasn't doing well. She tried to mask it, but Marla knew she was in a great deal of pain even with the medication. Sometimes after taking the pain killers, Gale would hallucinate. She wouldn't know Marla, or where she was. Occasionally she would have mild seizures. More often than not she talked about things that Marla guessed must have been from her childhood: a cat named Dog, a farm—probably her grandparents', a favorite dress covered in pink and yellow roses with a lace collar. Stu called her every night from wherever he and Neal were staying. Through it all, Marla tried to remain upbeat and cheerful. She was determined to not let her friend down.

When Gale was too exhausted or in too much pain to talk or sleep, Marla told her about the Cottage and the island.

"When you get a little stronger, we will go to Portsmouth Island," Marla told Gale. "Just the four of us. You and Stu, and Neal and me. I want you to hear the birds at dawn. There is nothing else like it."

I would like that. Does Neal ever do any fishing?"

"Sometimes. He and Stu can go fishing, and we'll listen to the birds."

Marla had brought Gale home with her for the day thinking a change would do her some good. Gale hadn't left her house since getting out of the hospital. She had hardly even left her bedroom. Neal had called the night before telling Marla that he and Stu were cutting their recruiting trip short and would be returning the next morning. Something had come up at the University, and they would be busy once they got in. But he would come home as soon as he could. Gale talked to Stu and told him that she would be at Marla's.

The two women were sitting on the sprawling wooden deck over-looking the large backyard dense with pine trees, sycamores—or gum balls as Marla liked to call them, maples and oaks. Gale watched a gray squirrel bite off a tender branch from one of the maples, strip its leaves with its teeth, and carry it high up in a tall pine where it was building a nest. Even though it was warm, Gale was wearing a heavy wool sweater and had a quilt thrown over her legs. Somewhere nearby two blue jays were screeching at one another, arguing over territorial rights.

"Why don't I make us some hot tea. I have a box of mountain apple that I haven't tried yet, but it's supposed to be good.

"That would be nice, Marla."

Marla tucked the quilt more closely around Gale's legs and went inside. It had been a good idea to bring Gale home with her. Gale seemed to be feeling better. She took down two cups and saucers from the kitchen cabinet and opened the box of herbal tea. She was so intent on what she was doing, she didn't hear the back door open. She put the teabags into the cups, filled the cups with water, and put them into the microwave oven. Then she got out a loaf of raisin bread and a bread knife and began slicing it.

"Hello, Marla."

Marla turned around, and it were as though she had been sucked back into the past that she had been trying so hard to forget. Neal, her home, the National Championship—none of it existed. Instead, she was somehow locked in the same horrible nightmare. It could even have been the same kitchen. Martin, smiling, so sure of himself. Knowing the power he had over her. Knowing he could paralyze her with fear.

The timer on the microwave went off, but Marla didn't move. She looked into Martin's eyes. It was Martin, and yet it wasn't. Just as before, there was nothing behind the eyes. No light, no conscience, no soul. Martin Andrews was no longer there. Instead, there was this unfeeling, irrational and totally insane stranger. And Marla knew without any doubt that his only purpose in being there was to hurt her.

* * *

Neal's and Stu's seven o'clock flight was delayed two hours. It had rained during the night and the temperature had dropped—one of those unpredicted late spring freezes—causing a thick sheet of ice to form on the runway. Leaving from Baltimore, it took one hour to fly to Raleigh-Durham, and then another forty-five minutes to drive to the campus. Stu dropped Neal off in front of the administration building and then went to find a parking space.

"Glad you made it, Coach." The secretary smiled at Neal when he rushed in. Elizabeth Wall had been the Chancellor's secretary forever. Many considered her a permanent fixture of the University—an ageless, well-groomed woman who decided who should or should not have access to her boss. Others thought of her as the power source behind the Chancellor who knew everyone and everything and who also influenced whatever decisions were made in the head office. Neal liked her. He also felt a little sorry for her, and he wasn't sure why. Maybe it was because before he met Marla, his life had been so narrowly focused, and he saw the same thing in Libby Wall. But she was dependable and efficient. She had always been helpful those times when he needed something from the head office. He had repaid her by making sure she got season tickets and a parking pass to all the home basketball games. "Here is that information you wanted. It's up to date as of five o'clock yesterday afternoon. You can go on in. The Chancellor is waiting for you."

"Thanks, Libby," he said, kissing her on the cheek. "I'm sorry about calling you at home so late last night."

"That's quite all right. I'm glad I could help."

He glanced at the sheet of paper she handed him and put it in his briefcase. Then without knocking he opened the door to the Chancellor's office and went in.

"Neal. How good to see you." Frank Boyd got up and went over to shake Neal's hand. "Charlie told me you were out of town and couldn't be here this morning, but then Kevin came and told us you were on your way. So we've just been having a good old rehash of that tremendous game your team won in Albuquerque."

Neal ignored Morgan who had stood up when the Chancellor did. Other than Kevin, Tom Reynolds, Chairman of the Athletics Council, was the only other person there.

"I just got in," said Neal. "And I certainly didn't want to miss a discussion that's going to determine whether Piedmont State is going to have a basketball program or not."

There was a knock on the door and Stu walked in.

"How are you, Stuart?" The Chancellor motioned to an empty chair next to Kevin and then pressed a button on his intercom. "We'll have that coffee now, Mrs. Wall."

Morgan fixed a smile on his face. "It's not like that, Neal. We just want to make a few changes in the academic procedures."

Mrs. Wall came in carrying a tray with several cups of coffee already poured. She offered it to the Chancellor first, then to Neal.

"Now, Charlie, nothing has been decided yet." The Chancellor went back to his desk and motioned for Neal to sit in the chair nearest him. Neal finished pouring two sugar packets and three creams into his cup before sitting down.

"I think I can clear up a few misconceptions here in a hurry so we won't have to waste any time."

Mrs. Wall served the others and left.

Neal spoke directly to the Chancellor. "If you go along with what Morgan is proposing, there is no way in hell we'll be able to be competitive—either in our own Conference or outside of it. And whether you like it or not, winning is what draws students to the University as well as financial support. Since the NCAA finals, the Seawolf Booster Club has received the highest number of pledges in the history of the school. Also, these figures came from the Admission's Office. They are the applications of new students who want to come here this fall." He pulled out the piece of paper from his briefcase and handed it to Boyd. "That figure represents the applications received just since the National Championship."

Boyd adjusted his reading glasses and glanced over the figures. "I haven't seen these figures. According to this, applications are up by thirty percent over last year at this time."

"And it's still early yet. As you know, Chancellor, the biggest surge of enrollment applications usually hits in late July and early August." Neal sipped his coffee and put his cup down on a nearby table.

"It's not the general enrollment we're concerned with, Coach." Charlie squirmed slightly in his chair. "It's the fact that our athletes—especially our basketball players—have done so poorly in academics. It's abysmal, and, quite frankly, I'm embarrassed to be associated with such a negative message. After all, we are an institution of higher learning."

Neal looked at Morgan. "Then maybe you should disassociate yourself from this University."

"The basketball team does have a poor academic record, Neal." Boyd took off his glasses. "I understand only two of your seniors will graduate with their class. The other three seniors will have to repeat several courses in the fall."

"That's true." Neal sat forward. "But you have to remember, these kids were admitted to the University under the old rules—before Proposition 48. And even though it's going to take them a little longer, they will graduate. Considering how far they have come, I think it's pretty remarkable. If it hadn't been for basketball, and these kids being able to attend State on an athletics scholarship, they would probably be out on the street somewhere—or worse. They might not be Dean's List students, but they are a hell of a lot better off having attended State as poor students than not having attended at all."

"I think that's debatable." Morgan fidgeted with his cup and uncrossed his legs. He immediately crossed them again.

Reynolds, who hadn't said anything since Neal arrived, cleared his throat. "I think Neal is right."

Stu glanced over at Kevin, raised his eyebrows, and sipped his coffee.

"Now that we are under Proposition 48, of course," Neal continued, "we have tightened our requirements. We don't even look at a kid to recruit unless he has a solid C average in high school. And all of the other colleges are playing by the same rules in their basketball programs. If you break rank like this and impose harsher guidelines for us to follow, it will be the death of our basketball program. And I don't say that casually, Chancellor. Neal stood up and walked over to the door. Stu and Kevin got up and followed him. "It will also mean that you will have to find yourselves a new head basketball coach."

* * *

"What do you want, Martin?" Marla felt the counter top press into her back. She heard the blue jays squawking outside. She noticed the checkered pattern on the tile floor made by the late-morning sun streaming in through the window. She could smell the aroma of apples and spices coming from the microwave.

"Looks like that jock you married has done all right for himself." Martin smiled at Marla. "All of this and a National Championship title, too. Tell me, does he know how much you like to fuck in the shower?" He moved toward her.

"Marla, can I help with anything?" Gale came in from outside dragging the quilt with her. She stopped when she saw Martin.

For a moment Martin didn't know what to do. It was obvious he hadn't expected anyone else to be in the house.

"That's all right, Gale. I can manage. Martin is just leaving."

Gale's eyes widened when Marla mentioned Martin's name.

It took Martin only a moment to focus his thoughts. "Why don't you just go back to wherever it was you came from." His eyes strayed from Gale's face to the quilt and back to her face. "The coach's wife and I need to discuss something in private."

Gale didn't flinch. "I think you are the one who needs to leave—before I call the police."

Martin moved toward Gale and stared at her. Unblinking he struck out and knocked her to the floor. The gold chain with the red coral amulet broke and flew across the room. "I said to get out of here, you bitch." Gale tried to get up, but couldn't. Blood dripped from her nose and mouth.

From somewhere Marla heard a terrifying scream—her scream—and she lunged at Martin, hitting him in the chest. When she hit him once, she couldn't stop. All of those times he had hurt her, and all of those times she had lied for him, protecting him so no one would find out. After all, he was a professional man, a doctor. He could be ruined if something like that got out. The good, kind doctor. He took care of people. He took care of her. She was one of those pitiful, unfortunate people who seemed to always have accidents. Bruises on her face and body, cuts. It was so nice she was married to such a good doctor. Everyone admired him—such a wonderful man. But he didn't hurt them. Only her. And now, Gale.

The screaming continued, and she kept hitting him. It were as though a part of her felt all of the bitterness and anger and terror from those years for the first time, while another part of her, separate and somehow apart, watched and listened to what was happening. She could feel Martin's shirt as she struck him. She could feel the warmth of his skin, and smell his cologne. And all the while, the other, separate part of her looked on, watching and listening—the clothes, the skin, the screams that wouldn't stop. And everywhere was the color red.

It was only when Gale managed to pull herself up and throw her arms around Marla that Marla finally stopped. It was only then that she no longer heard the screams. And it was only then, as she and Gale collapsed onto the kitchen floor clutching each other, that Marla realized she had stabbed Martin to death.

* * *

"What do you think Boyd will do, Coach?"

Kevin, Stu, and Neal were riding back to the basketball office. Kevin, sitting in the backseat, had asked the question.

"I honestly don't know," answered Neal. "The Chancellor seems to lose all judgment when it comes to Morgan. I can tell you this, though," Neal glanced at Kevin and Stu, "I didn't spend the last twenty years of my life building a first-rate basketball program at State just to have Morgan wipe his ass with it. Kevin, when we get back to the office, I want you to call Bill Camp's office and try to get me an appointment to see him some time tomorrow. As President of the Consolidated University System, Bill Camp has the ultimate and final authority over the chancellors from all the various schools in the system. We go back a long way. I have a lot of respect for him. And he owes me a few."

"Fuck. Nothing like going to the top." Kevin scratched a note to himself on some paper.

Bill Camp and Neal were roughly the same age and had started working for the University System the same year. When Camp's college-age son got into trouble during his freshman year, Neal helped him get through the worst part by letting him work in his summer basketball camp. Over the years, the two men had built a strong friendship.

"Stu, I know you want to go home to Gale now. But tomorrow when you get to the office, I want you to start calling the major Seawolf donors. I think it's time they found out what Morgan is up to. Make sure you mention that there's a possibility that Morgan is responsible for spreading those stories against the team."

"You got it." Stu pulled his car in next to Neal's that was parked in the reserved space in front of the basketball office where he had left it.

"And I think I'll pay a little visit to our business manager first thing tomorrow morning. I noticed that Morgan turned a little green around the gills at that last meeting we had in his office when I told him I was going to discuss his tickets and expense accounts with the press. Who knows. Maybe I stumbled onto something there."

Kevin climbed out of the backseat and headed for the office to make his call to Bill Camp's secretary.

"I'll see you at the house," Neal told Stu. Stu backed out and Neal got in his car. He wouldn't bother going into his office to check his messages. He'd do that tomorrow. Right now he wanted to see Marla. He had been ten days on the road, and he needed her. As soon as Stu collected Gale, he and Marla would have the rest of the day and evening to themselves. He thought of her with her hair piled on top of her head sitting in their large bathtub and covered in bubbles. He could feel himself getting aroused. Tomorrow he would deal with Morgan, but tonight he wanted Marla.

* * *

Gale pried Marla's fingers off of the bloody knife and wiped the handle of it on the quilt that was entangled around her legs. Marla's screams had been replaced with sobs.

"Listen to me, Marla. You have to get hold of yourself."

The two women hadn't moved from the floor. Marla had her arms around Gale. She was shaking and crying. Gale pulled her other hand loose, the one without the knife, and shook Marla as hard as she could.

Marla immediately stopped crying and stared wildly at Gale.

"Now listen to me and do as I say. This is important. Are you listening?"

Marla nodded her head.

"You didn't kill Martin. I did. I came into the kitchen to fix some tea and he attacked me. I grabbed a knife and stabbed him. You came in when you heard the commotion." Gale looked at Marla. "Do you understand?"

"Gale, I killed him." Marla looked with horror at the gruesome scene around her. "My god, I killed him."

113

Gale struggled to keep from passing out from the pain ripping through her body. She knew Martin had cut her. She could feel the blood on her face. But that's not what hurt. It was that horrible disease eating her up inside that was causing her so much pain.

"No, Marla. Listen to me. When they ask, tell them I killed him. Believe me, it's better this way. What can they do to me? Nothing. I am already dying."

"Gale, I can't . . ."

Gale shook Marla. "Now you listen to me. The Seawolfers accepted you as long as they thought you were the one who had been wronged. But if they find out you killed him, no matter what he did to deserve it, they will never forgive you. They will make a circus out of this. Think of Neal and what he has worked so hard to build. Do you think kids will want to come play for a coach if his wife has killed someone? Do you think their parents will let them? Believe me, Marla, I know what I am talking about. Now do as I say."

Gale started to get up off the floor, but Marla grabbed her. "Please, Gale, don't leave me." She was hysterical again. Gale leaned back against Marla, too weak and in too much pain to move. Somewhere she could hear a door opening, the sound of footsteps, and Neal calling his wife.

Chapter Ten

Charlie Morgan was in a foul mood when he returned to his office following the meeting with the Chancellor. He also had another one of his headaches. Boyd had all but told him to lay off Neal. Neal had built up a lot of support over the years. He was a good man, a winning coach, and people just liked him. "I have no doubt whatsoever that what Neal tells me about a winning basketball program bringing in more students and increased revenues is true," Boyd repeated for the third time to Morgan as he was leaving. "I'm afraid, my friend, that if a choice had to be made today between you and Neal—knowing what I do about how the Seawolf fans feel, you would lose. If I were you, I'd find a way to work with him." At that point Boyd had put his arm around Morgan's shoulders. "We're all on the same team here," he said, "and I think you could learn a lot from Neal if you just give him a chance."

That had ripped it, as far as Morgan was concerned. Frank Boyd giving him a pep talk like he was a goddamn moron or something. Here he was supposed to be in charge of the whole fucking Athletics Department, and the Chancellor was telling him he could learn something from some half-witted jock. Well, he would just show Boyd who was boss. He would show them all.

Ray followed Morgan into his office and closed the door. He knew Morgan was seething. In fact, he had never seen anyone so pissed.

"I want you to find out the name of that woman who had the hots for Connors before he got married. It's Jean something. Then I want you to arrange a time and place for me to meet with her. Not on campus. Somewhere private where we won't be seen or recognized."

Ray shook his head and looked down at his feet.

"Well, if you have something to say, say it, goddamn it!" Morgan slammed his briefcase down on the desk.

"I really think you are barking up the wrong tree there. Nothing ever came of it. She's just some crazy fan who occasionally drinks a little too much at the games. When she does, she thinks she is in love with the coach."

"You know her then?"

"Yes. I know her." The truth of it was that Ray had been seeing Jean. No one knew about it, of course. After all, he was married. But he had a good thing going. In fact, it was the only thing he had going. His wife hadn't had anything to do with him since Albuquerque when he stayed out all night trying to meet that low life to pay him off. He had told his wife he was with Morgan, but she had called Morgan's suite to check up on him and found out that Morgan hadn't seen him. At least Jean was better than nothing, so he sure as hell didn't want Morgan messing it up by bothering her about something that had happened before Connors got married to Marla.

Morgan ignored Ray's reluctance. "Good. Then fix up a meeting with her. Tomorrow."

"Tomorrow is Thursday, Charlie. You're meeting with the Board of Directors all day."

"I said tomorrow!"

Ray walked out leaving Morgan staring out of the window behind his desk. This whole goddamn business was getting out of control. Morgan hadn't told him, but earlier in the week Ray had seen him looking at the Administrator's Handbook, a manual written up for all of the department heads in the Consolidated University System. Morgan had been reading the section on "Dismissals." Later, when Morgan wasn't in, Ray had gone into his office to see what it said. Basically it said that any employee of the administration, faculty, or coaching staff with tenure, or who had been employed within the University System for a total of fifteen years, could not be fired or dismissed from his or her position unless he or she had been convicted of a felony or immoral behavior. Apparently Morgan was going after Neal on an immoral behavior charge.

Ray sat down at his desk and put his head in his hands. Lately he had been thinking he never should have left New Hampshire. He had always known that Morgan was a little off balance in his view of the world. Everything in life had to be one big competition, and he didn't like being second to anyone. But he was totally irrational about it. In fact, if Morgan hadn't come to State to take over as Athletics Director when Boyd asked him to, Morgan probably would have gotten fired from the University of New Hampshire where he was Chairman of the Department of Animal Husbandry. He had made a lot of enemies there by surrounding himself with yes-men, which made it impossible to have a successful program in anything. The few men who had tried to offer suggestions and make changes had ruined their own chances of any promotions or advancement. Most had moved on to other schools and new jobs after a couple of years. Ray had stayed with him, however, not because of any good feelings between him and Morgan or a misplaced sense of loyalty, but because Morgan had been generous to him, rewarding him with gifts and promotions and the promise of more if he stuck around. It had been a pretty good deal for Ray. Up until now. Now this business with Connors had already gone way beyond the line of competitiveness. It was like a sick obsession with Morgan, and Ray was in it right up to his ass. He wasn't sure the rewards were worth it. Not any more.

He couldn't stop worrying about Albuquerque either—about the fact that the guy had seen his face. Maybe the guy didn't get a good look at him. But what if he did? And what if he found out who he was, which was quite possible since Morgan had insisted on including all of those goddamn photos with those goddamn stories he spread about the basketball team taking drugs. He sure as hell wasn't going to take the blame for that one. That had been all of Morgan's doing—finding some drug dealer to set up one of the starters on the Seawolf basketball team. Ray only agreed to get the money to the guy.

Ray rubbed the back of his neck and slumped back into his chair. After a few minutes he grabbed the phone and began dialing Jean's number.

* * *

Stu followed Neal into the house all smiles. "Where are they?"

But Neal had already heard Marla's uncontrolled sobs. He pushed through the swinging doors leading from the dining room into the kitchen. What he saw paralyzed him—but only for a moment. He rushed over to where the two women were still clinging to one another on the floor. "Stu, get in here."

"Did you find them?" asked Stu following him in to the kitchen. And then he saw the grisly scene.

Neal picked up Marla and carried her to the living room. Stu bent over Gale, taking her in his arms, and rocked back and forth.

"Stu, I need my pain medicine, darling. I left it outside on the deck."

He helped her into the living room and eased her down in a chair. Then he rushed out to the deck to get her bottle of pills. When he returned, she immediately put two capsules into her mouth. Stu found a glass in the bathroom and brought her some water. He didn't want to go back into the kitchen.

After Gale gave him a brief account of what had taken place, Neal called his attorney, Walter Ferris, and told him roughly what Gale told him: Martin had entered the house uninvited, found Gale in the kitchen and attacked her when she asked him to leave, and she stabbed him. Marla didn't say anything. Then Neal called the police. He was friends with one of the detectives, someone who had worked with him on getting one of his ball players out of a jam a few years back, so he talked to him directly. Both Ferris and Detective Bob James arrived at the same time. Someone from the coroner's office, the police photographer, and several other people connected with law enforcement arrived a short time later along with a throng of reporters.

"How in the hell did they find out about it so fast?" said Neal when he saw a TV mobile unit pull up in front of the house.

"They monitor the police reports as they come in," said Ferris. "Don't worry. I'll handle it."

"I think it's open and shut, Neal." Bob James glanced over at Stu. "A clear case of self-defense." Stu was holding up remarkably well considering his wife had just admitted killing someone. "I will need to get a statement from Mrs. Connors, too, of course. And then I'll turn over my report to whoever the prosecutor is assigned to the case."

Marla had stopped crying, but she couldn't stop shaking.

"Would tomorrow be soon enough to finish up? I think it would be better." Neal had his arm around Marla. "Gale and Marla have had a terrible shock."

"Certainly," he said getting up. "I'll come back tomorrow morning. Say around ten o'clock?" He stood looking at Marla for a moment and then went into the kitchen where the medical examiner was finishing up.

"All I can say is, the poor bastard must have scared the hell out of whoever killed him. There are at least fifteen stab wounds. I'll know more when I do the autopsy."

Detective James narrowed his eyes and nodded. He had been a member of the Raleigh Police Department for thirty years, twelve of those years as a detective. During that time he had developed a number of good qualities. He was an excellent judge of character. He was thorough. And he had unfailing instincts. And his instincts were telling him that Mrs. Simmons didn't kill Martin Andrews.

Marla and Neal went home with Gale and Stu after Ferris made a brief statement to the reporters. Until the police finished their investigation of the crime scene and they could get it cleaned up, they wouldn't stay there. At first they were going to get a hotel room, but Gale insisted that they stay with them. They had that basement apartment, and Neal and Marla would have all of the privacy they needed. "And we can give each other moral support," Gale had argued. She was right.

Marla stood under the hot shower, letting the water run over her hair, her face, and her body. Her mind was blank except for one thing. She would not be able to lie about what had happened. No matter what the outcome or repercussions, she would have to tell the truth.

Finally she turned off the water. She opened the shower door. Neal was sitting on the edge of the tub holding a large bath towel. Tenderly he dried her off and wrapped her in it. Then he held her close to him. Marla pressed her face against his chest, listening to his heart beat, and feeling the strength of his body flow into her own.

"Neal, I killed him," she whispered.

Neal continued holding her. "I know, honey," he said quietly. "I know."

Later in bed Marla told Neal what had happened. How she had left Gale on the deck while she went into the kitchen to make them some tea. She had started slicing the bread when she realized Martin had come in. She remembered being afraid and then seeing Gale. And she remembered Martin hitting Gale and knocking her to the floor. The next thing she remembered was sitting on the kitchen floor with a bloody knife in her hand and Gale beside her.

"We'll get through this, Marla. I promise you, it will be all right."

Marla went to sleep in Neal's arms. For the first time since her divorce from Martin, she didn't have the nightmare. That nightmare was over. What Marla didn't realize was that the other nightmare, the one that had caused her to sense fear for so long, was just beginning.

Chapter Eleven

Stu woke Marla early the next morning. Gale was nauseous and in severe pain. "The pills aren't doing any good, and Gale won't let me call the doctor. I don't know what to do," he said helplessly.

Marla put on her robe and slippers and went to Gale's bedroom. Neal got up and went to the kitchen with Stu to make some coffee.

Marla was stunned to see how sick Gale looked. During the time Marla had been staying with her, Gale had started looking better. Marla thought she might even be improving. After all, doctors occasionally made mistakes. Seeing Gale now though made Marla realize the doctors had been right. Gale would never get better. Of course, with everything that had happened, it was no wonder. She wiped Gale's face with a cool, damp washcloth and sat down next to her, holding her hand and stroking her arm.

"I don't think I can go with you to the Cottage, Marla. Not this time around anyway."

"Of course you can. We'll go there now."

Marla wiped the tears from her eyes and looked out the window. It was just getting light—that first gray light that comes with a promise of a colored, vibrant brightness to follow.

"We are in the motor boat and crossing the channel that runs between Morehead City and Portsmouth Island. It is still dark, because we want to get there before dawn. That way we can see and hear everything come alive." She continued holding Gale's hand, gently stroking it.

"The water is calm this morning, and there's a slight breeze. Our hair is blowing and the salt-water spray covers our skin with little droplets of mist. Neal pulls the boat up to the dock and hands Stu the rope.

Stu gets out and ties the boat to the dock. It's just a short walk through the sand flats. You can smell the Jobellflowers. When it gets light, you will be able to see their beautiful orange-yellow color, but right now you just smell them."

"What do they smell like, Marla?"

Marla thought for a moment. "You know that mock orange bush in the corner of your yard? Well, they smell a little like that, except sweeter. Once we get past the sand flats, we walk on the wooden planks around the marshy area. The frogs are croaking. Scores of them. We hear several splashes as some of them jump into the water.

"Then we get to the yard proper of the Cottage. We walk through the moss-draped oak trees. The grass is soft and spongy, and damp with dew. We can see the Cottage. It's a rambling two-story, white frame structure. There is a peaked roof and lots of big windows trimmed in faded blue looking out to where we have just come.

"It's almost dawn now, but not quite. There is still time to make a pot of coffee. When it's made, we take our coffee out on the veranda. It's a huge wrap-around porch, and we sit in some wooden rockers, watching, listening, and sipping our coffee."

Neal and Stu came in as Marla was talking. Neal sat down in a chair across the room next to the window, and Stu lay down next to Gale on the bed.

"The first light is gray. It is the defining moment. It lets you identify shapes and forms off in the distance—the live oaks, the saw grasses, the Devil's cane. They are starting to come into focus now. And somewhere, not too far away, a single bird begins to sing. Tentatively at first, and then with a happy eagerness as other birds join in.

"Looking across the marshes and beyond where the ocean waves break, the first color of dawn appears on the horizon."

"What color is it?" Gale looked out of her bedroom window.

"It's a soft pink, almost salmon, still muted by the gray. Gradually other colors appear—yellow, violet, orange—and as they do, more and more birds begin singing. The seagulls and grebes, marsh sparrows and egrets. A flock of pelicans flies overhead in formation.

"You can see the Jobellflowers now. A carpet of yellow-orange spread out across the sand. A soft dew covers everything, and as the sun rises higher in the sky, a kind of gentle evaporation takes place which makes you feel like you are seeing everything through a lace veil. Everything glimmers, because it's a silver dawn—that perfect time of day when everything is fresh and new."

Gale's breathing was coming rapidly. "It's so beautiful," she whispered.

Marla got up, unable to hold back her tears. Neal took her out of the room leaving Stu alone with his wife. He was still with her when she died later that morning.

* * *

Charlie Morgan threw the egg and the dish that it was in against the dining room wall, shattering both and staining the blue-flowered wall-paper. He had just cracked open what was supposed to be a two-minute-thirty-second boiled egg, which his wife had deliberately cooked for four minutes. "You'll get salmonella poisoning eating raw eggs," she reminded him. He didn't want raw eggs. He did want them runny, however. And a four-minute boiled egg was definitely not runny. As always, it had put him in a bad temper when he bashed the end of the eggshell with the back of his spoon expecting it to ooze yellow yolk and instead finding it solidified. However, his temper went completely out of control when he opened the paper and read the headlines.

The lead story on the front page described in great detail the killing that had taken place in the Connors' home the day before. There were also the black and white photographs showing in rather graphic detail a cloth-draped body and several dark areas on the Connors' kitchen floor, presumably blood.

The story explained how Gale Simmons, wife of assistant coach Stuart Simmons, had been visiting the wife of Piedmont State Head Basketball Coach Neal Connors, when an intruder entered the home and attacked Mrs. Simmons. "The intruder was dead when the police arrived, apparently stabbed to death by Mrs. Simmons with a nine-inch bread knife. Coach Connors was out of town on a recruiting trip when the incident occurred, but arrived home a short time later. The person killed was identified as Dr. Martin Andrews, the former husband of Marla Connors," the story said.

"Dr. Martin Andrews was a prominent physician from Red Oak, North Carolina, a small rural town located fifty miles west of Raleigh. He had practiced medicine in Red Oak up until two years ago. He gave up his practice at that time, but continued living in the area." Then there were the usual quotes from people who had known him. Colleagues, former patients, neighbors. All of them expressed shock and disbelief.

Morgan tried to keep his hands from shaking. His body was hot and clammy and he felt short of breath. He had difficulty focusing his eyes as he read the story for a second time. He doubted very seriously if Gale Simmons killed Martin. After all, wasn't she supposed to be sick with cancer? No, it must have been Marla. She had the fire, as he had found out in Albuquerque. But even if she hadn't done it, he sure as hell could spread enough doubt around where it would make people believe she had.

Now if he could just get that woman who had made a fool of herself over Connors to cooperate. Of course, he would make it look like he hated to dismiss an employee who had such an outstanding record in the field of collegiate basketball. But certain things couldn't be tolerated, such as unethical and immoral behavior. Possibly felonious behavior where his wife was concerned. And it was his job as Director of Athletics to insure that the highest standards were maintained within the department and within the University. Even the Chancellor would have to agree with that, no matter what the fuck the Seawolfers thought. He would destroy Marla Connors and everything she loved—just like he promised.

Morgan crushed the newspaper and threw it where he had smashed the egg and dish earlier. Taking several deep breaths, he pushed himself up from the table and stalked out of the house.

* * *

Ray hurriedly dressed and drove to the Athletics Department as soon as he read the morning paper. The story about Gale Simmons killing someone in the Connors' home was all over the front page. He couldn't even guess how Morgan would react to the news.

Ray unlocked the door to the office. None of the secretaries had arrived yet. He quickly glanced through the stack of messages on his desk and then went to the supply cabinet looking for the coffee filters so he could make a pot of coffee. The phone in his office rang. It was his private line. Thinking it might be Morgan, he ran back into his office to answer it.

"Well, aren't you the early one, heh?"

Ray didn't recognize the voice. Only that it was a man. "This is the Department of Athletics. I think you have the wrong number."

126

"Oh, I don't think so, heh," the man answered.

It was the impudent manner in which the man talked and the odd way he ended everything he said with "heh." Ray had heard it before. Suddenly he remembered where. His lower intestine immediately went into a spasm and his heart started pounding. He took a deep breath, trying to ease the cramping in his stomach. "What do you want?"

"We still have some unsettled business—like the rest of the money you owe me, heh."

Ray could hear him blowing into the receiver. He must have been smoking a cigarette.

"Plus interest since you didn't pay me on time, heh."

"You got paid what you were supposed to. You were to get the rest only if State lost the game."

"That was when you were a Houston fan." The man laughed hoarsely into the phone and then coughed. When he finally stopped, he said, "But the Director of Athletics and his assistant at Piedmont State University still owe me money. I'd sure hate to have to tell the press that the Seawolf Athletics Department didn't pay its debts." Once again Ray heard the coughing. "I want fifty thousand dollars, cash, small bills, in one of those Seawolf duffel bags. You know that pizza joint, Two Guys, on Hillsboro Street?"

"Look, there's no way . . ."

"Shut up and listen. Meet me there eight o'clock Saturday night with the money. Come alone, heh."

"I don't know if I can get the money."

"You'll get it. Eight o'clock Saturday night. Two Guys."

"How will I recognize you?" Ray was practically doubled over from the pain in his stomach.

The man laughed hoarsely. "You won't have to. I'll recognize you, heh." The phone went dead.

Ray slammed the phone down and headed down the hall for the men's room. Just then Morgan came in.

"I want to see you in my office," Morgan said walking on past Ray.

"In a minute, Charlie."

"Right now, Ray."

"Go to hell," Ray muttered under his breath. He had other things to take care of *right now*, and all of them involved being in the men's room.

* * *

Detective James' good qualities stopped when it came to punctuality. Instead of showing up at ten o'clock the next morning, he arrived at the Simmons' home at two-thirty in the afternoon. It was just as well, with everything that was going on. Earlier Marla explained to Stu that she had killed Martin and not Gale, but it didn't seem to matter to him. Instead, he surprised Neal and Marla by becoming once again his take-charge self. He offered to help her in any way he could, and then immediately launched into taking care of all of the thousands of details that needed to be taken care of in preparation for Gale's funeral. Later that morning he went to the funeral home to complete the arrangements.

Neal called the basketball office and informed Kevin what had happened. Of course everyone had read the morning paper, and the campus was literally buzzing with talk. Bill Camp was out of town, Kevin learned, when he had called the day before, but he made an appointment for Neal to see him on Monday of the following week.

Neal in the meantime would be taking a few days off until they could get everything settled. He told Kevin when the funeral for Gale was scheduled so he could notify everyone. Gale and Stu had made a lot of friends over the years, on campus as well as off. People would want to know about it. Of course, there would be something in the paper as well. Kevin would take care of things in the office and alert Neal if anything urgent came up.

It was at that point that Detective James arrived. Neal led him into the living room where Marla was waiting with Walter Ferris. Neal sat down beside her and put his arm protectively around her. "My wife would like to give you that statement now, Bob."

It really wasn't that difficult once Marla started talking. Gale's death, and the suddenness of it, made everything else seem insignificant. Marla repeated most of Gale's story except for the part where Gale had said she killed Martin, and she told him about the troubled marriage they had until she finally left him.

"I don't see where this is going to change the outcome of my report. It still looks like self-defense," offered Detective James. "I'm afraid there's nothing I can do about keeping it out of the papers though."

"We understand," said Neal.

Detective James scribbled a few more notes into the well-worn brown notebook he was using. When he got up to leave he turned around and looked at Marla. "Did you ever file a complaint with the police any of those times Andrews assaulted you, Mrs. Connors?" It was almost too casual, the way he asked.

"No. I was just so ashamed. And afraid that people would find out. Since he was a doctor, he did whatever was necessary to," she hesitated, looking for the right word, "do damage control."

Detective James nodded.

"Is there anything wrong, Bob?" asked Ferris.

"I don't think so." He walked to the door. "I'll let you folks know when you can return home. Hopefully, it will only be another day or two."

After he left, Ferris looked at Neal and Marla. "We might have a problem."

Chapter Twelve

Ray leaned back on the plush blue and pink sofa cushions, put his hands behind his head, and closed his eyes. He loved getting a blow job, and Jean was a master at it. He felt her ample breasts press against the inside of his thighs and her warm wet tongue take his head into her mouth, playing with it and teasing it. Then she sucked his whole cock into her mouth, moving up and down on it when she did, pressing the head of it gently with her tongue and soft lips.

He didn't try to hold back. He didn't have that much time to spend with her, and he had really come to talk to her about Morgan. As he had expected, Morgan was beside himself over that story in the newspaper. In fact, he was acting like a crazy person. He wanted to meet with Jean that day, no matter what. Ray wasn't sure how she would react when he asked her to meet with Charlie, but for now he was going to enjoy the hell out of getting eaten.

"Did you like it?"

Ray stood up to rearrange his boxer shorts inside his trousers and sat back down, pulling her down next to him. "Best thing I've had all morning," he answered, kissing her. He could taste himself on her mouth.

"I want you to do something for me."

She cocked one eyebrow and looked at him. Jean was easy and overweight. She drank too much, and she liked to flaunt her wealth. But she wasn't stupid. She could sense when something was up.

Jean had been married and divorced four times. Everyone knew she was looking for husband number five. She thought she had a sure thing with Neal, but she hadn't even been able to get him alone with her, let much less go to bed with her. Heavens knows she gave it her best shot. She donated twenty thousand dollars to the Seawolf Club for a basketball athletics scholarship, and attended every one of the games—at home and away. She even bribed a maid to let her into Neal's hotel room in Charlotte where he was staying during the Atlantic Coast Conference Championship. He found her there wearing a negligee and drinking her third glass of champagne—which she had charged to his room. It wasn't one of her finest moments. She wasn't used to being turned down. After all, she wasn't that old. Fifty-nine could even be considered young. She had money. She had worked hard at trying to keep her figure looking good. And plastic surgery could do wonders these days. But he hadn't been interested. He gave her ten minutes to dress and get out of his room. He also gave her the half-empty bottle of champagne to take with her.

It had really hurt her feelings. And then she got angry, once she sobered up. She didn't like being turned down. She didn't like thinking she had made a fool of herself either. And she knew she had. It didn't help any when word of what she had done got around among the Sea-wolfers. They kept adding to the story, making it worse than it really was. She'd never hear the end of it.

What really got her was when Neal surprised everyone by marrying the Chancellor's new young administrative assistant a few months later. Jean was furious. As long as Neal was unattached, the sting of his rejection was easier to live with. She could tell herself that if he weren't so wrapped up in coaching, she would be the woman he would be interested in. But she could no longer tell herself that when he married Marla. What made things even worse, there were no other future husband prospects on the horizon. So she had settled for Ray Knox, even though she knew he was married and nothing would ever come of it, and even though she knew he was little more than a lap dog for the Athletics Director.

"Charlie would like to have a private meeting with you. He has a little problem he thinks you can help him with."

Jean had noticed that whenever Ray got tense, a nerve twitched on his right eyelid. It twitched now.

"What kind of problem?"

She wondered if Ray had been talking to Morgan about her. She knew Morgan was married to that frumpy, doormat of a wife, but she hadn't heard of any problems between them.

"I'd rather he told you himself. Of course, he doesn't know about our—involvement."

So it wasn't sex Morgan wanted. And it couldn't be money. She knew pledges were up with the Seawolfers, and besides, she had given that twenty thousand dollars. It would be a long time before she gave any more money to the Seawolf Club for all the good that had done her. The only other thing she knew about that had been going on in the Athletics Department since the National Championship was all of that mess that came out in the papers about the players using drugs. But that had been cleared up—at least she thought it had.

"So when does he want to meet?"

"As soon as possible. Today if you can. I thought maybe he could come over here. That way you won't have to worry about being seen or overheard."

Jean thought about what she had planned for the day. Shopping at Bloomingdales in the morning for a baby gift. Everyone she knew was becoming a grandmother. And she always had lunch on Thursday's with her friend from the University at Cobblestones. She liked long lunches, so that would probably take at least a couple of hours or more.

"How about four o'clock this afternoon?" She had already planned to wear her new pink Channel suit, so she would still be wearing it when Morgan got there. He would see just how classy she was, and how rich.

"That will be fine." Ray got up to leave. "I'll call you soon," he said, kissing her lightly on the lips.

Jean stood with her hand on the door for a moment after Ray left. He was worried about something. That was for sure. She went into the kitchen, spooned some freshly ground coffee into her silver percolator and turned it on. She listened until it began its somewhat obscene internal grunting noises and burps and then picked up the morning paper which she hadn't had a chance to read yet. There in big black bold print she read, DOCTOR KILLED IN COACH'S HOME.

* * *

It was unusual for Walter Ferris to be awake before nine o'clock in the morning, especially on a Thursday morning when he normally didn't schedule any appointments. He didn't even open his eyes before his third cup of coffee—freshly ground Arabica, black and strong. But something about the way Detective James had asked Marla if she had filed any police reports regarding her ex-husband's abuse raised an alarm inside his head. That alarm along with the headache he felt coming on because he had missed his normal intake of morning caffeine had him at the courthouse bright and early. From what he could find out, Tom Cochoran was the assistant prosecutor who had been assigned to the case. Cochoran had already sent his own team of investigators over to the Connors' home to collect evidence and had been nosing around the University questioning people who knew Marla. He had also driven to Red Oak to talk to former patients, neighbors, friends, employees—anyone who had known Andrews and Marla during the time they were married.

134

Ferris didn't like what he was hearing. Cochoran sure wasn't wasting any time. He was young, hard-working, and ambitious. Being assigned to a high-profile case like this one could mean a promotion for him if anything came of it. Ferris went to the courthouse snack bar and got a cup of coffee hoping that would cure the pain in his right temple. It wasn't the strong stuff he normally drank, but it would have to do. He needed to talk to Marla as soon as possible. The funeral for Gale Simmons was scheduled for Saturday. He would see Marla there and arrange a meeting. In the meantime, he would contact that private investigator he had used on special cases in the past.

* * *

Jean decided to cut her lunch short. After all, she could visit with her friend by telephone later if she wanted to. The more she thought about it, the pink Channel really wouldn't be appropriate to wear in her own home to meet with the Athletics Director. Her red floral silk dress would be much better, red being State's color and all, with opaque stockings and low pumps. And she needed to get home by no later than two-thirty to give herself plenty of time to change. Her friend didn't help matters any by showing up at Cobblestones twenty minutes late. By then Jean was on her second vodka martini and feeling quite flustered in spite of it.

But once they ordered she began to relax. And the glass of wine—an exceptionally good Chablis—was delicious with the chicken fettuccini and garlic bread she ordered. Jean's friend, who also happened to be close friends with one of the secretaries in the Athletics Department, was able to tell Jean some things that hadn't been reported in the newspaper. "Apparently, Marla is a ball-buster." Jean's friend eagerly gulped the scotch-on-the-rocks the waiter had brought her when she first arrived and just as eagerly launched into what she had learned. "She destroyed Andrews' career as a doctor when she divorced him. He never could quite get over it. But that wasn't enough to satisfy her. She decided to lure him to her home and murder him, making it look like he had attacked her. Of course, there was only her word that he had ever abused her since there were never any charges filed against him with the police." She paused long enough to order another scotch.

"She thought Coach Connors was going to be out of town another week. He's recruiting, you know."

Jean nodded.

"It was just a fluke that he came back early. Can you imagine walking in on such a horrible thing?" The two women stared at one another blurry-eyed. "I mean, there must have been a tremendous amount of blood. How in the world do you get blood stains off tile floors? And I also heard," the friend leaned closer to Jean's left ear, "and this has to be kept just between us."

"Oh, of course. You know I'd never repeat anything you tell me." Jean drained her glass of wine and refilled it from the bottle that she had asked the waiter to leave on the table.

"Well, it's being said that she had planned to blame Gale for the murder. That's why she had Gale over at her house. Isn't that awful? Gale Simmons. That poor defenseless woman already dying of cancer and having something like that to face. And that was why it was reported wrong in the newspapers. Marla told the police that Gale had done it. Can you believe it?"

Jean clucked her tongue and shook her head. As a matter of fact, she couldn't believe it, even after two vodka martinis and three glasses of wine. But it did make for interesting conversation.

"There's no telling what Marla had in mind for Coach Connors. I mean if she killed one husband . . ."

Jean's mind started racing. If she played her cards right, she might become Coach's wife after all. She would have to give this a lot of thought, though. No more surprise visits in hotel rooms. That was too aggressive for Coach's sensibilities, apparently. No, she'd have to come up with something a little more subtle.

Jean managed to return home safely without any mishaps by driving extremely slow. People seemed to drive so reckless these days. The rich cream sauce on the chicken fettuccini had made her feel headachy, but she fixed herself some seltzer and aspirin when she got home and put on a fresh pot of coffee in case Charlie wanted some. She certainly did. Then she quickly changed into the silk dress she already had laid out on her king-size bed. She had some difficulty getting the opaque panty hose on—one stocking leg kept wanting to twist the wrong way. But eventually she got it straight, at least straight enough, and after a quick look in the mirror she decided she had never looked better.

She wondered if Ray was coming, too. He hadn't said. Just then she heard the doorbell.

* * *

Charlie smiled and took Jean's hand. "It's so nice of you to take time out of your busy schedule to see me. May I call you Jean?" he asked, still holding her hand. Ray wasn't with him.

"Why of course, Charlie." Jean returned his smile. This was going to be interesting. It had been a long time since anyone had tried to do a snow job on her. And Morgan was trying to do a major one now. She led him into the living room.

"I was just getting ready to have a cup of coffee. Will you join me?"

"That would be nice, if it isn't too much trouble. Do you need any help?"

She almost laughed out loud, but stopped herself. She wondered when the last time was that he offered to do anything for anyone. Not since before he reached puberty, she was willing to bet.

"No, I can manage. But thank you." She brought in the silver tray with two cups of coffee, cream, and sugar and set it down on the butler table in front of the sofa where he was sitting. She sat down next to him.

"Do you take cream or sugar?"

"Both," he answered. He continued smiling at her.

Jean spooned in some sugar and poured the cream. Luckily the headache medicine she had taken earlier was starting to take effect. Her hands weren't shaking too much, and she was feeling a little more alert than when she first got home. She handed him his cup.

"I believe you know how to spoil a man, Jean." He sipped the coffee.

"Yes, well. As they say, practice makes perfect." She watched him take another sip of coffee and swallow.

"Mr. Knox mentioned that I might be able to help you with a little problem you're having."

He settled his cup back in its saucer. "Yes. I suppose you've heard about the murder that took place in the Connors' home?"

"Such a tragedy." Jean hoped she sounded sincere. Also, she noticed he had used the word "murder." "I read it in this morning's paper. Such a tragedy," she repeated.

"Yes. I'm going to be completely open with you, Jean. I know I can trust you to keep what I am going to tell you confidential." He moved slightly closer to Jean. "I have felt for some time that

Connors—and now his wife—is not creating the proper environment for our student athletes."

His emphasis on the word "student" didn't get past Jean. She sipped her coffee.

"Our basketball team is a disgrace to the University. We will be lucky if two percent even pass this year. And I blame the head coach. He's the one responsible, after all, for bringing them in. Out of the ACC schools, State's basketball program is on the bottom for graduating athletes."

Morgan swallowed some more coffee and studied Jean's face. He wondered just how much of what he was saying was sinking in. The smell of liquor was strong on her breath, and her eyes looked rheumy. He continued.

"I feel it is my job as Director of Athletics to get the basketball program back on track where it should be. And," he reached out and held Jean's fleshy hand, "I simply don't believe I can do it with Connors as coach."

Jean left her hand where it was. So that was it. Morgan wanted to dump the coach. She wondered what his real reason was for wanting to get rid of Neal though. She didn't buy for an instant his cock-and-bull story about grade point averages and graduation rates. Not only that, the man had to be just a little deranged to want to fire a coach who had just won the National Championship.

"I understand what you are saying, Charlie, but I don't see where I can help you."

"How can I put this as delicately as possible?" He glanced around the room as though expecting to find the words he was searching for hidden somewhere behind the furniture. "I thought you might have a reason for wanting to see him leave as well. From what I understand, he behaved in a very ungentlemanly way toward you. I think if the truth were told—not that garbage the Seawolfers have spread around—that there would be immoral grounds on which I could have him dismissed." Morgan noticed Jean's body tense slightly. He had definitely struck a nerve. "You would have to let it be known how he tried to force himself on you. Of course, no one would blame you. And he would get what he deserved." He paused for her reaction. When he didn't get one, he continued.

"Suffering, as I am sure you have, it would only be right for me to provide you with two season tickets to all of the athletic events as well as access to the Director's Box at the home football games from now on. You have certainly proven your loyalty to State with that generous twenty-thousand-dollar gift. Would you like that?"

Charlie was running out of things to say, and he wasn't getting a clear reading on the woman. Maybe she was smarter than he had given her credit for. Either that, or her liquor-stupored brain was beyond comprehending.

"Let me get this straight." Jean pulled her hand free and put her cup and saucer back on the silver tray. "You want me to say that Coach Connors tried to rape me, and in return, you'll give me two season tickets to all the athletic events and a standing invitation to the A.D.'s Box at all the home football games for as long as I want?"

Morgan flinched at her use of the word rape and the tone of her voice when she said it. "Well, yes. I guess that's what I am saying."

Jean looked at the man sitting next to her. She had done a lot of stupid things in her life, things she wasn't the least bit proud of. But this wasn't going to be one of them. She needed time to decide on how to handle the situation though. Morgan was dangerous. She would have to be very careful.

"Let me think about it, Charlie," she said sweetly. I'm sure you understand."

"Of course I do." He stood up. "Don't take too long though. I need to act on this as soon as possible." The smile was gone, and his eyes were stone gray—threatening. Usually Jean wasn't easily intimidated. But the tone of his voice, and those god-awful eyes—she felt chilled and she shivered involuntarily.

After Morgan left Jean mixed some more seltzer and aspirin.

"Goddamn," she muttered to herself. "What in the hell have I gotten myself in to?"

Chapter Thirteen

The University chapel was overflowing with people and flowers. Everything was red and white except for one yellow day lily resting on the body in the coffin, the day lily Gale wouldn't be able to see. Marla had placed it in the coffin herself the night before when she and Neal had gone to the funeral home with Stu.

Marla and Neal stood at the back of the chapel greeting people when they came in and directing them into the room where the body was being viewed. Marla had already said good-bye—when she placed the flower. She wouldn't view the body again. Gale was no longer there.

It was amazing how many people turned out. When all of the seats were taken up inside the sanctuary, more chairs had to be set up in the entrance foyer. Since there was no family other than Stu, Marla and Neal sat with him in the front pew when the minister gave the eulogy. It was quite nice, as far as funeral services go. A graduate student from the Piedmont State Glee Club sang some hymns. And Dr. Edwards, the minister delivering the sermon, had known both Stu and Gale for many years, so he was able to relate personal experiences about Gale as well as read biblical scripture.

Afterwards, everyone filed into the recreational hall for refreshments and to sympathize with one another, although it soon became evident that what everyone was talking about wasn't Gale. The furtive glances, the whispers and raised eyebrows, and the sudden pauses in conversation when Marla came near made it obvious that Martin Andrews' death was foremost in everyone's minds. Since Marla's confession of what actually transpired the day Martin was killed, the newspapers had printed front-page, headline news, complete with pictures every day. Marla hadn't realized how many pictures were taken of Martin's body that day. Now, it seemed, the newspaper had prints of all of them as well as photographs of Neal and, of course, her. It had started—just as Gale said it would. People were questioning and placing judgment before they even knew what was involved. Marla wouldn't win this one. She didn't mind for herself. But she couldn't stand the idea of Neal getting hurt.

The afternoon drug on, and through it all Marla stayed close to Stu, at least close enough so he wouldn't feel alone, pressing his hand when she thought he needed it, telling him how beautiful the service was, and saying all of those things that one says when there simply is nothing to say.

"Are you all right?" Neal put his arm around Marla. She looked up into his dark brown eyes. He felt so strong.

"Neal, they . . ."

"I know," he said glancing around the room. Try not to let them worry you."

Walter Ferris came over to them. "We need to talk, Marla. Will you be available Monday morning?"

Marla nodded.

"What is it, Walter?" Neal pulled Marla closer.

"The assistant prosecutor is starting to dig, and I think we just need to be prepared. I hate surprises." He looked at Marla. "I need to find out more about Andrews and your marriage."

Several people had moved closer to where Walter was talking to Neal and Marla, obviously intent on trying to overhear their conversation. He lowered his voice. "We can't talk here. Will nine o'clock be all right? In my office?"

"We'll see you then," Neal answered. He kissed the top of Marla's head. "I promised you we will get through this, and we will."

Marla wanted to believe him. But she had seen the people looking at her. She had heard their whispers. She took a deep breath. This wasn't the time to think about it, she told herself. She would think about Gale. And then, later, she would decide what to do.

* * *

Ray walked up to Two Guys and pushed his way through the crowd, all of them college students, and all of them seemingly having a good time. Ray was neither a college student nor was he having a good time. In fact, he had never been so mad. First having to make up excuses for Morgan not attending Gale Simmons' goddamn funeral, and now this. This was the last time he was going to do Morgan's shit for him—and he had told him so. He also pointed out to Morgan that the guy's demand for money was blackmail, and more than likely he wouldn't be satisfied with just this one payment. But, as usual, Morgan hadn't listened.

Since it was Saturday night, Two Guys was mobbed. Ray nervously checked the zipper on the duffel bag with the fifty thousand dollars in it. Morgan had taken it out of a shoe box in the back of one of his filing cabinets. Where in the hell Morgan had gotten that much money, Ray had no idea. He didn't ask. He just wanted to deliver it to the guy and get the hell away.

People were lined up out the door waiting to get seated inside. Someone from the restaurant was going around writing down names and assigning numbers on a seating list. There was a twenty-minute wait, she told everyone. Ray ignored her when she asked for his name and the number in his party and pushed to the front of the line. "Someone is holding a table for me inside," he said when several people complained.

It was fairly dark in the restaurant except for the lighted candles on every table. It was noisy—loud music, everyone talking and laughing, and the clattering of dishes and pizza pans from the kitchen. Ray stood near the cashier trying to avoid being in the way of the people wanting to pay their checks. He glanced nervously around the room letting his eyes adjust to the dim light, not knowing what the shit else to do. The guy said he would know him. Ray had hoped he would see the guy first, that he would remember something about his face from that night in Albuquerque. But the guy had been wearing a scarf and that stocking hat, and it was so dark that night, just like it was dark in Two Guys. Ray didn't recognize anyone.

The girl who had been taking names outside came in and looked at Ray. "Are you Ray Knox?" she asked.

"That's right," answered Ray.

"A guy outside asked me to give you this." She handed him a piece of paper folded in half and went back outside.

Ray opened it. *Meet me in alley behind Two Guys*, it said. It was scrawled in pencil. Ray crumbled the note and stuffed it into his pants pocket. "Jesus Christ," he muttered. He could feel his lower stomach muscles start to tighten, a sure indication that he would have to find a bathroom soon.

Ray left the restaurant and started walking around the block toward the entrance to the alley. A slight breeze had picked up and he was shivering. Once again he felt the zipper on the bag. It was still closed.

"So, we meet again, heh." The guy was standing near a garbage dumpster. *How appropriate*, thought Ray. Unceremoniously he shoved the bag at the guy.

"Here. It's all there. Count it if you like, but don't expect me to wait around while you do." Ray started walking away. The nerve over his right eye was twitching like crazy.

"We'll keep in touch, now, heh." The man started laughing and coughing.

Ray wondered if that was some kind of veiled threat for more money. Shit. He didn't care. He just wanted out—away from Morgan and away from Piedmont State. And by god he was going to get out just as fast as he could.

Chapter Fourteen

Neal and Marla spent all day Sunday cleaning up. The assistant prosecutor decided the police wouldn't need to go back to collect any more evidence and left word with Walter Ferris that the Connors could return to their home. Neal told Marla he would hire someone to come in and take care of things, but Marla insisted on doing it herself. As terrible and grim as it was, she needed to do it in order to help her deal with what had happened. With the loss of Gale weighing so heavily on her, she hadn't taken the time to let the other horror sink in yet. It still seemed like part of the nightmare—distant, unreal, and intangible. Cleaning the blood stains from her kitchen brought the reality of what happened sharply into focus.

Stu came over early and spent the day helping. He said he wanted to stay busy. Later that evening, after they had finished, Marla cooked a pot roast and vegetables for dinner. Cooking relaxed her and gave her the sense of relief. It allowed her to reclaim her kitchen—to use it and see it as it was meant to be. Hopefully now she could erase the images in her mind of what had happened there just as she had erased the stains of blood from the floor.

"I've got that meeting with Bill Camp tomorrow afternoon," Neal reminded Stu. "But tomorrow morning when Marla and I finish up at Walter's office, I want you to go with me to talk to the business manager."

"I'll be there," answered Stu. "Why don't I pull all of the records we have on ticket sales and receipts. That way you will know exactly who got how many tickets and where the seats were located."

"That's a good idea, Stu. I have a funny feeling about this."

Marla listened to the two men sitting at the kitchen table discussing over coffee their plans as she washed up the dishes. When she finished, she sat down with them.

"Stu, would you like for me to go through Gale's clothes and things tomorrow. I'm sure we could find a charity to donate them to—or maybe give them to the church."

"That would be a tremendous help, Marla. I wouldn't even know where to start." He played with his cup. "It's really hard seeing her things just where she left them, thinking she is coming back, and yet knowing she isn't."

"I think I understand." Marla felt her eyes tearing and looked away. She missed Gale tremendously. It was going to be difficult having to dredge up the past for Ferris. And she dreaded being by herself when Neal went back to the office. Worse still, she couldn't shake that other feeling of dark fear. It was still with her and she couldn't understand why. After all, Martin was dead. She was probably just tired, and so much had happened. Working with Gale's things and taking care of them would help take her mind off whatever it was that was frightening her. She would feel like she was doing something for Gale. It would be comforting. But first she would have to get through the meeting with Walter Ferris.

Chapter Fifteen

The offices of Walter Ferris, attorney at law, P.A., were located in an older residential section of Raleigh where massive oaks and beautiful wrought iron lamp posts lined the winding streets. A few years earlier when the commercial downtown district of Raleigh had been renovated and changed into a pedestrian mall, most of the successful attorneys moved into the beautiful new offices that had been built for the purpose of attracting more business to that six-block area. Since the courthouse was located within the same area, it was convenient and ideally suited for lawyers. The modern new office buildings filled up rapidly.

But Walter Ferris elected to remain where he had been practicing law since the beginning of his career some forty years earlier in an antebellum home that had been built in the mid-1800s. Its stately appearance and manicured lawn, as well as the other large homes surrounding it, gave anyone seeing it a feeling of security and well-being—and wealth. In addition to his own large office and the reception area, the old mansion housed the offices of three paralegals, two secretaries, a law library, and a conference room. Upstairs there were various office machines set up as well as an enormous area for storage and files.

Ferris had done extremely well over the years, having represented at one time or other most of the wealthy families in Raleigh. He had long ago quit taking cases simply for the high fees he could charge. He no longer needed to. Instead he was more likely to accept a case that presented an interesting challenge. His years of experience had taught him to never be surprised by what people are capable of doing. He always expected the unexpected, and he believed in being well prepared. And once he took a case, he didn't want to lose.

Walter had known Neal ever since he first came to Raleigh as a young coach from New York. He had represented him on a number of occasions—most of them trivial—and in return Neal had seen to it that Walter had good tickets to any of the Piedmont State basketball games he wanted to attend. It was a good trade-off as far as Walter was concerned.

But this business with Marla was a whole different matter. And from what he had already learned from the private investigator, the situation was definitely taking on the earmarks of an interesting challenge. Walter liked that.

"I'll tell Mr. Ferris you are here." The receptionist smiled warmly at Marla and Neal. They were early. In a few minutes Walter came out of his office and greeted them.

"Marla. Neal." He kissed Marla on her cheek and shook Neal's hand. "Would you like some coffee? Tea?"

Marla shook her head. "We just finished breakfast," explained Neal. "Thanks just the same."

They followed him into his office. Everything had a rich golden glow of old mahogany. The paneling, the furniture, even the crown moldings on the ceiling. The dark undertones of the wood were softened by pale yellow, floor-length draperies and cornices covered in the same yellow fabric. Walter steered them to a sofa, also covered in soft yellow, that was part of a seating arrangement defined by an old, but obviously very valuable, Persian rug. An M. Charles oil painting of the Outer Banks, one from the artist's early period, hung on the wall over the sofa.

"Marla, I know you said you never told anyone about the physical abuse you suffered from Andrews." Ferris wasn't going to waste any time finding out what he could from Marla. "But is there any chance someone could have seen marks left on you after one of his attacks?

Did anyone ever ask you about the bruises or cuts—anything like that?" Walter was seated in a maroon leather arm chair opposite Neal and Marla. He had a notepad and pen resting on his knee.

Marla thought for a moment. Neal took her hand. "Once when I went to my gynecologist for my annual exam my whole left side was bruised. When he asked me about it, I told him I had been horseback riding and had fallen."

"O.K. That's good. That's what I need. What was the doctor's name?"

Marla told him. "Of course, the people I saw on a regular basis, like where I went grocery shopping, the pharmacist, the lady in the post office—they would occasionally ask how I got a cut or bruise, but I always made up something. They must have believed me because they usually laughed about it." Marla took a deep breath. "And I got pretty good at covering up marks with makeup. I really don't think people noticed that much."

Walter made a few more notes.

"What about your family?"

"My parents are in a nursing home and haven't been able to travel in years. I would go to visit them, usually in July around my birthday. Of course, I never told them anything about it. They thought the world of Martin. It would have hurt them so much to know what he was really like. It was hard enough on them knowing when we divorced."

"What about in-laws? What was his family like?"

"I never knew Martin's family. He told me he had been born when his mother was in her forties, and that his parents had both died a few years before we were married. He also told me he was an only child."

Walter stared thoughtfully at Marla and then scribbled down some more notes.

"Did you have any photographs taken during those years you were married—maybe something that would show an injury?"

Marla shook her head. Martin was camera-shy. And he was careful about there not being anything that would make people ask questions."

Walter put the pad and pen down on the table next to his chair. "How long had you been divorced before you and Neal got married?" He leaned back in the chair and smiled.

"Not quite a year." Marla laughed. "I had decided to swear off all men, but, of course, that was before I met Neal."

"You were working in the Chancellor's office, I believe?"

"That's right. As soon as my divorce was final, I moved to Raleigh and began working as Frank Boyd's administrative assistant. It was a good job. I was responsible for writing grants and filling out applications for State funding—that type of thing. I also filled in for Elizabeth Wall, the chancellor's private secretary, whenever she needed time off."

"How did you and Elizabeth Wall get along?"

Marla was a little surprised by the question. "We got along very well. Some of the other women in the office resented her, I think. But she was always nice to me. Maybe because I didn't mind working extra hours when something needed to get done. I was just so thankful to have the opportunity to work at the University. It meant a new town, a new job, and a new life. After eight years of living in an abusive relationship, I just wanted to get control of my life. Of course, the last thing I wanted was to get married again."

"Why was that?"

"I just couldn't get over the fear that Martin was still out there somewhere watching me and waiting for me to do something that would trigger his violent behavior. I was afraid that getting involved with someone, even though I was divorced, was just the thing that would send him over the edge."

Neal reached out and took Marla's other hand.

"But Neal was so charming and attentive—and patient. I could tell him things I had never been able to tell anyone before."

"Well, I'm a patient kind of guy." Neal leaned over and kissed Marla.

Walter laughed. "I'm not sure the basketball officials would agree with that."

Marla looked at Walter thoughtfully. "I know people have made a great deal out of our ages, but I feel, if anything, the difference in our ages helped. Neal is so confident and sure of himself. He has helped me get over many of my own insecurities. I feel safe with him. I guess that's one reason why I agreed to go out with him in the first place."

Walter nodded. "I think Charlie Morgan took over as Athletics Director about that same time, didn't he, Neal?" The question was matter-of-fact. One friend making pleasant conversation with another.

"That's right. Marla and I were married the first week in March, right before the start of the ACC Tournament, and Morgan arrived on campus two weeks later. I remember he and his wife invited us over for dinner at their house. They weren't even settled in yet, but Morgan said he wanted to meet my bride. Remember, Marla?"

"I remember it wasn't a very pleasant evening. Anne, his wife, must have been exhausted from all of the unpacking. There were still boxes everywhere. I felt guilty even being there."

Walter picked up his pad and pen.

"Well, I think that's all I need right now. I'll let you know if I hear anything more from the assistant prosecutor's office. Marla, if you think of anything at all—no matter how unimportant you think it might be—call me. If I'm not here, you can leave a message with my secretary." Walter walked Neal and Marla to the outer office. "By the way, Marla, why do you suppose Andrews gave up his practice after your divorce?"

"I honestly don't know. He had a good practice going. Some of his patients he had been taking care of ever since he opened the office in Red Oak. He had talked at one time about wanting to do research, but nothing ever came of it. I don't know this, but I always suspected he had inherited quite a bit of money from his parents."

"Enough to live on without practicing medicine?" asked Walter.

"I saw a bank statement one time from a bank in New England somewhere. I didn't recognize the account, but it was in Martin's name, and it showed a balance of over five hundred thousand dollars. Since he had never told me about it, I felt it best not to say anything to him."

Walter nodded and looked directly at Marla. "Since your divorce from Andrews, did you ever see him or talk to him, even briefly? Until he showed up at your house that day, that is."

"No. Never. I never wanted to see or hear from him again. Although," Marla hesitated, "there were times when I thought I saw him. When we were in Albuquerque for the NCAA Finals, Gale Simmons and I had gone shopping and I thought I saw him there. But I'm sure it was just my imagination. We were all pretty keyed up over the games by then."

On the way to the car Neal stopped. "I forgot to ask Walter about some tickets. I'll only be a minute." Marla opened the car door and got in.

Walter was back at his desk reading something when Neal walked in. "O.K., Walter. What's going on with all the questions about Morgan?"

Walter looked surprised.

"Come on. You didn't ask about Morgan just to make conversation."

"Neal, I can't discuss it yet. But I promise you, I'll tell you just as soon as I know something definite."

"I think maybe you need to know, I suspect Morgan has been selling tickets illegally, not to mention padding his expense accounts. I also think he was the one responsible for spreading those rumors about the team using drugs before the Championship game. Does any of that tie in with what you think you have?"

"Neal, I don't know what we have here, but be careful."

"Is the assistant prosecutor going to charge Marla?"

"I don't know. Cochoran is working hard trying to dig up evidence against her. You know these young Turks. Anything to make a name for themselves."

"I just don't want any of them trying to make a name by using my wife. She's already been through enough."

"I know, Neal. Believe me, I know."

After Neal left, Walter opened the file he had been looking at earlier. He glanced through several papers until he came to a Photostat of a birth certificate. In the space provided for the name was typed CHARLES MORGAN ANDREWS.

Chapter Sixteen

Jean hadn't been able to sleep at night since Morgan's little visit. She had been through four husbands and enough lovers that she couldn't even remember them all. She thought she knew men. But she had never met anyone like Charlie Morgan, and, quite frankly, he scared the shit out of her. It wouldn't do any good to talk to Ray about it. He would only run back and tell Morgan. She realized now that Ray was afraid of him, too.

Being put down by Neal had been insulting and humiliating. But when she really analyzed it, he had only been truthful with her. He wasn't interested in getting involved with her. Period. If she thought he was, it wasn't because of anything he had said or done. It was because of her own mental gyrations, which after a couple of drinks could get quite imaginative. If she claimed that Neal had tried to rape her, she would be laughed right out of Raleigh—probably right out of North Carolina. And yet, she had definitely felt threatened when Morgan told her to make her decision soon. He expected her to go along with it. The tickets and use of the Director's Box were an obvious bribe. But if she refused to do what Morgan wanted, bribe or not, she hated to even think about the consequences.

Jean dumped an extra heaping spoonful of coffee into the percolator and listened to it burp, hiccup, and grown as it struggled to heat the mixture. By the time she had drunk her fourth cup of coffee, she knew what she must do. Still wearing her nightgown and robe, she lumbered into the living room. There on the desk was her address and telephone book. Flipping through the pages she soon found the number she wanted and dialed. The voice on the other end of the line sounded young, efficient, and alert.

"You have reached the office of Walter Ferris. May I help you?"

* * *

The ticket voucher information Stu pulled from the computer was only the beginning. He found out that Morgan had received ten books of tickets from the Athletics Department for the Atlantic Coast Conference Tournament the past year. In addition, he had received five more from the Seawolf Booster Club, making a total of fifteen books of tickets. Technically, all of the Athletics Directors in the ACC were supposed to be allocated the same number of tickets to the tournaments for personal use: two books.

By identifying the locations of the tickets, it was just a simple matter of making a few phone calls to determine who had used each of those tickets, how much they paid for them, and where they purchased them. Over and over again, the name Ray Knox surfaced. It wasn't difficult to figure out that Ray was selling the tickets for Charlie Morgan since he had been given the tickets to begin with. By the time Stu finished making the calls, he had discovered that of those fifteen books of tickets, thirteen had been sold for an amount in excess of twenty-five thousand dollars. To sell any ticket to a collegiate sporting event over its printed value was illegal. And this was just the ACC Tournament. Stu hadn't even started looking at the regular season tickets or the NCAA Championship games.

When Neal walked in, Stu could hardly contain himself. "Wait until you get a gander at this." He waved some papers in Neal's face.

"That good, huh?"

"Even better than that."

The two men went into Neal's office and shut the door. When Stu got through showing Neal what he had discovered, Neal leaned back in his chair and whistled softly through his teeth.

"This alone is enough to send the son of a bitch to prison."

"I know." Stu grinned.

They spent the rest of the morning with the business manager going over expense records. When they finished, there was little doubt that Morgan had turned in false expense reports.

"Christ, he didn't even try to be careful about it." Stu pulled out the hotel bill from where they had stayed in Albuquerque. "Look at this. You, Chancellor Boyd, and Morgan all had identical suites. You and the Chancellor were charged the rate of $125 a night, and that's what you put on your expense sheet. Morgan's expense sheet shows he was charged $225 a night. I mean, how dumb can you be?"

Neal nodded. "I have a feeling that the illegal sale of tickets and padded expense accounts aren't all we are dealing with here." Neal then told Stu about the meeting with Walter Ferris and his questions concerning Morgan.

"I wonder what Ferris is on to."

"I don't know. Walter said he would tell me as soon as he has something definite. In the meantime, I'd better get going if I'm going to make my meeting with Bill Camp on time."

Stu started gathering up the papers he had been showing Neal. "Do you want to take any of this with you?"

"No. There will be plenty of time later to document any accusations we make. I mainly want to make sure Bill knows what is happening over here. By the way, I dropped off Marla at your place on the way in from Walter's office. She wanted to get started on Gale's things."

"I really appreciate her doing that." Stu looked down at the floor.

"She wanted to, you know. Gale was her best friend, and she's going to miss her. We all will. Anyway, would you mind checking on her if I'm not back from my meeting with Bill—say by four o'clock. I don't want her to think I've forgotten her."

"I'll check on her."

Neal straightened his tie and grabbed his sports coat from the rack where he had hung it that morning. This damn thing with Morgan was going to be a mess—and on top of everything else. He climbed in his car and headed for Chapel Hill where the offices of the Consolidated University System were located. Neal had already made his decision. He had known even before he won the National Championship. Even if none of these other things had occurred, it wouldn't have made any difference. It was time to get out of coaching—before he got too god-damn old to enjoy Marla and what little time they had left together.

* * *

Marla sat barefooted in the middle of the floor surrounded by piles of dresses, slacks, blouses, underclothes, and shoes. On her head was the Western hat Gale had brought back from Albuquerque. It still had the price tag dangling off the leather band. Knowing Gale, she had probably worn it to Anne's party like that after the Championship game just to give Anne something else to talk about.

Marla had emptied everything out of Gale's closet and chest of drawers. After sorting through the things, she made a list of what could be donated. Then she put them in big plastic bags. Some of the things she wasn't sure about—like Gale's jewelry. Gale had always loved pretty jewelry, and she had collected some beautiful pieces. Marla decided she would ask Stu about it before doing anything.

Seeing Gale's things had brought back so many memories. Like Marla, Gale had always worn red and white to the games. The red polka-dotted dress Gale wore to the Carolina game when Marla got sick. That was right after she and Neal had gotten married. They lost that game, and as far as Marla knew, Gale never wore that dress again. The red corduroy pants suit she wore to the Alaska Shoot-Out. Marla had just become a hall walker then. It was a three-day event held over Thanksgiving in Anchorage. It was the first time she or Gale had been out of the lower forty-eight states. The host arena only seated about 5,000 fans, but the games had been broadcast nationally on ESPN. Gale wore her corduroy pants suit to each of the games as long as the Seawolves kept winning, afraid if she didn't, it would bring bad luck to the team. The Seawolves won the tournament.

Marla finally finished bagging up the last of the clothes and shoes. It had taken her most of the day, and she hadn't eaten anything. She still needed to do something with all of Gale's personal things like makeup and hair brushes. There was also a stack of papers and letters that Marla had found in one of Gale's drawers. All of this was a lot more difficult to deal with than Marla thought it would be. She thought of Stu. He would never have managed it. It was better for him to be back at the office.

She went to the bathroom and washed her face. Then she went into the kitchen to see if there was anything to make a sandwich with when she heard the doorbell rang. Two uniformed police officers stood on the front porch.

"Mrs. Connors?" They both glanced at the hat still on Marla's head and then down at her bare feet.

"Yes."

"We have a warrant for your arrest. We need you to come with us."

Just then Stu drove up.

"What's going on?" He got out of the car and walked briskly over to Marla.

Marla didn't move. She was too stunned and too weary to say or do anything.

Chapter Seventeen

It was after lunch before Jean finally got hold of Walter Ferris. Apparently he had some business downtown at the courthouse that had taken all morning. She didn't leave a message with the efficient-sounding person who answered his office phone. She didn't want anyone to know who she was or why she was calling. She only wanted to talk to Walter Ferris—and as soon as possible.

Of course, Walter knew who Jean was once she gave him her name. There probably wasn't anyone who was associated with the athletics program at Piedmont State who didn't know her. He was surprised to hear from her though, and that she needed to see him so urgently. "A matter of life and death," she had said. After juggling his schedule a bit, he told her he could meet with her at two o'clock that afternoon.

Jean in the meantime dressed and tried to pass the time by watching television. Her phone rang several times, but she didn't dare answer it, thinking it might be Morgan.

What she needed was a good stiff belt of whiskey to calm her nerves, but she knew if she got started drinking, she might not be able to stop. And she didn't want to go see Ferris half sloshed. By one o'clock she was in such a frantic state, she got in her car and just drove around, thinking she would be better off away from the phone and away from the house just in case Morgan decided to stop by. She got to the attorney's office at one-thirty.

Walter finished with his one o'clock appointment earlier than expected and only kept Jean waiting a few minutes. She spied the liquor cabinet the minute she walked into his office and told him to fix her a bourbon, straight up. He poured some Wild Turkey into a cut crystal glass and handed it to her. It had been a long time since he had seen anyone so frightened. When she finally got her story out, he could understand why.

"That man is crazy," Jean repeated for about the tenth time. "I'm afraid to be in the house alone. Can't you get a restraining order against him or something?"

"Not unless he does something to make you think your life is in danger. Right now all we have is that one conversation, and as far as I can judge from what you told me, he didn't actually threaten you."

Jean looked longingly at the liquor cabinet.

"Do you have a friend you could stay with for a few days or who could stay with you?"

Jean shook her head. "I don't know."

"Jean, I know how you feel. But I honestly don't think you have anything to worry about. It's Neal Connors Morgan wants—not you."

Walter stood up. "If he does contact you again, though, I want you to call me immediately. It's important. Will you do that?"

"Yes." Jean pulled herself out of the chair she was slumped in. "Maybe I'll just go out of town for a while."

Just then the intercom buzzed on Walter's desk.

"It's Mr. Stuart Simmons on the phone, Mr. Ferris," his secretary informed him. "He says it is urgent."

Walter opened the door for Jean. "If you go out of town, let my secretary know how I can get in touch with you, Jean. I'll look into this and let you know what I find out. In the meantime, try not to worry."

Jean smiled weakly and left.

Walter walked over to his desk and pushed the button on his phone console that was blinking.

"Hello, Stu. What can I do for you?"

* * *

The meeting with Bill Camp took a lot longer than Neal had anticipated. It had been a while since the two men had seen one another. They had a lot of catching up to do. Of course, Bill wanted to talk about the Seawolves winning the National Championship. He was sorry to hear about Stu Simmons' wife. And he asked about Marla. He carefully avoided mentioning anything about what the newspapers were full of: Andrews' death.

Neal followed the conversation along as Bill directed it. He knew that Bill would eventually get around to asking him why he had come to see him. And he did.

"How is Charlie Morgan these days?"

"Actually, that's why I wanted to see you."

Bill grunted. "I thought it might be." He opened a desk drawer and pulled out a large stack of papers. "These are all letters from the Seawolves' largest contributors wanting me to can his ass."

Neal smiled. Apparently Stu had found time to make those phone calls.

Neal told Bill his suspicions regarding the false stories that had been published in the newspapers about the team using drugs, and about the meeting that had taken place in Morgan's office.

"So you think Morgan planted those stories just so he could fire you?"

"Yes. I do. I don't know if he's just trying to get rid of me or if he's wanting to destroy State's basketball program."

"It's one and the same as far as I am concerned," said Bill.

Neal then told him how Morgan had tried to push through new rules regarding academic requirements for the athletes, among other things. "If I hadn't been out of town recruiting, he never would have gotten the

Athletics Council to go along with it. But the fact that he did shows you what kind of pressure he's willing to apply. Fortunately I found out about it and was able to convince Chancellor Boyd that it would be a huge mistake."

"Boyd told me about it. Not only would it have been a mistake, it would have been insane."

"That's why I wanted to talk to you directly. I just want to be sure you know what's happening. Chancellor Boyd and Morgan go back a long way. Sometimes it's hard to use good judgment when a close friend is involved."

"I don't think you have to worry about Boyd. The fact that he told me about what Morgan had done indicates to me that he is regretting his decision naming Morgan Athletics Director. I'm sure, too, he has received just as many letters as I have."

"There's one more thing I want to talk to you about. I haven't announced it yet because I wanted to tell you first."

Bill raised his eyebrows. "You wouldn't do anything in haste, would you?"

"No. I've given this a lot of thought. It's time I stepped down as head coach. Nothing is going to top the year we've just had—winning the National Championship. Next year will be a rebuilding year. It's time someone else took over."

Bill shook his head. "I was afraid you were going to say that."

"You are too good a friend to say anything about it, but you know the state my personal life is in right now. It can't be good for the basketball program or the University. But even if none of it had happened, I would still feel like it was time to get out."

"This makes me sad, my friend. I think I understand how you feel, but it makes me sad all the same. I pity the man who tries to take your place."

"You already have someone."

Bill looked surprised.

"Stu Simmons." Neal waited for Bill to think about it. "He's dedicated, loyal, honest, the players respect him, and he's a good recruiter. And he's been around long enough to know what kind of basketball the Seawolfers want. He's a good man, Bill."

"I know he is, Neal. But can he get the job done? Can he make the tough decisions when they need to be made?"

"At one time I would have doubted it. But now, after seeing how he's coped with his wife's death, I think he can handle anything that comes along—certainly just as well as I could. Maybe even better. And he doesn't want to retire any time soon. It would give our basketball program a continuity. That's good. And he also knows the new recruits who are coming in this fall."

Bill nodded and for a moment silence filled the room. Bill clasped his hands together. "Neal, would you not announce your resignation just yet? Give me a couple of weeks to deal with Morgan. That way, any decision involving a new basketball coach can be made by Boyd."

"I understand. I'm not sure if we have two weeks though." Neal told Bill what he knew about the assistant prosecutor's investigation.

"I'm not worried about that as far as the school goes. I just hate that you and Marla are having to go through such a terrible ordeal. You told me Walter Ferris is handling this matter for you. He's a good man. But if you need any more help, the University legal counsel is at your disposal."

"Thanks, Bill. I really don't think it will go that far, but I appreciate the offer."

When Neal left the President's office, it was with the understanding that he would announce his resignation the first of May. That would give Bill the time he wanted. In the meantime, Neal would only tell

Marla about his decision. As far as Stu being offered the head coaching job, Neal had made his recommendation. Now it would be up to Bill Camp and Frank Boyd to decide.

Neal felt good. He would feel even better once his decision was made public. But for now, he felt good. He pulled into his parking space at the basketball office. Stu must have been watching for him because he came running out of the building before Neal could even get out of the car.

"Neal, Marla's been arrested."

Chapter Eighteen

It had been three days since Morgan had talked to Jean. He tried calling her several times, but didn't get an answer. Either she was one of the busiest, goddamn women he had ever known, or she wasn't answering her phone. He hoped it wasn't the latter. After all, he thought he had handled the situation pretty well. Offering her tickets and an invitation to sit in the Director's Box was no little thing. Seawolfers who had contributed hundreds of thousands of dollars over the years didn't get that much. Good tickets were hard to come by and reserved for only those who gave the most, either to the Athletics Department or to the Seawolf Booster Club. Getting an invitation to join the Athletics Director in his private box during the home football games was a prestige thing. There was an open bar, a luncheon buffet, or dinner if the game was being played at night, plush chairs to sit in while watching the game, a big-screen television to watch the replays if the game was being televised, or to keep up with other games being played at the same time. Everything was state-of-the-art and designed for the purpose of providing luxury to those who were willing to pay for it. And here he was offering it to Jean for nothing. He picked up the phone and dialed her number again. When he got no answer, he buzzed for Ray on the intercom and told him to come to his office.

"Have you heard from your friend lately?"

Ray stood in the doorway. "What friend is that, Charlie?"

Morgan motioned for Ray to come in and close the door. "Jean. Do you know where she is?"

"I haven't talked to her since I asked her if she'd meet with you. Why? Is there a problem?"

"No. She was supposed to get back to me about something and she hasn't done it." Morgan played with a paper clip on his desk.

"She's probably just busy. If she said she'd do something for you, I'm sure she will." Ray was getting more than a little concerned over Morgan's behavior. Ever since that story had come out about that Andrews guy getting killed, Morgan had been acting crazy—even more so than usual. Yelling at everyone and throwing things. His secretary had quit, and no one else in the Athletics Department wanted to be around him. And the office gossip had it that even Anne, his wife, was fed up and didn't want to stay in Raleigh. Ray wondered if it wasn't because of the way Charlie had been acting.

Ray, in fact, hadn't tried to contact Jean since that day he was at her house. He had been too busy himself. After discussing it with his wife, he had made a few discreet calls to former associates back in New Hampshire. If things worked out, he would be returning to his old job the first of the month. He just couldn't take being Morgan's errand boy any longer. Not only that, he had gotten wind that the school auditors were looking into ticket sales and expense accounts in the Athletics Department. He sure as hell didn't need to stay around for that.

"You're awfully closed-mouth." Morgan looked at Ray. "What have you been up to?"

Ray felt the nerve start to twitch over his right eye. "I've been busy with baseball and track lately. Of course you know that the Russian track team is coming over for the exhibition meet in a couple of weeks. There's a lot to do to get ready for it." Sweat started to form on Ray's forehead and upper lip. Morgan had been so paranoid lately, it would be just like him to figure out that he was planning to leave. Ray walked over to the large window behind Morgan's desk overlooking the football practice fields and track. "There's still a lot to do to get the track in good shape." He hoped he sounded convincing. He could feel

Morgan's eyes on the back of his head. "Which reminds me, I have a meeting with the grounds crew in ten minutes. I'd better get going. Did you need anything else?" Ray walked back over to the door.

"No. Go on to your meeting." Morgan flipped the paper clip with his finger and watched it land on the carpet across the room.

Morgan thought he had everything worked out. It had been so easy. Once he convinced Boyd to give him the job at State as A.D. it was just a matter of time when he would ruin Connors and, along with him, Marla. Sexy Marla. He had seen her in the hotel lobby, looking like a well kept whore. So sweet, so loving. Or so everyone thought. Once he got through with her, everyone would know what kind of bitch she really was. How she had left her husband and didn't even have the decency to tell him. She just left. When Martin came home from the office, she was gone. No note. Nothing.

Martin had called him late one night right after that—crying like a baby. Morgan hadn't heard from him since they were kids. Just before the two of them had been farmed out to families in the area because their mother had left them. Their father didn't want them either.

They were only half brothers, but they should have been allowed to stay together. Martin's new family moved away a short time later, and Morgan didn't know what had happened to him—until he called that night, crying like a baby.

Morgan could feel himself losing control again. He was doing that a lot lately. Even over little things, like those goddamn four-minute eggs his wife insisted on feeding him. It was getting so he didn't trust anyone. Boyd wanting him to work with Connors. What a joke. The employees in the Athletics Department were all against him, too. He could feel it. Even Ray was acting secretive. And Anne. She was threatening to leave. But even if she did, she'd come back. If she knew what was good for her.

Morgan took several deep breaths trying to relieve the pressure building up in his head. He forced himself to stand up. If only Martin had waited. Morgan promised he would take care of things, just the way he always had when they were kids. Martin had come crying to him then too when his mother started screaming and sobbing. They couldn't see what was happening. They were always in Morgan's room with the door closed. But they could hear what was happening. The loud crashing noises, things falling and breaking, their father yelling. And there were the other noises. Always the other noises. That was the worst part of all of it. Morgan had only been eight years old at the time, three years older than Martin. But he didn't cry. Not like Martin. Martin was impatient then, too. He didn't wait for Morgan to take care of things. And because of it, they got separated and sent to live with strangers. And now when Morgan said he would take care of things with Marla, Martin still didn't wait. And Marla had killed him because of it. Well, he would still take care of things. He had already talked to the assistant prosecutor on the case, telling him how sweet, innocent Marla had thrown herself all over him that morning in Albuquerque. And once that woman Jean told her story of how Connors tried to rape her, he wouldn't need to do anything else. The press and the courts would do the rest.

Morgan walked the perimeter of his office still feeling the pounding in his head. He stopped in front of the antique chair. The worn, velvet-covered, wing-back chair that had been in his family for generations. At least that is what his mother had told him. That was all he had left now. His mother was gone. His father was gone. Martin was gone. There was no one else. Just an old chair. Morgan reached out and raked his fingers across the grain of the velvet feeling its soft texture. Then he picked it up and hurled it through the window.

Chapter Nineteen

Walter Ferris canceled the rest of his appointments for the day and rushed downtown to the police station as soon he hung up from talking to Stu. He had expected Cochoran to issue a warrant for Marla's arrest, but not so soon. He had misjudged the assistant prosecutor. He wouldn't do it again. By the time Neal got there, Walter was already meeting with Cochoran.

"How ya doin', Coach?"

Neal looked at the sergeant on the desk. He had never seen the man before, but Neal was used to people recognizing him and speaking.

"I'll be a hell of a lot better when I find my wife. Do you know where she has been taken?"

"I'll get someone to show you." He motioned to a woman in a uniform sitting nearby. "Take Coach Connors to room 5-E," he instructed.

"Thanks," said Neal and he followed the woman down a hallway. Three doors down the woman stopped and knocked. Another uniformed officer opened the door from the inside. Neal went in.

Marla was sitting at a table next to Walter. A couple of other men in civilian clothes sat across from them. When Marla saw Neal, she jumped up and rushed into his arms.

"Oh, Neal. I am so sorry."

Neal held her tightly against him and stroked her hair. "It's all right. Walter will take care of things."

"Hello, Neal." Walter nodded.

One of the men across the table got up and extended his hand toward Neal. "Tom Cochoran, assistant prosecutor. And this is Larry Alverez, my associate."

Neal shook hands and continued holding Marla. "What's this all about?"

"I'm afraid we've uncovered enough evidence to suggest that the murder of Martin Andrews wasn't self-defense." Cochoran motioned for Neal and Marla to sit down.

"And what evidence is that, Tom?" Neal could feel his heart pick up speed.

"That's what I was trying to determine," said Walter. "From what I can gather, Tom seems to think Marla asked Andrews to come to the house while you were on your recruiting trip for the purpose of killing him."

"I would never do that—I couldn't have. I didn't want to ever see him again." Marla held onto Neal's hand.

"We found the letter you wrote to him, Mrs. Connors."

"Letter? What letter?"

"I'd like to see it if you don't mind." Walter clasped his hands together on the table. Cochoran opened the file folder in front of him and pulled out a piece of white paper. There was an envelope paper clipped to the back of it. "The cancellation stamp on the envelope corresponds to the date on the letter," said Cochoran, handing it to Walter.

Walter glanced over the letter. Supposedly it was from Marla telling Martin how much she enjoyed being with him in Albuquerque and that she was looking forward to seeing him again soon. "It's a bit obvious, don't you think? This letter has been typed. Anyone could have sent it."

"Perhaps. But we haven't found anyone else with a motive."

Neal read the letter. "And what could Marla's motive be for crissake?"

Walter put his hand on Neal's arm.

"Mrs. Connors is the only person in her ex-husband's will." Cochoran looked at Marla. "She stands to inherit over a million dollars."

Marla gasped. "A million dollars! But I never knew. How could I? He never discussed finances with me."

"It was money that had been set up in a trust by his mother."

"When was the will drawn up?" Walter asked. His voice was calm and even.

"Five weeks ago. It was signed and dated Monday, April 4, a week before she wrote the letter."

"April 4?" Neal looked at Walter. "That was when we won the National Championship."

Cochoran smiled and nodded. "I know. Ironic, isn't it?"

"That means Marla had been married to Neal for almost a year when the will was made out. She wouldn't have known about it." Walter sounded as though he were instructing a six-year old on how to bait a fishing hook. "I think it's apparent that you're dealing with a very sick person here. Someone who has, or thinks he has, a reason to hate Mrs. Connors. Whoever it is has gone to a lot of trouble to make it look like she killed Andrews for some reason other than defending her own life. There was a history of abuse, and she feared for her life. It was self-defense, but certainly not intentional murder."

"Of course, we only have her word that she was abused. There are no police records to substantiate that. On the other hand, if she had been seeing him, it's quite possible the subject of the will came up in conversation." Cochoran looked at Marla. "And as far as I am concerned, that alone would be motive."

Walter glanced at his well manicured nails and then back at Cochoran. "Is that all the evidence you have?"

Cochoran grinned, the left side of his mouth turning up higher than the right. "More or less."

Walter knew what that meant. Cochoran was hiding something—something that Cochoran felt would probably win his case and that he wasn't ready to reveal yet. Walter continued looking directly at Cochoran and sat forward. "If I were you, I'd give it a lot of thought before filing charges against Mrs. Connors."

Cochoran blinked and stuffed the letter and envelope back into the folder. "Oh, I have."

Walter leaned back in his chair. He had known people like Cochoran all of his life. Too wrapped up in their own agendas to recognize or even care about the truth. It was like a game of chess. Walter would plan his game strategy and work towards that end, making adjustments when necessary. If Cochoran was true to character, however, his game plan would be to aggressively attack. Walter would have to handle him carefully. If he came on too strong, Cochoran would dig in deeper just to prove he could do it. And if Walter appeared to acquiesce, Cochoran would try to crucify him. He wouldn't be the first young lawyer to try to win a case from the venerable Walter Ferris just to make a name for himself. But Cochoran also had another motive—something the others didn't. The lead State prosecutor was retiring at the end of the year, and Cochoran was in the favored position to take over. The scuttlebutt around the courthouse was that it could happen even sooner, especially if Cochoran won a case like this one.

Walter felt the thrill of the challenge once again surge through his body as he thought about what Cochoran had uncovered—the letter and the will. And something else he wasn't revealing yet, whatever that was. Walter had been weaned on young attorneys like Cochoran. He wasn't intimidated. In fact, he welcomed the challenge. At this stage in his life, it was one of the few enjoyments he had left. And no matter what, he sure in hell wasn't going to let him win.

"Could we go to your office for a few minutes, Tom?" There are some things I need to go over with you." Walter stood up with his briefcase as though there were no doubt Cochoran would do as he asked. "This won't take long, Marla." Walter patted her on the back reassuringly. "Just sit tight."

* * *

It was dark when Marla and Neal got home. Walter had managed to get Marla released on a fifty thousand dollar bond. The charge against her was first-degree murder. Cochoran wouldn't drop it or reduce it. Walter had told him some of the things he had learned concerning Charlie Morgan and his relationship to Martin. But when he realized Cochoran wasn't going to change his mind, he decided to keep the rest of the information to himself. He would present it in front of the judge where it would be given a more objective appraisal. Besides, he didn't want to reveal all of his moves too soon. He would enjoy playing the element of surprise on Cochoran just to see the disappointment on his cocky, impudent face.

It took some maneuvering, but Walter managed to get the probable cause hearing scheduled for one o'clock the next day. One advantage of being a trial attorney in Raleigh for over thirty years, and a good one at that, was that a lot of people in high places owed Walter favors. And the favor he wanted was to get this case concluded as quickly as possible. Dragging it out would only give the press time to build up negative feelings against Marla from the general public, and there was already enough of that. Of course, Marla had pleaded not guilty.

Neal called Stu as soon as he and Marla got home so he could bring him up to date. After he hung up the phone, he went to find Marla. He found her already in bed. "How about a sandwich or maybe some soup? We'll have a picnic in bed."

"I'm really not hungry, Neal. I think I just want to go to sleep."

"Popcorn then. Or maybe a bowl of ice cream?"

Marla shook her head and turned away.

Neal undressed and got in the bed, pulling Marla into his arms when he did. "You don't need to worry about any of this. Walter is on top of it. Believe me, O.K?"

He could feel Marla nod her head.

But Marla wasn't convinced. Somehow without realizing why or when, she had lost control of her life, just as she had when she was married to Martin. Like then, no matter what she did, there was a negative force working against her. At least when she had been married to Martin, she knew that the force was him. She knew what it was she had to fight. But now the force was invisible and all-consuming. And it was evil. She didn't know how to fight it because she didn't know what it was. The only thing she knew was that she couldn't put Neal through it. She loved him too much. Even if the charges were dismissed, there would always be people to blame her. Gale had been right. The Seawolfers would never forgive her. But they didn't need to blame Neal. And if she were no longer around, they wouldn't. She would insist that Walter prepare the divorce papers as soon as possible. She just hoped that would be enough to save Neal and his career.

Marla turned her back to Neal. Already she was trying to prepare herself for the separation. Even when Martin had been his cruelest and Marla couldn't move because of the physical pain she was in, it was nothing compared to the pain she felt knowing she was going to leave Neal, the one person she loved more than her own life. It felt like death, only worse, because she would have to go on living.

* * *

Even though it was after seven Walter returned to his office when he left the police station. The private investigator he had hired was supposed to have delivered something to him. Walter hoped he had left it at the office.

Marla had surprised him when he first arrived at the police station by asking him to start divorce proceedings between her and Neal. She had also made him promise that he wouldn't tell Neal. She wanted to tell him. Walter knew why she was doing it. She felt the scandal would somehow hurt Neal and his career. What Walter tried to explain to her without success was that the Seawolfers would talk about it for a few months and then forget about it. There would be some other new item of gossip to distract them.

But she had been adamant. She wanted the divorce as soon as possible. Even uncontested and with no custody of children involved, it would take a year by North Carolina law. If she went out of state, however, which she intended to do, she could get it in six weeks. He had finally agreed, but only because he was afraid if he didn't, she would go to another lawyer who would do as she asked. At least this way, he could hopefully drag it out long enough until she changed her mind. As far as he was concerned, a divorce would be a terrible mistake. If ever two people were meant to be together, it was Neal and Marla. He wouldn't tell Neal since he had promised Marla he wouldn't, but he wouldn't prepare the divorce papers either. Once this other thing about Martin's death was resolved, he was certain she would change her mind.

Walter unlocked the door and turned on the light. On his desk was a large brown envelope. Walter opened it and pulled out a handful of papers. Without sitting down he quickly scanned over them. When he had finished he shoved everything back in the envelope and placed it next to the large file marked CONNORS in the top drawer of his desk. He locked the drawer and then on his way out hurriedly wrote a note to his secretary: *Need to talk to Dan (PI), ASAP.*

The envelope contained some of what he was hoping for, but it still wasn't enough. At least not enough to get Marla off at the probable cause hearing tomorrow. With this new information, he figured he had about a thirty percent chance, tops, of keeping the case from going to trial; that is, if he was in good form in front of the judge. And he planned to be. But those odds weren't good enough as far as he was concerned, no matter what kind of form he was in. He would have to dig deeper for other evidence, and now with this new information the private investigator had uncovered, he had a good idea of where to look.

One mistake lawyers like Cochoran frequently made in their zealousness to win a case was to overlook the obvious. Instead, they focused on what they believed to be the sensational, something that would put their name in the headlines. In this case, Cochoran was being distracted by name recognition and the personalities involved—Neal and Marla Connors. He would lose the case because of it. Maybe not now, and maybe not at the hearing tomorrow, but eventually he would lose.

* * *

Ray drove slowly around the Athletics Center, the building that housed the offices of the Athletics Department. The parking lot was empty, but he wanted to make sure no one was around. The damn coaches were always showing up at odd hours, and the last thing he wanted to do was to get caught up in a conversation with one of them about why he was clearing out his office. They were as bad as a bunch of gossipy old women. If one of them found out he was leaving, the whole campus would know before he could even get out of town.

Satisfied that the building was empty, he parked in the loading zone out back. That way he wouldn't have to carry his stuff so far. Using his master key, he unlocked the door and went in, turning on only one light in the hallway. He didn't want to attract any attention by having a lot of lights blazing. He walked up the stairs and down another hall to the administrative offices where he unlocked the door and quickly closed it behind him. There were empty boxes kept in the storage closet. He picked out several sturdy ones and hastily filled them with files, computer discs, and personal items. He didn't have much. When he had finished, he carted everything out to his car.

The Personnel Director at the University of New Hampshire hadn't been able to give Ray a definite answer as to whether he could have his old job back. In fact, he had been pretty evasive when Ray tried to get some information from him. But Ray couldn't risk it by waiting around any longer. Too much was happening. It was just a matter of time before that sleazy drug dealer would show up wanting more money. And Morgan's business with Jean. Who knows how that would turn out. And even though no one in the business office was talking, he was sure the auditors had already been in and had probably completed their report. There was no question that Morgan had mishandled Athletics Department money, and if the auditors wanted to, they could easily accuse Ray as well. He sure couldn't depend on Morgan to stand up for him either, not the way he had been acting. No. It was better if he just left. He would take his chances at getting a job at the University in New Hampshire. He wouldn't even have to get his old job back, if that was a problem. He could do something else at the University. At this point, he wasn't going to be particular.

Ray fit the last of the boxes into the trunk of his car and slammed the lid closed. He had only packed a few of his clothes—whatever he thought he would need for a week or so. His wife would bring everything else once he found them a place to live. In the meantime, when anyone asked, she would just say that he had a family emergency and she didn't know when he would get back. The important thing was that Morgan not find out where he had gone. If he knew that Ray had left for another job, especially back in New Hampshire, it would be just like him to try to ruin it for him.

He went back inside to lock the office and turn off the light. Morgan's office door was open. Apparently Morgan hadn't bothered to lock up when he left earlier in the day. Ray went inside and noticed the shattered window behind Morgan's desk. He also noticed that the chair Morgan was so peculiar about was missing. Oh well. That wasn't his problem. Not anymore. Ray started to walk out when he remembered the file cabinet and the shoe box that was hidden in the back of it. He had watched Morgan count out fifty thousand dollars in one hundred dollar bills from the money that was in the box, and there had been a lot left. Unless Morgan had used it for something, it would still be there. Ray opened the drawer and felt in the back. The box was there. Inside were several bundles of cash. Ray closed the drawer and left, taking the box with him.

"Just think of this as that bonus you promised me, Charlie," Ray said to himself smiling as he climbed into his car. He put the box on the floorboard next to the driver's seat. Fifteen minutes later he was leaving the Raleigh city limits and headed north.

* * *

Jean unlocked her front door, turned on the light, and scooted her large suitcase inside with her foot. A pile of mail was stacked on the small cherry table in the foyer where her neighbor had put it. There was also a stack of unread newspapers on the floor. Usually whenever Jean went away, she asked her neighbor to throw the newspapers away. But this time she wanted them saved so she could read what had taken place about the killing. She would also get the latest news from her friend at lunch on Thursday at Coblestones.

She glanced at her watch. It was eight o'clock. Ferris might still be at his office. He had told her to be sure to keep him informed where she was. She needed to let him know that she had decided to come home. She didn't like being away, even for only a day or two, unless she was with the Seawolfers following the team somewhere. Going anywhere by herself was too lonely. All she did was drink, eat, and sleep. She had probably put on ten pounds, and it had only been two days.

Besides, after thinking about it, she probably over-reacted to what Morgan said anyway. He had hoped to bribe her into lying for him. She would simply tell him she didn't want to get involved, even though his offer of tickets and the invitation to sit in the Director's Box was extremely generous. She was sure he would understand. She would tell him in a nice way, of course, and that would be the end of it. He might even invite her to sit in the Director's Box anyway. After all, she had donated that twenty thousand dollars.

She picked up the phone and dialed the office of Walter Ferris. When his answering service answered, she hung up.

Chapter Twenty

After talking to the private investigator early the next morning, Walter drove over to the assistant prosecutor's office. Cochoran wasn't there, but Walter managed to find out from an especially chatty and helpful paralegal in the assistant prosecutor's office that the mystery evidence Cochoran had was another letter, also typed, supposedly from Marla to Martin telling him she had received the copy of his will naming her as the beneficiary. In the letter she invited him to visit her while Neal was out of town. It was dated one week before Andrews was killed. Walter was able to get a copy of the letter with the assistance of that same paralegal. Since he already had a copy of the other typed letter, it was easy enough to compare them, and when he did, Walter had no doubt they had been typed on the same machine.

Following his instincts, Walter waited until he thought Morgan had already left for his office in the Athletics Department and then went to pay his wife, Anne, a visit. He had to step over several suitcases when she invited him in. He couldn't have caught her at a better time. Anne was obviously upset. Her mascara was still smeared under her eyes from where she had been crying. She and Morgan weren't getting along, and she was leaving to go stay with her family for a while—maybe forever. She didn't explain to Walter what had happened, but whatever it was, it must have been pretty bad. Without asking why Walter wanted to know, she gave him the account information on a trust fund that had been set up in Morgan's name. If he had asked her, she probably would have given him the names of Morgan's psychiatrists and the institutions where he had been admitted, but he didn't need to bother her about that. Dan had already traced that information down for him.

What Walter did want was Morgan's typewriter from his home office, and Anne gave it to him when he asked for it. If he was right about this, the typewriter was all Walter needed to validate his suspicions. He had just enough time to stop by the forensics lab downtown and still get to the courthouse by one. If his friend, Mike, was working in the lab this morning, Walter knew he could count on him to drop whatever he was doing to take a look at what Walter had. He had done rush jobs for Walter in the past, and he was reliable.

The two letters had to have been typed on Morgan's typewriter by Morgan. That piece of evidence backed up by a forensics expert would destroy Cochoran's theory that Marla had lured Andrews to her home while Neal was out of town in order to kill him for the inheritance. Walter believed Marla when she told him she had not been in touch with Andrews since their divorce. He was pretty sure who had though. Out of all of this, one thing was certain. With everything Walter had found out so far, Charles Morgan Andrews was certifiably and legally insane. Whatever his reasons were, Morgan was trying to destroy Marla, and along with her, Coach Connors. Walter was glad Jean had decided to go away for a while.

* * *

Anne Morgan turned left off of DuBois Street onto Western Boulevard. She didn't see the blue pickup truck swerve to avoid hitting her. She didn't hear the driver either when he yelled and honked his horn angrily as he screeched past her from the turn lane.

The front and back seats as well as the trunk of the white Lincoln Continental she was driving were crammed with suitcases, boxes, and plastic bags—everything she owned. She didn't own the Lincoln. It was one of two courtesy cars that the University provided the Athletics

Director. Charlie preferred driving the small red Mazda sports coupe. She would have to figure out how to return the Lincoln to the University later. Right now all she wanted was to get away from Charlie and get away from Raleigh. Since she didn't have any other means of transportation, she was driving the Lincoln to Pennsylvania.

She took the clover leaf turn to the right that put her on Hwy. 70 North. It was five hours driving time to Washington, D.C. and another seven, if she made good time, to Harrisburg. She would drive straight through. Otherwise, if she stopped somewhere, she might be tempted to go back. And she simply couldn't. Not this time.

She reached into one of the boxes in the seat next to her and pulled out a tissue, throwing the one crumpled in her hand on the floor. Then she swiped at the tears running down her cheeks and blew her nose lustily. Thinking back on it, it wasn't that she had wasted thirty-five years on a bad marriage that had forced her to finally make the decision to leave. After all, most of her friends—what few friends she had— were unhappy with their marriages as well. She could have put up with her marriage, such as it was. Putting up with Charlie's craziness was more difficult. The drugs, the commutes in and out of sanitariums and mental health clinics, the constant worry and fear that he would have another "episode," as the psychiatrists termed it, and trying to keep all of it secret consumed pretty much her entire life. But even as bad as that was, the lies and deceit and the tremendous amount of stress that left her completely depleted of energy or motivation, she had dealt with it. Even when Charlie turned his anger and rage toward her. Even as bad as all of that was, she still had managed, and no one ever suspected.

She hadn't expected life to be perfect when she married him. After all, she had her faults too. She was overweight, a fact that Charlie constantly reminded her of. She was never what you could call pretty, or even attractive, no matter how much she spent on makeup and beauty salons and clothes. She wasn't especially smart either. If her father hadn't been on the Board of Trustees at the small liberal arts college she attended, she would have flunked out her freshman year. But, she learned early in life that money and power could get her just about anything she wanted.

Those were the things that probably got her Charlie. As an unattractive twenty-five-year-old still living at home and with no future to speak of, she decided that Charles Morgan was what she wanted. She had met him at a mixer her senior year at college. He was a freshman at the University of Pennsylvania, and even though he was younger, she was immediately attracted to him. And she was willing to wait for him until he graduated, if that's what it took. Besides, there was no one else. Heaven only knows how much her father had to shell out to get him to marry her.

She was able to overlook the true reason behind Charlie's interest in her because, at the time, she was convinced she could make him love her—eventually. She would do anything, no matter what, just to make him happy. Now, after thirty-five years of trying she suddenly realized she had failed. She was tired of trying. She would never be able to make Charles Morgan happy. And that was what hurt the most. In all that time never once had she felt as though she had pleased Charlie or made him proud of her. As hard as she worked at being the good little wife, a loving companion, a gracious hostess, and someone Charlie could depend on to do everything for him just to make his life easier no matter how much of an inconvenience it was to her, she had failed.

She had seen the "episode" coming. It had been building for weeks, even months. The headaches, the temper tantrums, the mood swings. The prescription drugs were no longer effective, and Charlie absolutely refused to seek medical help. It was all a familiar pattern to her. It was just a matter of time now when Charlie would lose all control. This latest episode seemed to have been triggered by Coach Connors and for some reason his wife, Marla. She didn't know what it was, and at this point, she didn't care. She simply didn't have the energy, the interest, or the strength to go through another one.

She had waited until Charlie left for work that morning. If she had said anything to him, it might have caused him to have another fit. Like the ones he had over those stupid poached eggs he insisted on eating raw. It was just easier all the way around not to tell him that she was leaving. She had quickly thrown her things together and loaded them into the car, not caring how neat or organized everything was. Even so, it had taken her most of the morning. And that attorney, Walter Ferris, had delayed her for a while by stopping by, not that it mattered. Right now all that mattered was that she was going home—to the family home. Her father had retired some time ago, but he still had his health, and he carried a great deal of influence with the people who mattered the most. He would help her just as he always had. She would stay there with her father and mother until she could figure out what to do with the rest of her life—what little bit was left. That was as far as she had gotten with her plans. She would just take her time and try to figure it all out. And she would try to figure out how to return the white Lincoln Continental to the University. Her father would help her with that, too.

* * *

Frank Boyd and Bill Camp sat at the large table in the president's office. Papers were strewn across its surface.

"My god. What did he think he was doing?" Bill looked at Frank.

"I don't have an answer for you. All I know is, he must be completely out of touch with reality. When this gets in the papers, there's no end to the damage it will do to the University."

"For starters, you can forget collecting on all of those pledges you have gotten since Neal won the NCAA Championship. People don't like it if they think their donations are being mishandled. It will take years to erase the stigma of something like this." Bill was angry. For the past hour he had been reading the University auditor's report on the Piedmont State Athletics Department; namely, the director's office. Thousands of dollars had been stolen outright by Charlie Morgan. Now an outside audit would have to be made, and when that happened, the State Attorney General would become involved. And there was absolutely nothing he could do about it. The damage was already done.

"Just how well did you know Morgan anyway when you recommended him for the job as Athletics Director?" Bill was trying to keep a cool head about all of it, but damn it, someone was going to get blamed for this god-awful mess, and ultimately it would have to fall on him. Here he was three years away from retirement—not even that—and some shit like this had to happen.

Frank shook his head. "Not well enough, apparently. We roomed together in college. Morgan didn't have any family, so when he wasn't going to visit someone else, I usually invited him to come home with me over the holidays—Christmas, spring break, that sort of thing. He had money because he drove fancy cars and he always took my mother expensive presents. She liked him."

"Well, that's a hell of an endorsement."

Frank ignored the sarcasm. "After we graduated, we kept in touch off and on for a while. He married into a wealthy family and seemed to settle down into a good job. And then I didn't hear anything from him—I guess for fifteen years or more. One day out of the blue he called me about the A.D.'s job. He said he was ready for a career change. Quite honestly, I thought he would be good for the program and for the University. He had always been so driven and ambitious in college. He worked hard, and from everything I could find out, he had made a name for himself at the University of New Hampshire." Frank shook his head again. "I guess you never really know a person."

Bill looked at the report scattered in front of him. "Well, we need to take some steps to get rid of him. You hired him, you fire him— today. I want him out of that office and off campus immediately. I'm positive once the Attorney General gets involved, there will be criminal charges made against him. I don't want him around the University when that happens.

"We are already bathing in this shit. If we are going to keep from smelling like shit, we need to do something to keep the Seawolfers' faith in us. Talk to the school attorney. See what can be done about recovering the stolen money from Morgan. If we can't get it back, then look into your discretionary funds. If you have to, use them. That missing money is to be replaced. I don't want the Seawolfers to think their money has been lost."

Bill got up and walked over to his desk. "Go ahead and set up a search committee for a new A.D. I want to go strictly by the book on this. Is that clear?"

"Absolutely." Frank had fucked up by circumventing a search committee when he hired Morgan. He wasn't about to make that mistake again.

"I might as well tell you this now. You're going to find out in the next few days anyway. Neal is resigning."

"Oh damn." Frank slumped back in his chair. "Because of Morgan?"

"Partly, I think. But also he says he's ready to get out of coaching."

"The Seawolfers aren't going to like this."

Bill nodded. "I know. But it's his decision. I asked him to wait until May 1 before announcing it. That only gives us a few days to do some damage control over Morgan."

"We'll need to set up a search committee for a head basketball coach, too."

"That's right," said Bill. "But wait until Neal makes his announcement. And when you do set up your committee, I want the Athletics Council involved. As far as that goes, get them involved in the search for a new Athletics Director as well. I have a feeling we have a lot of angry people to appease because of Morgan."

Frank was only too aware of the complaints that had been coming into his office daily about Morgan—not only from the Athletics Booster Club supporters, but from people on campus who had a connection with the Athletics Department. Frank had just put them off thinking it was because Morgan had a different way of doing things. It was always difficult for someone new coming into a job—especially when the person he was replacing had been in the job for twenty-five years. Now, too late, he realized he should have paid attention to those complaints. Frank crammed the report back into his briefcase and stood up to leave.

"Incidentally, Neal has recommended Stu Simmons as his replacement. You should mention that to the Athletics Council and the search committee when the time comes."

"I will," said Frank. He wasn't about to question anything the President said. He and he alone was responsible for hiring Morgan and for this crap the Athletics Department was in. He'd better get it squared away or there would be another search committee looking for a new Chancellor to replace him.

Before returning to Raleigh, Frank called his secretary, Mrs. Wall, and told her he wanted to see Charlie Morgan at one o'clock in his office. Then he told her to notify campus security. He wanted them to come to his office at twelve-thirty. There was no need to take any unnecessary chances. Considering the things Morgan had tried to pull, he was obviously a lunatic. For all Frank knew, Morgan might become violent when he learned he no longer had a job.

Frank's hands were damp with perspiration when he hung up the phone. One of the President's assistants spoke to him as he walked to his car, but Frank didn't even hear him. He was thinking about the meeting scheduled that afternoon for one o'clock.

Chapter Twenty-One

"This is just a hearing for the judge to determine if there is sufficient evidence for the State to go forward, Marla. It shouldn't take more than a couple of hours, unless the judge gets tied up on another matter."

Walter and Marla were seated at a table in the courtroom. Neal was sitting directly behind them. The rest of the courtroom was packed with spectators and reporters. Already the death of Martin Andrews and Marla's involvement had become the news event of the year. The Raleigh Police Department was strained to the maximum with extra work coming out of the assistant prosecutor's office, and the State Highway Patrol had been brought in to help direct traffic and control parking during the hearing. It was a circus—just as Gale said it would be.

"We might not get it dismissed today, Marla. It's going to be a close call." Walter patted Marla's hands as she clenched them tightly in her lap. "So I don't want you to be upset or disappointed if the judge decides there is probable cause. We are going to win this. All right?"

"Who is the judge, Walter?"

Walter looked back at Neal. "Jim Green. Do you know him?"

"Yes, I do. I get him tickets occasionally."

Walter nodded. "I knew he was a Seawolf supporter. That's good. It certainly can't hurt."

Just then Tom Cochoran came into the courtroom carrying two large briefcases. Two of his assistants, carrying file boxes, followed behind.

Marla looked at the briefcases and file boxes. "Oh, my gosh."

"Don't let that concern you." Walter smiled. "Cochoran is just trying to hot dog it. All he will get for his grandstanding is a hernia."

They only had a short wait until Judge Green got there. As soon as the clerk finished reading the case number and the names of the parties involved, Walter immediately stood up.

"With your permission, Your Honor, I would like to request a conference in the presence of Your Honor and Mr. Cochoran in the judge's chambers."

Cochoran's eyebrows shot up, and immediately he and his assistants began conferring in rather emotional whispers punctuated with a lot of arm flailing.

"Mr. Cochoran, do you have any objections?" Judge Green peered over his silver-framed, half-rimmed reading glasses at the assistant prosecutor.

"I would like just a moment to confer with my associates, Your Honor."

Cochoran was rattled, and Ferris knew it. Calmly he remained standing. He had known Jim Green a long time. They had gone to Duke Law School together. They had even argued the same side in moot court their senior year. He knew Judge Green didn't have the patience for game-playing and one-upmanship. He watched Judge Green fidget with a pen. Then his reading glasses. When he reached for the collar on his robe to adjust it, Ferris knew the judge had reached his limit.

"Mr. Cochoran, if you have so much to talk about, I am quite sure the rest of the court would like to hear it."

"I apologize, Your Honor. If you can give me just a couple of more minutes."

Ferris glanced back at Marla and winked. Cochoran was getting off on the wrong foot with Judge Green. When Cochoran finally stood up to offer his objections to Ferris' request for a conference, Judge

Green wasn't in any mood to hear them. Instead, he called a recess and adjourned with the two lawyers to his chambers.

"Keep your fingers crossed," Walter said to Marla and Neal, and he left the courtroom.

Everyone began talking. A few people stood up, but no one left. They were afraid they would miss something. Marla thought about Gale and the hall walkers and wished they could meet her now in the hall.

"I love you, Marla." Neal leaned forward and put his hand on Marla's shoulder.

Marla turned toward him. "I know."

"It's going to be all right." He smiled at her.

"Oh, Neal. I love you, too." But it wasn't going to be all right. Marla's heart thumped wildly in her chest. She would have to tell him soon about the divorce. Then he could put all of this behind him, and somehow she would have to find the courage to go on, alone.

* * *

At one o'clock Chancellor Frank Boyd was sitting at his desk staring at a memo. He had no idea what it said. It was just something for his eyes to stop on. Two security guards stood by the door inside his office and two more were stationed just outside the door. The intercom buzzed.

"Mr. Morgan is here for his one o'clock appointment," his secretary told him.

"Send him in." Frank's eyes moved from the paper on his desk to the door.

"Hello, Frank. It's good to see you." Charlie, smiling, crossed the room in long strides and stopped in front of the Chancellor's desk with his hand outstretched.

"Have a seat, Charlie." Frank ignored his hand. "I won't take much of your time."

The smile on Charlie's face slowly vanished and he glanced back at the door noticing the two uniformed men for the first time. "What's up, Frank?"

Frank pulled out a copy of the auditor's report and tossed it on his desk in front of Charlie. "You have been stealing, Charlie, from the Athletics Scholarship Fund. You have sold tickets illegally. And you have cheated on your expense accounts, which is stealing from the University. In short, you no longer have a job at this institution. You are to vacate your office by five o'clock this afternoon—sooner, if possible."

Charlie felt his chest heave and the ever-present pressure in his head swell to the point that he thought it would explode.

"I don't know what you're talking about." He didn't look at the bound audit report Frank had thrown at him.

"I'm not going to play games with you, Charlie. And I'm not going to let you sit there and insult my intelligence. You have made me look like a fool and you have jeopardized my career. It will take me years to get over this, if I ever do. I expect you, at the very least, to leave without any further conversation." Frank glanced at the two men standing at the door. When he did, they walked to the middle of the room and stopped.

"What am I supposed to do now? Admittedly I have had a few family problems. But I'm taking care of them. If there is some foul-up on an expense sheet, for crissake, I'll correct it. How bad can that be?"

"This isn't open for discussion, Charlie. Give me credit for having a little bit of sense. I'd appreciate it if you would get out of my office—now."

The two men moved directly behind the chair where Charlie was sitting. This was more than Charlie could stand. Anger filled his body. Someone had to be blamed for this. Someone would be punished.

"Well, fuck you. I'll sue your ass. You can't just get rid of me like this. And if you try, I'll take you and a lot of others with me—like that great basketball coach you are so fond of. I'll make your life miserable. I know all about you and the doting Mrs. Wall. How you've been having an affair for years. Letting the State pay for her travel expenses just so you could have her around to play with when you went out of town for meetings. How convenient. I don't think that would sit too well with the University Board of Governors, knowing that their Chancellor is screwing his secretary and they are paying for it, do you?"

Frank felt as though he had been struck over the head by a hammer. How in the hell did Charlie find out about him and Libby. They had always been so careful. He fought to maintain his composure. He had always heard the expression, it didn't pay to get into a pissing contest with a skunk. Now he knew what that meant, especially a skunk that was as crazy as Charlie Morgan.

"Charlie, you'll be lucky if you don't have to spend the rest of your life in prison over this." Frank spoke calmly. No matter what, he couldn't let Charlie get the upper hand. If Charlie thought for a moment he could control Frank with fear, it would be disastrous. "Even if the University decides not to bring criminal charges against you, the State will. So if I were you, I wouldn't talk about suing anyone."

"You cocksucker!" Charlie rose unsteadily and headed for the door, now eager to get out of the room and the building.

Frank stood up when Charlie did.

"There are two security guards waiting at your office to watch you pack your personal belongings only. If any University property gets mixed in with your things, they have orders to arrest you on the spot."

Charlie was ashen white. He slammed the door behind him, but it was hardly enough to express the desperation and isolation that enveloped him. He had lost everything—his family, his wife, now his job. Everything was gone. And it was all because of one person. Marla Connors.

Back in his office Frank instructed the security guards to follow Charlie to make sure he left the campus after packing his things. When they were gone, he collapsed in his chair. Perspiration soaked through his clothing and his hands were shaking. He hoped that was the last he would see or hear from Charlie Morgan, but somehow he knew it wouldn't be. Frank waited a few minutes trying to calm himself and collect his thoughts. He straightened the pile of papers in front of him, even though it didn't need straightening, and lined it up with the edge of his desk. He rearranged all of the pens in the white alabaster box, making sure the ends were pointing in the same direction. He picked up the silver framed photograph of his wife, two daughters, and son and stared at it. Then he positioned it back on his desk making sure to angle it just right from the corner of his desk. After taking several deep breaths, he pushed the button on his intercom.

"Libby, would you come in here please."

* * *

"Before we get started, counselors, let me make something clear because I want there to be no confusion on this." Judge Green rocked back in his oversized black leather chair. "I'm not going to tolerate any theatrics in my courtroom—especially in this case. I have enough to worry about as it is with all of the publicity without the two of you using my courtroom as a stage for your amateur acting debuts. Do I make myself understood?"

"Absolutely. I couldn't agree with you more." Walter glanced over at Cochoran who was squirming noticeably in his chair.

"Well, you don't have to worry about me, Judge," Cochoran said defensively. "I'm not the one playing games here. Ferris is the one who called this meeting before we even got started. So if anyone is doing an acting job . . ."

Walter interrupted. "Tom, you do know, don't you, that when new evidence surfaces—and it has—then it is the obligation of the attorney in possession of that evidence to make the evidence known to the opposing attorney?"

"Of course I know that," Cochoran snapped. He reached for the knot on his tie.

"Good. It is my intention to save you and the court a lot of time by presenting some new evidence now. I mean, why argue something when the evidence shows that there simply is no basis for the case to be presented in the first place."

"Oh, I doubt that. I doubt that very much."

"O.K., gentlemen. That's enough." Judge Green leaned forward and picked up a pen to write with. "Walter, let's hear what you've got."

Walter pulled the copies of the two letters from his briefcase and placed the first one on the desk in front of Judge Green. "This letter, collected as evidence by the prosecution, was supposedly written by my client roughly three weeks before Andrews' death. In it my client confesses her love for Andrews, among other things." Walter pulled out the second letter and watched Cochoran blanch. "This second letter, which I am sure the prosecution intended to disclose to me as evidence collected for this case but forgot to do so, was also supposedly written by my client." Walter stopped and looked at Cochoran, wanting him to agonize a little over what he was going to say next. Walter knew he had Cochoran by the balls. Walter could issue a complaint then and there against Cochoran for failing to provide complete disclosure and possibly have Cochoran fined at the very least or even thrown off the case. But he wouldn't. He handed the letter to Judge Green. "In this letter she states that she has received a copy of Andrews' will naming her beneficiary and tells him she wants to see him while her husband is away. Both letters were typed on the same typewriter, and Mike Cohen from forensics is prepared to testify to that fact."

Cochoran was beside himself. "So what, Walter? All that says is that your client typed both goddamn letters on the same goddamn type-writer. What in the hell does that prove?"

"The typewriter belongs to Charles Morgan. His wife will swear that the typewriter was never taken out of the house. Therefore, the letters had to have been typed in Morgan's house." Walter glanced over at Cochoran and smiled. "Reasonable doubt, counselor. That's all I have to prove. Reasonable doubt. Marla Connors never intended to murder Martin Andrews. It was self-defense, just like she claims. He had abused her throughout their entire marriage, and she believed he was going to harm her the day he showed up at her house unexpectedly. He threatened her with bodily harm, and that was why she killed him. These letters are phony. They were typed by someone, probably Morgan, who wanted it to look like Marla planned to murder Andrews."

Judge Green peered at Cochoran over his glasses. "Counselor?"

Cochoran picked up the two letters and looked at them. "I'm not ready to drop the charges. We don't know that she didn't type them while she was visiting Morgan in his home. It is his testimony that she was all over him anyway, constantly trying to get him alone. Making all kinds of sexual advances. Maybe they were in on it together. I don't know. If that's true, then that would give me all the more reason to find your client guilty." Cochoran was nervously glancing from the judge to Walter while he talked. Walter had thrown him when he produced that other letter. He had planned to show Walter the letter, but later, after he got his case on a more solid foundation. Cochoran didn't know how in the hell Walter found out about it, but if he got it from someone in his office, that person would be out of a job and on his ass—and damn quick. Cochoran tossed the letters back on the desk. "I'd say all this does is strengthen my case, Ferris."

"Does the fact that Charlie Morgan has spent time in and out of mental institutions over the past twenty years change your mind?" Walter asked. "And that he and Andrews were half brothers and as children were brought up in the same dysfunctional home until they were separated to go live under foster care? In fact, as Andrews' only living relative, Morgan would be the legitimate heir if Marla were found guilty of first degree murder."

It was obvious from his reaction that Cochoran didn't know about Morgan's history.

"But there is nothing that proves that Morgan and Andrews even kept in touch with one another. And besides. Morgan isn't the one on trial here, is he, Ferris? It's Marla Connors. And I have enough evidence to prove that she murdered her ex-husband in order to inherit the money. It was premeditated, and it was deliberate."

Walter looked at Judge Green and shook his head.

"Unless you can prove she didn't type those letters, Walter, I'm afraid I have to rule in favor of the prosecution at this time. We'll have to go forward with the hearing."

"I understand." Walter gathered up the papers and his briefcase. "Let's get this show on the road then, shall we?"

Cochoran bolted toward the door, obviously impatient to leave.

"Mr. Cochoran."

"Yes, Your Honor."

"I am willing to accept Mr. Ferris's judgment on the matter that certain evidence was unintentionally withheld from the defense. But if I find out differently, or if it is discovered that there is other evidence involving this case that has been withheld from the defense, I will personally see to it that you never practice law in the State of North Carolina again."

Cochoran nodded and left.

"I simply can't tolerate these overly ambitious, smart-alecky, know-it-alls the law schools are turning out these days. Christ. We weren't like that, were we?" Judge Green leaned back in his chair.

Walter laughed. "Probably. But it was so long ago, we've just forgotten."

"I'm sorry, Walter. I wish I could have come down in your favor."

"That's all right, Jim. It was a long shot. I'm going to win this one. It's just going to take me a little longer, that's all. Are we still on for golf Thursday morning?"

"You bet. I even went out and bought a new graphite putter and it's a beauty. Nice head on it. So you'd better watch out."

Walter smiled and went back into the courtroom.

* * *

Elizabeth Wall left work early, which wasn't all that unusual. After all, when you have dedicated your life to one job for as many years as Mrs. Wall, you are entitled to certain privileges. No one ever questioned her. Besides, she was the Chancellor's private secretary. For all anyone knew, she was taking care of some important matter for Chancellor Boyd.

She slid into her black 500 SL Mercedes Benz, a gift to herself on her fifty-eighth birthday. It was the only extravagant thing she had ever bought for herself. Even though the weather was hot for this time of year, the tan leather seats felt cool to her back and legs because as the Chancellor's private secretary she was given one of the special covered parking spaces near the Administration Building. It had taken her ten years to earn that parking space. Ten years of faithfully reporting to work on time and putting in a full eight hours—often more—each day, of being dedicated and loyal to the University, and of always being above reproach. She was also extremely bright. It had paid off, for along with the parking space came a promotion naming her the Chancellor's private secretary which placed her above all of the other women who worked in the Chancellor's office. At the time of her promotion, she was attractive, widowed, and still fairly young. Her new position in the Chancellor's office also gave her the enviable possession of power. And like her youth, beauty, and widowhood, she handled it well.

Of all the women who worked on campus, Elizabeth Wall was the one to emulate. Her dress, her conduct, her reputation, and her ability to handle people allowed her a coveted place next to the Chancellor that no one else had. In the years following her promotion, she developed the Chancellor's trust and his dependency on her that not even his wife shared. More often than not, it was her judgment that he relied on. It was her opinions on which he based administrative as well as personal decisions.

Because her position with the Chancellor and the University at large put her in a sort of nebulous zone, above the general staff but below the administrative-faculty level, she was sought after by both camps for advice and guidance, or the hope to gain her favor toward some personal benefit. Therefore she knew everything that took place on campus. She was discreet and could be trusted with the most sensitive problems involving the University and its employees, including the Chancellor's personal life. It was only natural that over time she would become his lover as well.

There never was a time that she thought Frank Boyd would leave his wife for her. It simply wasn't discussed. Elizabeth Wall wouldn't have considered it anyway. She had found out early on that Frank Boyd didn't have the intelligence or strength of character she wanted in a man—certainly not in a husband. He was a typical academic administrator who looked good in the role, wearing his tan trousers with a navy blazer and silk tie, or on special occasions his three-piece Armani suit, but who relied on others to insure the quality and correctness of his performance. In his case, it was Elizabeth Wall he depended on. That was why she could control and manipulate him so easily. Therefore their relationship was one of passionate convenience, and giving to each other as long as it was within certain boundaries which never extended into his marriage or into her activities beyond the University.

All of her life, Elizabeth Wall had carefully thought out her every act and deed. No decision was made in haste. Now at age fifty-eight, she was looking forward to just three years' time when she could start drawing her Social Security survivor benefits based on her claim as a widow. With that money together with whatever her State pension allowed for a full retirement, she would be able to live comfortably.

Having worked at the University for almost thirty years, eighteen of those years as the Chancellor's private secretary, gave her a sense of security and a level of self-confidence that came with knowing she was the best. She had worked hard and prepared all of her adult life just so she wouldn't be faced with financial worries in her later years. She didn't delude herself into thinking Frank Boyd would help her. Nor was there anyone else she could depend on. She had only herself. And now all of that, twenty-eight years of hard work and planning, was about to be destroyed just because of one man. Charlie Morgan.

She drove the big black car into her driveway and pushed the automatic garage door opener. The door rattled and groaned. Finally after several false starts, it opened. This irritated her. She had already called the repairman twice about fixing the stupid thing. Elizabeth couldn't stand for things to be messy or out of place or not working properly. Like her own appearance and manner, she surrounded herself with perfection. A hesitating garage door was simply unacceptable.

One of the first things Elizabeth was going to do once she started receiving her retirement and the Social Security payments would be to sell her house and buy one of the pretty garden homes in the new Cross Creek development across town. She had liked her house when she first bought it because it was so near the campus. But now it was getting old, and too many things were starting to break down. She wouldn't have to worry about such things as faulty garage doors at Cross Creek since all of the maintenance was included in a monthly association fee. She had already figured out her payments, and by the time she retired, she could easily afford them. Plus she liked the location. Near a nice mall and all the convenience stores. It would be ideal for her. A new home for the new life she would be starting as the retired personal secretary to the Chancellor. She unlocked the back door and went into the house.

"I'm home, Gladys," she called out. A large calico cat suddenly appeared, purring and wrapping its furry body around Elizabeth's legs. After changing out of her navy linen suit into a pair of brown slacks and matching tunic top, she went into the kitchen and poured herself a glass of apple juice. She carried it out to the small screened porch and sat down in a wicker rocking chair with Gladys beside her.

"Frank thinks I should resign." Elizabeth stroked the large cat. "Even though it would mean losing a large chunk of my State pension by not working until retirement, as well as destroying my reputation, my position within the University, and everything I have worked for, he thinks it would be best if I resign, before there can be a scandal."

Gladys shifted her large feline body so that Elizabeth's hand could knead her neck. She purred loudly and began flexing her front paws rhythmically.

"Of course, as usual, Frank is wrong. Always making the wrong decision and not thinking things through. What in heaven's name would he have done without me all of these years. And how would he manage without me if I did suddenly resign with no notice? No, my resigning will never do. Not when I have only three more years before reaching full retirement. We'll just have to come up with another solution. Won't we, Gladys?"

Gladys growled with pleasure and flicked her tail backwards and forwards.

Elizabeth sipped her juice. She had always felt that everyone on campus knew about her involvement with the Chancellor. Why shouldn't they? She knew everything about them. It was amazing, really. It was almost as though there were some primitive telepathic communications system within the walls of the University. The knowledge of every word and deed was somehow transmitted to the collective consciousness of all who worked there. The people employed on campus spent most of their days gossiping about everyone else. But they weren't going to say anything about Elizabeth Wall or the Chancellor—not if they valued their jobs. Charlie Morgan, on the other hand, had nothing to lose. He was bitter and angry, and, Elizabeth suspected, more than a little insane. He and he alone was the problem. If he were eliminated, there would be no reason why she shouldn't be able to work out her remaining three years and take a full retirement.

Frank wouldn't do anything. It was obvious from his conversation with her that he was scared. And whenever he got scared, he became even more weak and ineffectual than he normally was. No, as usual, she had only herself. She would have to find some way to handle it.

After a few moments, Elizabeth looked at her watch. It was three o'clock. Morgan wouldn't have had time to pack all of his things yet. He would still be at his office. She finished her juice and got up, dumping the cat to the floor. She went into her bedroom closet and moved several neatly stacked boxes around on the top shelf, eventually pulling one small box down. She carried it back out to the porch where she opened it and carefully sorted through layers of white tissue paper. Carefully she wrapped her hand around the small, black handle and lifted the gun out of the box. It had never even been fired.

* * *

Frank Boyd wrenched the top off the plastic bottle of antacid tablets, dumped two round white discs into his hand, and popped them into his mouth. He had already eaten three tablets, but they hadn't done the job. He still felt the terrible burning sensation in his stomach, chest, and throat. He tried to chew the two tablets, but instead of dissolving, they stuck to his dentures. Christ! What a fucking mess in had gotten himself into. He thought back over the conversation he had just had with Libby. As usual, she was calm about the whole thing, even when he told her he wanted her to submit her resignation effective immediately. He was the one who was frantic, but, shit, he had a right to be. He might lose everything. His job was already in jeopardy as it was because of Morgan, and if Morgan let it out that he had been having an affair with his secretary, he might as well kiss his job and a healthy State pension good-bye. But that would only be the beginning. Bill Camp, as President of the Consolidated University System, would have to call a special meeting with the University Board of Governors and Board of Trustees where a vote would be taken to dismiss him. Even if the meeting were protected by the Sunshine Law as a personnel matter, the publicity would be brutal. And because of the sensitive nature leading up to his dismissal, there would also be a full audit of all the financial records in the Chancellor's office probably dating back to when he was first named Chancellor. He hadn't been as careful as he should have been—especially with the discretionary fund. Each time he had taken money from it, it hadn't seemed like that much. But over the years it had added up. He had already seen what the auditors could do when they went looking for something from what they had turned up in the Athletics Department. Even if he wanted to pay it back now, he couldn't. It amounted to too much. And now Bill Camp was expecting him to use the funds from that same account to replace what Morgan had stolen. He just hoped that between what was left in the account and what was in his own personal savings, it would be enough.

Frank Boyd got up from his desk and paced back and forth. Not only that, what in the hell would his wife say? Shit! She wouldn't say anything. She would just throw his stinking ass out. And then he would be no better off than Charlie Morgan. Christ! What a mess.

He couldn't think why he ever got involved with Libby anyway. He had told her that he loved her, but they both knew that wasn't true. And they had been doing it so long, it had almost become as routine as when he was with his wife. But he had kept arranging times and places where they could be together. Using money from that damn discretionary account. Secret meetings, a quick fuck. All of it was one cheap thrill. And for what? When it got right down to it, it was his damn ego. He liked thinking he could get some snatch on the side. It made him feel more like a man. That he had something other men didn't have. And he liked it even better because he thought he could get away with it.

Well, he had given Libby two days to think it over. That was more than fair as far as he was concerned. He had wanted her to resign right then, but she told him she wanted two days to think it over and try to come up with a solution. So he had given them to her. Now he wished he hadn't. With Morgan running around like a fucking maniac ready to blab everything he knew, they didn't have two days. Christ! They probably didn't even have two hours.

He looked at his watch. It was after five. Morgan should already be off campus. His wife had told him that morning to try to get home early. She would be expecting him for dinner. He didn't know if he could face her—not with all of this on him. Maybe he could call her and tell her he had to work late. That had always worked in the past. Only this time, he really would be working late.

Chapter Twenty-Two

Walter took Marla and Neal out for an early dinner when they left the courthouse at a little Italian restaurant just down the street. The hearing had taken most of the afternoon. Each thing Walter brought up, Cochoran argued against. There was the record from a psychiatric hospital where Martin had spent most of the time as a patient following his divorce from Marla. He had been diagnosed as bipolar with strong schizophrenic tendencies. There were the birth certificates of Charlie Morgan and Martin Andrews, proving they were half brothers. There were depositions from former employees and co-workers at the University of New Hampshire where Morgan had worked before coming to State swearing to his violent tendencies, and Morgan's own medical record showing he had also spent time as a patient in a psychiatric hospital although the reasons were kept confidential since the file was still active. There were depositions from Marla's gynecologist in Red Oak testifying to her bruised body, as well as a dentist testifying about Marla's broken tooth and cut mouth. The private investigator had dug that one up on one of his fact-seeking trips to Red Oak.

Even though Walter presented strong arguments, in the end, the court ruled that there was enough evidence to support the assistant prosecutor's claims against Marla. The fact that Marla had never filed any charges against Martin for abuse hurt her case. Especially since the assistant prosecutor provided a list of character witnesses who were willing to testify to the fact that Dr. Andrews was a kind and gentle doctor and a loving husband. The case would have to go to trial.

"I just can't believe that Martin and Charlie Morgan were half brothers. Although I don't know why that should surprise me. Martin was always so secretive about his past." Marla pushed the food on her plate with her fork without eating anything.

"From what my private investigator was able to find out, the mother set up a trust fund for each of her sons as soon as she was financially able. Apparently there was a history of mental illness in the family and she wanted to be sure that Morgan and Andrews would be taken care of in the event that they needed treatment. I'm sure she felt a lot of guilt, too, abandoning them the way she did when they were so young.

"It's bizarre, isn't it? Everything about this case points to Morgan and his involvement. And yet it's his testimony that's keeping this whole thing from getting thrown out." Walter reached for the chilled mug of beer in front of him and took a long drink. "It's too bad Gale died when she did. As an eyewitness she could have disputed his story."

"Do you mean in his deposition where he says that Marla made sexual advances toward him in Albuquerque?" Neal filled Marla's glass with wine, then his own.

"Yea. I just need to find something that will discredit his testimony and link him to Andrews in a more recent time frame. From what I have been able to find out from people who knew the family and from a couple of the psychiatrists who treated Morgan, Morgan always felt more than a reasonable sense of responsibility for his brother. I think those feelings carried through when Marla divorced Andrews, and Morgan was still trying to take care of Andrews by destroying Marla. Even though I can prove they were half brothers, I don't have anything showing they were still in touch with one another. Morgan, of course, denies that he even knew where Andrews was and insists that they lost all contact with each other when they were separated as kids and went to live in foster homes." Walter took another drink of beer and set it down on the table thoughtfully. "That's the key. Finding something that proves they were still in contact with one another. After that, everything else should fall into place."

"I still don't understand what that will prove," said Marla. "What difference does it make if they were in contact with each other?"

"I think that Andrews contacted Morgan some time around your divorce. Just like when they were young boys, Andrews wanted Morgan to take care of everything. In Morgan's warped mind, taking care of everything meant destroying you—which he set out to do when he took the job as Athletics Director at State. Even after Andrews got killed, Morgan still felt it was his responsibility to complete what he had started. By making it look like you killed Andrews deliberately for the inheritance, he could accomplish that. The funny thing is, I think Morgan is so insane, I doubt very much if he even realizes that if you were to be found guilty, he would then inherit Andrews' share of the trust fund."

"But this is all just speculation, Walter," said Neal.

"For now, that's true. But there are a lot of things to support it. We'll get there." Walter watched Marla pick at the food on her plate. "Marla, you need to eat something and not worry about this. For one thing, I never defend a client who is guilty. For another, I never take on a case I can't win. We will win this. I can promise you that."

"I know you think you can, Walter. But right now from where I am sitting it doesn't look like it. Judge Green didn't rule in our favor on anything today."

Walter smiled and took another gulp of beer. "I know. That doesn't bother me. It's just part of the legal posturing that goes on in courtrooms. Fun and games. Right now Cochoran is thinking he has won the moon and is feeling pretty bright-eyed and bushy-tailed about it. Actually all he has won are a bunch of little meaningless objections which I deliberately raised knowing I wouldn't get sustained. But the big objections will come, and when I make them, you can be assured Jim Green will rule in my favor."

It was raining when they came out of the restaurant. Walter waited with Marla while Neal went to get the car.

"Have you had a chance to prepare the divorce papers, Walter?"

"Marla, I really haven't. I don't know why you want to rush into this. Even if you do go out of state to file, you have to do it yourself. In other words, you have to physically be there to file. In some places like Los Vegas and Reno you even have to set up residency and actually live there for six weeks before you can get a divorce finalized. So it isn't quite so easy as just preparing the papers and signing them. I really think that until we get this trial behind us, you need to wait. Then, if you still want to divorce Neal, I promise you I will have those papers ready for you."

"Don't you understand, Walter?" Marla started crying. "It will be too late then. Neal needs to be free of me now, before I can do any more damage to his reputation and his career."

Just then Neal drove up. "Get in, Walter, and I'll take you to your car," he said opening the door for Marla.

Nothing else was said about the divorce, but Walter knew that Marla was running out of patience with him. He just needed a little more time. He hadn't said anything to Neal and Marla because he didn't want to get their hopes up prematurely. But if the private investigator found what Walter wanted, there was still a good possibility that the case wouldn't go to trial. And that's what Walter was counting on.

* * *

When Walter got back to his office, Stu Simmons was waiting for him.

"Stu, it's good to see you." Walter quickly glanced through the phone messages his secretary handed him. "Come on in. I hope you haven't been waiting long."

Stu went into Walter's office. "No. I just got here a few minutes ago, and your secretary told me she was expecting you at any time. How did it go in court today?"

"About what I expected. The judge found in favor for the prosecution but I still think we stand a good chance of preventing it from going to trial." Walter went over to the sofa and sat down. "Make yourself comfortable and tell me what I can do for you."

Stu sat opposite Walter and pulled out a sealed, letter-size envelope.

"I found this in Gale's papers. I'm afraid I am just getting around to sorting through them."

Walter nodded. "It takes time."

"Apparently she intended to mail it to you because it is stamped. And it's marked confidential. I don't have any idea what it is or when she wrote it, but I thought I'd better hand deliver it in case it is something important."

Walter took the envelope. It was addressed to him. Walter knew Gale, of course, but he had never done any legal work for her. He was as perplexed as Stu was. Plus receiving something from the dead was a little unnerving. It had happened to him once before his first year out of law school. He was invited to a Christmas party hosted by several law firms in the area. He went expecting to make contacts and meet new people. A couple of days later he read in the newspaper where a young woman had been killed in a car accident. A picture of the wrecked car was printed on the front page. The story went on to explain how she had recently moved to the area to begin work as a corporate attorney. That same day, Walter received a Christmas card in the mail from the same woman. The strange thing was, he couldn't even remember meeting her. He could only surmise that he had met her at that party.

"Please sit down, Stu, and we'll find out what this is all about."

Walter slit the envelope open. Inside was a hand-written letter. It was dated two weeks after the National Championship Finals. Apparently Gale had written it while she was still in the hospital because she had used hospital stationery.

Dear Walter,

I was witness to an unpleasant incident that occurred in Albuquerque the morning before State played the final game in the National Championship. I am telling you because I know you will be discreet and that you will use this information only if in your judgment you feel it is necessary to protect or defend Marla Connors.

Gale went on to describe in detail how Morgan had tried to force himself on Marla in her hotel suite that morning and how Marla had repelled his advances. Gale had signed the letter and also had her signature notarized, probably by someone on the administrative staff in the hospital. She had been thorough.

Walter handed the letter to Stu. "Your wife has just given me what I need to discredit Morgan. She was a smart lady, Stu. And she must have thought a lot of Marla to go to all of this trouble."

Stu read the letter and smiled. "She always did say she had learned a lot over the years hanging around men's locker rooms. I guess she knew Morgan was no good."

"A lot of people are going to know once we get finished with this."

After Stu left Walter made a few notes to himself about some other things Stu told him concerning Morgan that had just happened. Then he sorted through the phone messages his secretary had given him earlier until he found the one he wanted. Dan, the private investigator, had told him he would get back to him in a couple of days, but apparently he already had some news. With any luck at all, Walter would be setting up another conference with the Honorable Jim Green and Prosecuting Attorney Tom Cochoran. Walter dialed the number written on the green sheet of note paper. "Hello, Dan. This is Walter. I just got your message. What did you find out?"

"It took some doing—in fact I almost missed it—but I found the record of a phone call made by Andrews to Morgan right before Morgan moved to Raleigh. You see, that's what threw me. I was looking through the records of calls Andrews might have made to Morgan in Raleigh. But this call was made to New Hampshire, right before Morgan was named Athletics Director at State."

"And you are sure?"

"Oh, I'm sure. Andrews was in contact with Morgan. I'll get copies of everything to you, but I knew you would want this information as soon as possible. There is one more thing. I spoke to a freelance reporter who covered the NCAAs in Albuquerque this year. His name is Nance. He is ready to swear that Morgan is the one who lied to the press about the Seawolf basketball team using drugs before the Championship game. And—you are going to love this—he recognized the photo of Martin Andrews I showed to him. He is positive he saw Andrews leaving Morgan's suite in Albuquerque right before he was to meet with Morgan for his interview."

Walter leaned back in his chair and folded his hands behind his head. This case had really been an interesting challenge, but now he was closing in. All of the pieces were finally starting to fit. He thought about Cochoran's impudent, smug-looking face when the judge had overruled his objections during the hearing. Now he was about to wipe Cochoran's ass with those overruled objections.

* * *

Cochoran closed the door, pulled out a bottle of Cutty Sark scotch, what he considered the "gentleman's drink," and poured three fingers into a Mickey Mouse coffee mug, a present from his office staff. Then he threw his feet up on his desk, loosened his tie, and slowly sipped his drink. It had been a good day. Except for his boss, everyone else in the office had already left, but Cochoran wanted to savor his little victories over the venerable Walter Ferris just a while longer before going home. God, how he had enjoyed watching Ferris jump up with his petty objections only to get shot down each and every single time. He had to have really been desperate, making all of those stupid objections like that. It wasn't particularly smart of Ferris trying to implicate Morgan in the murder either. Cochoran didn't like Morgan, but so far everything Morgan had told him had held up. It was just another one of Ferris' desperate ploys to move the burden of guilt away from Marla Connors. And it hadn't worked. Cochoran smiled and took another swig of scotch.

Of course, Cochoran told his boss all that had transpired during the hearing as soon as he got back to the office. The old man had been impressed; Cochoran could tell. Cochoran mentioned it to a couple of the other assistant prosecutors in the office as well, knowing it would make them green with envy. There was nothing that would prevent him from being named State prosecutor now once the old man stepped down. All because of this one case. And it had been so easy. It were as though the evidence had been handed to him on a silver platter. Once he got his promotion, he would move into the old man's office—the big one in the corner overlooking the Capitol and its beautiful grounds. He would get some new office furniture too. Not that State government issue junk that the old man was using.

The telephone on his desk rang, startling Cochoran out of his reverie. It was the clerk in Judge Green's office.

"Judge Green wants to see you in his chambers at the courthouse in fifteen minutes."

Cochoran put his feet back on the floor and sat up. "Can you tell me what he wants to see me about?"

"It's concerning the Connors case."

Cochoran hung up the phone, drank what was left in his mug, and straightened his tie. Then he made two quick calls to his assistants at their homes telling them to meet him at the courthouse. If Ferris was playing some kind of game, Cochoran wanted all the backup he could get. He grabbed up the two briefcases he had been lugging around all day, feeling more than a little pain in his right arm and lower back, and rushed out the door. Of course, there was always the chance that the purpose of the meeting was going to be something in his favor. But for some reason, he doubted it.

* * *

When Neal and Marla got home there was a message on the phone answering machine from Stu. He wanted Neal to call him as soon as possible at the office.

"I got your message, Stu." Neal watched Marla go into the bedroom.

"I just left Walter's office. How are you and Marla holding up?"

"All right, I guess. Green didn't dismiss the case, but Walter doesn't seem concerned. Walter is doing one hell of a job, by the way."

Stu then told Neal about Gale's letter.

"That is good news, Stu. Marla will be glad to hear it."

"Walter sure seemed to think so. I think he is going to turn Cochoran onto Morgan now."

"Really?"

"That's right. Morgan cleaned out his office and left here about an hour ago. Four campus security guards escorted him to his car."

"You mean he quit?"

"I don't know if he quit or if he was fired. He met with the Chancellor earlier. That might have had something to do with it. No one knows where Ray is either. Apparently he came in last night and cleaned out his desk."

Neal kept looking at the bedroom door. Marla hadn't come back out.

"Well, whatever the reasons, I hope those two are gone for good. Look, Stu, I have to go. We'll talk tomorrow."

"Right. Oh, and tell Marla congratulations for me. I know she's been through hell but it looks like it's going to turn out all right."

"Thanks. She'll appreciate that."

Neal hung up the phone and went into the bedroom. Marla was lying across the bed. Neal sat beside her. "Stu sends his congratulations, and he also had some good news." Neal told her about the letter Gale had written and about Morgan getting escorted off campus.

Marla nodded and tears filled her eyes. "Gale really was a good friend."

"Marla, is there anything worrying you? I mean other than what you've had to go through with the hearing and all? It will soon be over with and you won't have to ever think about it again. You know that, honey, don't you?"

Marla didn't say anything. Neal pulled her up into his arms. "Tell me what's wrong. You promised you wouldn't keep anything from me. Remember?"

"Neal, I want a divorce."

Neal held Marla away from him so he could look at her face. Maybe he didn't hear her. "What did you say?"

Marla started crying. She tried to pull away, but Neal wouldn't let go of her. "I want a divorce," she repeated.

"But why? Did I do something to make . . ."

"No, damn it. You didn't do anything except love me. I did it. I never should have married you. I want out."

Neal wrapped his arms around Marla and held her tightly against his body while she wept.

"I don't understand, but we can work this out. I'm not going to let you do this to us."

* * *

Jean was examining the brown spots on the leaves of her rhododendron and trying to decide what to do about them when Charlie Morgan drove up. He had seen her, so there was nothing to do but smile and wave.

"Hello, Charlie."

"Hello, Jean." He got out of the car and walked towards her. "I've been waiting for your call. You haven't forgotten what we talked about, have you?"

Jean glanced toward her neighbor's house. She had seen her leave earlier so that meant no one was home. The other neighbors, the ones who lived close by, all worked. They wouldn't be getting home for another hour or more. There was just that black Mercedes parked down the street, but there didn't seem to be anyone in it.

"Well, I've been on a little trip, you know."

Charlie looked at her with those cold gray eyes. "Would you invite me in for a drink? I'd like to talk about it now with you."

Jean's heart began pounding in her ears. No way in hell was she going to let this nut back into her home. At least outside she could run if she had to.

"Well, actually, Charlie, the house is in such a mess. I haven't even unpacked yet. You know how that is, I'm sure, with all those athletic trips you take."

Whatever smile had been on Charlie's face vanished. Now it was just those cold, penetrating eyes staring at Jean and causing her to shiver. "That's all right, Jean. We don't have to go inside if you don't want to. Just tell me what you have decided."

Jean stepped away from the bushes in the direction of the sidewalk. "Actually, Charlie, I'd really rather not get involved. As generous as your offer was—the tickets and the Director's Box—my goodness."

Jean didn't even realize he had moved, it happened so quickly. The first blow knocked her to the ground and stunned her. After that she didn't see or feel anything. Her neighbor found her when she returned from the grocery store. Jean was crumpled in a bloody mass in her rhododendron bushes.

* * *

Tom Cochoran had blown it big time, and he knew it. Ferris hadn't even waited until the next day to get in touch with Judge Green. Cochoran had hauled ass with his heavy briefcases and two assistants back to the courthouse for a conference in the judge's chambers. With the new evidence that Walter had uncovered, Cochoran had no choice but to drop the charges against Marla Connors. He had called his boss from the courthouse and told him what had happened. His boss said he wanted a full report back at his office when he finished up. He didn't sound particularly happy. Cochoran would go after Morgan now. It wouldn't be the career-advancing case he had hoped for, but it was better than nothing.

Corchoran returned to his office where he knew his boss was waiting for his report. He would have been the next State prosecutor if he had won this case. Now he wasn't so sure. Ramsey, who had moved from Texas last year, was starting to make a name for himself. He had been winning all of his cases, including the ones where he had been given little or no chance of doing so. Even Smith was starting to look good. Smith, who hadn't done anything in ten years, all of a sudden scored big on that Columbia drug-ring case. A lot of publicity and a lot of emotional involvement from the people. That's what Cochoran thought he had with the Connors case. But in his eagerness to win he had broken the cardinal rule: Never assume the guilt of someone until all of the evidence is in. Well, maybe his boss would understand. After all, he had lost a few big cases in his time.

Cochoran walked briskly down the hall to the State prosecutor's office. He took a deep breath, knocked, and walked in.

"What the fuck happened, Tom?"

Chapter Twenty-Three

Jean had three broken ribs. One had punctured a lung. Her face was badly cut and bruised. And she had a concussion. She would live. The first thing Jean wanted when she regained consciousness was to call Walter Ferris. At first the hospital staff was difficult with her. They wanted her to rest after her traumatic ordeal. Besides, she would have to talk to the police when they got there, and she needed to conserve her strength. But Jean could be difficult too when she wanted something. And she wanted to talk to Walter Ferris, even if it meant calling him at home.

"Is he there?" Jean asked the efficient-sounding person who answered the phone.

"Who did you say is calling?" the person asked for the third time.

"Jean." It was difficult for Jean to talk and, she realized, even more difficult for the person on the other end of the line to understand what she was saying with her face swollen twice its normal size—no matter how efficient the person was. Thank god she still had her teeth. Some of them were loose, but the doctor said they would tighten back up again.

"Hold on please."

The next voice she heard was Walter's.

"That goddamn fuck'n son of a bitch almost killed me. You said I didn't have anything to worry about."

Walter couldn't make out each word, but he understood enough of what Jean was saying to know that she was in the hospital and that Morgan had put her there.

"I want his ass. Even if I have to track the mother-fuck'n bastard down myself." Jean couldn't talk any more. Her head hurt too much. Her entire body hurt too much. What she wanted now was a drink.

Walter did find out which hospital she was in and the name of her doctor before she either dropped or slammed the receiver down. He left immediately after making a quick phone call to Detective James. He would plan to be present when the police questioned Jean the next day.

* * *

Morgan grimaced with pain as he drove down the road toward Connors' house. His ankle was probably sprained—a bone in his foot might even be broken—from kicking that fat bitch. Well, if she wouldn't help him, he'd take care of Marla himself. He should have done it sooner and not even tried to drag Connors into it. Then maybe Martin would still be alive. And maybe he'd at least still have a job. But Marla was tricky. She and that lawyer of hers must have figured out about the letters. It was probably Marla who had gotten him fired, too. She was to blame for everything. Once he got rid of her, things would be all right again. His mother would come back home and they would be a family, just like before—only better. Him, Martin, their mother, and their father. His mother would love him for fixing everything. He could see the glow of satisfaction on her face now. And she would let him sit in the special family chair just like before whenever he did something good. The big velvet chair. Things would be like they were supposed to be. But first he'd have to get rid of Marla.

* * *

"Talk to me, Marla. At least you can tell me why you don't want to be married to me." Neal sat next to Marla on the bed, holding her hand. The one thing that had concerned him the most when he married Marla was the fact that he was so much older than she was. Maybe she realized that now too, and that was the reason she wanted a divorce.

"Neal, don't you see. It's just like Gale said. The Seawolf fans will never forgive me. I killed my ex-husband. I killed Martin. If I don't divorce you, they will blame you, too. It will ruin your coaching career. I love you too much to let that happen."

Neal looked at Marla in disbelief. "My god. And I thought it was because I was too old for you. That you had decided you want a younger man." Neal laughed and pulled Marla into his arms.

"Listen to me, Marla, and listen good. I don't want you to ever doubt this now or in the future." Neal leaned forward and moved a strand of hair from her damp face. "There is absolutely nothing in my life more important than you. Nothing! Even if none of this had happened with Martin, I would be ready to get out of coaching. It's time. I want to. It no longer holds the excitement for me it once did. But you do. Good god, Marla, you are my life. Can't you see that? Nothing else matters. So if you can put up with having an old ex-jock underfoot, that's what I want."

Marla pulled Neal toward her and kissed him. That was what she wanted, too. More than anything in the world. Maybe they could get through this horrible nightmare after all.

Tenderly Neal kissed Marla's face. "You are my life, Marla," he repeated. "I love you."

Marla lay quietly with her head on Neal's shoulder, feeling his chest move up and down rhythmically as he breathed, listening to the beating of his heart. Through the open bedroom window they heard the tree frogs start singing their nightly serenade as the dusk slowly turn into darkness.

A loud cracking noise suddenly broke the stillness of their bedroom, silencing the frogs and causing Marla to scream. Outside someone yelled. And then there was the sound of someone running past the bedroom window. Quickly Neal got up and pulled on his clothes.

"Get on the floor and stay down," he said. "Someone is firing a gun at the house." He rushed out of the bedroom, closing the door behind him.

Marla grabbed her robe and put it on. There was another gunshot. This time the bullet ripped through the window screen, shattering the upper panel of glass, and lodged in the wall next to the bed. Terrified, Marla fell to the floor. She heard more yelling and what sounded like several people running.

The bedroom was dark, but reflecting under the door Marla could see a light on in the living room. If only she knew where Neal was. She crawled toward the door. When she got to it she stood up and pressed herself against the wall. Slowly she reached for the doorknob. Just as she did, the door was thrown open. The light from the living room flooded the bedroom. Once again the feeling, that evil force she hadn't been able to identify, poured through her entire body, pushing her life spiraling out of control. And she now knew what it was. It was Charles Morgan.

Marla watched horrified as Morgan limped toward her, his hand reaching out for her hair. Marla screamed. She tried to push him away from her as she fought to get out of the bedroom. He shoved something cold and hard against her face. It was a gun. Instinctively she clawed at him and bit his hand causing him to drop it.

"You whore! You filthy whore!" Morgan slapped her hard across the face causing her to fall to the floor.

"Neal!" she screamed as she scrambled to get up. "Oh, god, not again." She had to get away. But he kept coming toward her, grabbing at her, trying to touch her. He pushed her down on the bed and tore at her robe. Marla struggled to get away but his hands were choking her. She kicked and beat him with her fists, but he was too strong. She couldn't breathe. Everything was turning black. She wanted to fight back, but all of her strength was slipping from her body. In the distance she heard another gunshot. She felt Morgan fall forward, crushing her with all of his weight. Somewhere from behind him came other hands, the hands of a police officer, who yanked his limp body off of her and she watched Morgan as he slumped to the floor. Charlie Morgan had been shot. He was dead.

Neal ran to Marla and wrapped his arms tightly around her as two other police officers ran into the bedroom. "Oh, god, Marla. Are you all right? They got him, honey. He can't hurt you anymore."

"Sorry for the intrusion, Mrs. Connors." It was the taller policeman who spoke in a Southern drawl to her. "It's a good thing Mr. Ferris notified us that this guy might be on his way to Coach's house. Otherwise, we might have been too late. Are you O.K.?" He examined the red marks on her throat where Morgan had choked her.

Marla held on to Neal tightly. "Yes. I am fine."

He nodded. "Medics are on the way." Then, more pointedly, "Where is your gun, Mrs. Connors?"

"Gun? I don't have a gun. Charlie had a gun but he dropped it when I tried to push him away. I think it fell over there somewhere." Marla pointed toward the dresser.

"We don't even own a gun," said Neal.

"Well if you don't have a gun, who shot him?" The policeman looked at the other officers. "Morgan's gun must have discharged when he dropped it," one of the men finally said. Just then Detective

James, who had been listening outside the door, walked in, followed by Walter Ferris.

"Coach. Mrs. Connors. Looks like you have had some more excitement."

"Are you two all right?" asked Ferris, glancing around the room and spotting the shattered window, instinctively gathering evidence.

"I'd say we've had just about all the excitement we can stand, Bob." Neal held Marla against him. "It's all over now, honey."

"Yes, it is." Marla smiled up into Neal's face. Reflections from the red and blue flashing lights of the patrol cars flickered on the walls, floor, and ceiling of the bedroom. Strangely enough, in spite of everything, she felt calm. That undefined fear she had been carrying around inside her for so long was gone as though it had never existed.

Detective James bent over the body to examine the wound. "There is no doubt that he has been shot, and judging from the amount of damage, a hollow-tip bullet was used," he told Ferris. So the bullet hadn't come from police force issue. Thank god. If it had, that would have meant one of the officers would have been suspended until the completion of an investigation by the county law enforcement agency. They didn't need that. They were understaffed enough as it was. He walked around the room. Marla was wearing a robe with no pockets and it was spattered with blood. But she would have gotten that when Morgan fell on top of her. Neal just had on a pair of jeans. He could have been carrying a gun. But judging from the angle in which the bullet must have penetrated Morgan's skull, the person firing the gun had to have been standing outside the bedroom window. Would Coach have been able to shoot Morgan from outside the window and then run back into the house just as the officers were pulling Morgan off of Marla? He didn't think so. Other than Morgan and the police, there was no one else at the house. So who the hell shot Morgan?

Later, Marla and Neal watched from the window, the window that had been shattered by a bullet only a short time earlier, as the paramedics put Morgan's body into the ambulance and drive away. It was over.

"Neal, you and Mrs. Connors won't mind if I stop by here sometime tomorrow and have a look around outside, will you?" Detective James was just finishing writing his report in his brown notebook.

"Of course not, Bob. We'll be around here all day if you need to come back inside for anything."

"Let me know if you need anything," Ferris said and then left. It had been a long day, but he had one more stop before heading home. He would visit Jean in the hospital and let her know she didn't have to worry about Morgan any more.

Marla wrapped her arms around Neal and kissed him tenderly. It was really over. All of the evil was finally gone from her life. There would be no more nightmares, no more unexplained feelings of anxiety and fear. She was free.

* * *

Detective James found a second gun after further investigation. Actually, it didn't take much investigation. Detective James went back to the Connors' home the next day so he could look around the house in the daylight. When he noticed that some of the shrubbery outside the Connors' bedroom window had been mangled, he casually searched the area. He found the gun just to the right of the window where it had either been dropped or thrown. Forensics easily determined that it was the murder weapon used to kill Morgan. There were no fingerprints, so whoever had fired the weapon had either worn gloves or taken time to wipe the gun clean. Since the gun wasn't registered, there was no way of knowing who owned it.

One of the police officers told Detective James that he had been with Neal from the moment he came out of the bedroom when Morgan fired the first shots into the Connors' home until they burst into the bedroom after Morgan had been killed. At no time did he see Coach with a gun. Since they were on the scene immediately after the fatal shot was fired, Marla was still under Morgan's body. Pinned down like that, there wasn't any way she could have thrown the gun out of the window even if she had shot him. Besides, neither Coach nor Marla were wearing gloves, and they certainly wouldn't have had time to wipe their fingerprints from the gun. And Detective James believed Coach when he said he didn't own a gun.

No. This gun belonged to someone else. Oddly enough, those closest to Morgan who normally could have been considered as suspects weren't even in town when the murder took place. Ray Knox had cleared out the night before, Detective James had found out, and no one seemed to know where he had gone or why. No one seemed to particularly care either. And Morgan's wife had also left, apparently to go stay with her family in Pennsylvania one of the secretaries in the Athletics Department had told him. So there was someone else. Someone who wanted to see Morgan dead. Someone who was able to stand quietly outside the Connors' bedroom window unobserved and shoot Morgan, shattering his skull and killing him instantly. And Detective James didn't have the slightest fucking idea of who it was. He pulled out his cell phone and punched in the number for Walter Ferris. He would want to know.

Chapter Twenty-Four

Neal and Marla sat at the head table along with the Commissioner of the Atlantic Coast Conference and his wife, Frank Boyd and his wife, Bill Camp and his wife, and Stu. Neal had said he didn't want a retirement dinner, but Stu had begged so pitifully that Neal had finally relented. The banquet room at the Sir Walter Raleigh Hotel where it was being held was filled with Seawolf supporters, friends, and colleagues Neal had worked with at the University and in the Athletics Department. Sports writers and photographers from all over the state were also there circulating among the guests, collecting comments, and snapping pictures. The huge turnout even surprised Neal.

"You look beautiful," Neal told Marla once again. She smiled at him. She felt beautiful. For the first time in many years the darkness and fear that had been so much a part of her was gone. She hadn't known what it was until the full truth came out about Martin and Charlie. Somehow Marla had always felt that Martin was only a part of her fear. But she didn't know what it was or understand it. It all made sense now. The Seawolfers would never understand, of course, but that no longer mattered. She and Neal had each other. That was what mattered.

"Of course, I am sure I can speak for Frank and Bill as well when I say quite honestly we all were afraid that Neal, with the tremendous support he has from the Seawolfers, might take our jobs." Everyone laughed. The Commissioner, Frank, and Bill were taking turns lauding the accomplishments of Neal during his tenure as head basketball coach at State. "But I tried to comfort myself by saying that since there was no way on this green earth that Coach could win the National Championship, that might make him fall down in favor slightly with his fans, and at least I would have another year as Commissioner of the ACC. So what does Neal do? With a 103 degree temperature, no center on his team, and a bus driver who wrecks the bus en route to the Championship game with the entire team and coaching staff on board, Coach arrives at The Pit and beats the blazes out of the team with the longest winning record in NCAA history. I'm not so sure that his resignation isn't just a ruse to get my job." Everyone roared.

Then Stu got up. "All I want to say is, I couldn't have enjoyed working for anyone as much as I have with Coach. I love him like a brother."

Neal stood up and shook Stu's hand. "I'll just say a few words. I know you folks. Without an occasional slam-dunk to keep you awake, you lose interest. And I expect with all of this talk, your attention span has already reached its limit."

Everyone laughed. He waited for things to get quiet.

"This past years has been one of the happiest and most exciting in my life."

Everyone was listening now.

"Winning the National Championship was a dream come true."

People again began applauding and a few cheered. Again Neal waited for everyone to get quiet.

"But what made it even more rewarding was the fact that I had a very wonderful, brave, and beautiful lady to share that experience with me."

There wasn't a sound in the large room. All eyes were focused on Neal and the head table.

"My wife, Marla."

Neal reached down and took Marla's hand, pulling her up next to him at the podium. After a moment, someone began to clap, slowly. Others joined in. And soon everyone was on their feet applauding.

Marla smiled through her tears at the people who had supported Neal for so long. And now, in their way, they were offering her their acceptance and forgiveness.

"What are you going to do now, Coach?"

The dinner had long been over, but no one wanted to leave. Neal and Marla were trying to make their exit so they could go home. It had been a nice evening, but Neal had already stayed longer than he normally did at social functions. The question came from a reporter from the *Raleigh News and Observer*.

"Marla and I are going to take some time off, just relax at the beach. And then I might write a book—all about this year and how we won the Championship. I know someone who writes for a paper in Albuquerque and also does freelance work who might be interested in helping me with it. And after that, we'll just see. Right now, I just want to take my wife home."

"Marla?"

It was Elizabeth Wall. Marla went over to where she was standing alone, leaving Neal to answer another question from the reporter.

"Elizabeth. It is so nice of you to be here. I will always be grateful to you for being so kind to me when I worked in the Chancellor's office. And Neal has told me what a tremendous help you have been to him over the years."

Elizabeth smiled. "He was a nice person to help. In three more years I plan to do what he is doing. Retire and enjoy life. I just want to wish you all the best."

"Thank you, Elizabeth."

For a moment, Elizabeth continued looking at Marla as though she wanted to say something else. But just then Neal walked up to where the two women were talking and put his arm around Marla.

"Just think, Libby. You'll be able to take it easy now without me around pestering you."

"Believe me. You were no pest." The moment had passed. Whatever she had wanted to say was now forgotten, or at least buried. She leaned over and kissed Marla on the cheek. "Be happy," she whispered and she walked away.

* * *

Marla stood on the veranda at the Cottage overlooking the marsh and sandflats. She had just heard a bird sing his first notes of greeting to the new morning.

"I brought you some coffee." Neal handed her the cup and put his arm around her. Together they watched the first streaks of sunlight replace the gray light of dawn. Dew drops glistened on the carpet of grass spread out in front of them. Within minutes, the whole island was alive with song, color, and sweet scents.

"It's a silver dawn," said Marla quietly. And she leaned her head against the shoulder of the man she loved.

Coming Soon!

BARBARA CASEY'S

THE HOUSE OF KANE

Simultaneously wise and poignant, exotic and suspenseful, *The House of Kane* is a fascinating story of loyalty, treachery and the power of destiny. With an insider's view into the world of high stakes publishing, Barbara Casey weaves a masterful story that haunts the reader long after the final page.

"Barbara Casey's *The House of Kane* is a touchingly tender love story, set in an intrigue-riddled publishing industry. Her characters are interesting and varied. Her story is refreshing and engagingly told. Aspiring writers will want to read *The House of Kane* to tap her wisdom about getting into print." —John DeDakis, CNN Senior Copy Editor Author of *Bluff*

For more information
visit: www.SpeakingVolumes.us

www.ingramcontent.com/pod-product-compliance
Lightning Source LLC
Chambersburg PA
CBHW050509260626
47157CB00004B/1249